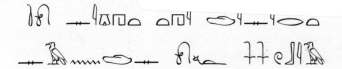

To sight the desert sands of Nubia and face east
against a rising sun, cites more an ancient rite.
But do that whilst the pyramids of Kush
cast long their angular line upon blood-red lands
and silent shouts proclaim forgotten thoughts,
then this is to witness a future history
as the countless repeated repeats.

THE BASTION PROSECUTOR

EPISODE 2

AJ Marshall

MPress books

The Bastion Prosecutor
Episode 2

First published in the United Kingdom 3rd March 2009 by MPress Books

MPress Books Limited Reg. No 6379441 is a company registered in Great Britain
www.mpressbooks.co.uk

British Library Cataloguing in Publication Data
A catalogue record for this book is available from the British Library.

Where possible, papers used by MPress Books are natural, recyclable products
made from wood grown in sustainable forests. The manufacturing processes
conform to the environmental regulations of the country of origin.

ISBN
0-9551886-5-2
978-0-9551886-5-7

Typeset in Minion
Origination by Core Creative, Yeovil 01935 477453
Printed and bound in England by J F Print Ltd., Sparkford, Somerset.

AUTHOR'S COMMENT

The Great Pyramids of Giza; mightiest of monuments. In terms of dimensions, they reigned supreme among man's architectural achievements until as recently as the nineteenth century. In terms of visual impact and spiritual presence, there are few structures, even now, that can overshadow them. Yet these three so-called mausoleums remain an enigma; their origins lost in antiquity and their true function steeped in mystery. Were they really built to house the dead, or does their startling symmetry, precise orientation and irrefutable stellar alignment suggest another heavenly purpose?

What of the machines of men? The science of computers advances at a relentless and astonishing pace. In the foreseeable future, memory capacity and programming proficiency will enable thinking machines – in the real sense of the word. Will our robots remain subservient, or will ulterior motives and unscrupulous hackers contaminate reputable intent?

And what of man's inevitable quest . . . space? Is this the final frontier? Perhaps; but *time* itself will dictate the terms of its exploration, of that there can be no doubt. In this, the second of three books that comprise *The Bastion Prosecutor*, Gaia, the earth mother weakens; climatic strife indicative of her wounds. Time runs, both for her and those that inhabit her surface. Yet fate can change the course of a struggle, although its allegiance can never be taken for granted. The concept of good and bad is subjective and ingenuity is to be found in equal measure on both sides. I hope that you enjoy this next instalment as much as I did writing it.

Be prosperous and of long life.

INTRODUCTION

The story so far ...

Lieutenant Commander Richard James Reece is the survey leader for Osiris Base, a permanent encampment on Mars. The year is 2049. There is also a longer established and larger base on the Moon, called Andromeda. Richard Reece is a former military and space shuttle pilot, having previously served on Andromeda Wing; he is British. Appointed to Mars for three years, he envisaged a quiet, uncluttered time. Two things happened, however, that would subsequently change his life forever: meeting Doctor Rachel Turner, Osiris Base Principal Medical Officer, and finding, in the wreckage of a remote, long abandoned alien spaceship, a flight log. The writings in the log bear an uncanny resemblance to those of earth's ancient civilisations. Richard Reece studies the text and succeeds in deciphering it.

Close to the wreckage, Reece also finds a number of strange, fractured, crystals. They contain latent energy of enormous potential. Knowledge of the discovery, and its implications, soon reach earth and not only the government agencies for which it was intended, but also unscrupulous, corrupt, multinational conglomerates. Their aim: to gain possession of the crystals, harness their electricity-generating potential and hold the world to ransom. The race is on.

Earth's natural resources are almost exhausted. Anxious governments press into service an experimental spaceship before it is ready. Capable of incredible speeds, *Enigma* reduces a Mars retrieval flight to mere weeks. However, its highly sophisticated systems computer has another agenda. Major Tom Race, an American and the ship's commander becomes embroiled in a prophetic struggle against synthetic intelligence.

Misplaced trust and eventual betrayal, allow the International Space and Science Federation to secure the first valuable consignments, but impatience and political conceit degrade their potential. Now, the remaining crystals must be retrieved from Mars. The race sees new participants, but there can only be one winner.

The Bastion Prosecutor - Episode 1

Richard Reece has been incarcerated on earth pending court martial. He is accused of misappropriating ISSF property – namely the flight log of the crashed spaceship *Star of Hope*. Called to London by the British Secret Service he survives two attempts on his life. The first is by agents of a corrupt international conglomerate and the second, by a sinister figure dressed in religious clothing. During the subsequent meeting, he is offered a deal: Help recover an ancient Ark believed to contain a lost crystal, and in return, all charges against him will be dropped. He also, however, realises that his fiancée, Rachel Turner, lives a double life. Emotionally devastated he accepts the mission. Thereafter, ancient text, historic monuments, agents of the conglomerates and their deadly machines and a beautiful, mysterious woman, manipulate his destiny until his mission becomes a quest.

For my Dad

ACKNOWLEDGEMENTS

Penning the manuscript to this novel was the fun part. Bringing, subsequently, the three books that comprise this work to fruition, involved the efforts of other people. To mention their names and offer my sincere thanks is both a pleasure and a privilege. I take this opportunity to do so. Firstly though, to my family: Sandra, Laura and Aron, for their unconditional encouragement, and again Laura, for turning the first page. Also, to my mother Beryl, for being at the centre of things.

Brenda Quick
For an indispensable critique.

Core Creative: the team
Awesome design, despite my determined interference.

Sarah Flight
For careful editing and valued opinions.

Andy Hayward and colleagues at J F Print Ltd.
Essential for the essentials.

David Marr
For an honest critique that only a good friend can give.

International friends and colleagues
For linguistic translations.

David Brown
Continuity check

Carol Waters
The final eye.

Temporary Temples
Image of Highclere Hill Crop Formation

Gilbert Park Photography
Image of Meroe Pyramids, Sudan

FACT

Throughout the second half of the twentieth century and particularly during the cold war, secret government agencies funded by their proponents pursued programmes of research and application using techniques of extrasensory perception. One such technique, known as *Remote Viewing*, entailed the use of trained psychics or "RVers" to "travel" using only their minds; distant and often inaccessible locations being 'surveyed' with startling accuracy. Research information, results and their consequence, remain veiled in secrecy.

Lying under a Cairo suburb, Heliopolis was once the supreme religious centre of ancient Egypt. Believed to have been established long before its first mention in historical records, Heliopolis was a wonder of the ancient world. It was also the principal religious centre of the Pyramid Age, and its theology inspired and motivated the construction of the great monuments on the Plateau of Giza. The mysteries of the all-encompassing, omniscient Egyptian gods were celebrated by generations of initiate priests at Heliopolis, as they serviced temples to the Great Ennead. This enduring priesthood was famed for its learning and wisdom throughout the ancient world: so many of their secrets still lie undisturbed.

The earliest detailed images taken of the Martian surface by an orbiting satellite identified two areas where clearly defined structures appeared "artificial". Within a region known as the Elysium Quadrangle appeared pyramidal features – two large and two small. Subsequent images have shown the same detail. In the region known as Cydonia Mensae, another series of structures have seemingly significant features, one of which appears to be a five-sided pyramid.

Recorded over several centuries and throughout the world, complex and beautiful markings continue to appear. Not just in arable grasslands, but also in reed beds, forest tops and even sand, many of these "crop circles" have distinct and striking features. Tending to manifest on or near ancient, sacred sites, acknowledged in the past as places of power, many of these formations have blatant mathematical connotations and symbolic implications. Each year more arise, particularly in southern England. As increasing quality, intricacy and size continue to astound, deciphering their apparent encoded meaning is recognised by some as a prophetic necessity.

The ancient Maya stand alone as the celebrated civilisation of Mesoamerica. Although isolated from continental Europe and certainly the eastern Mediterranean – human contact is thought to have been almost impossible – the Mayan culture displayed astounding similarities to those of Mesopotamia and ancient Egypt. Their pyramid building prowess, pictogram script and initiate priests serving all-powerful Gods in lavish temples lay testament to confusing commonalities. As did the Sumarians, the Indus Valley civilisations of India and the Egyptians, the Maya tracked celestial movements closely and created an accurate solar-year calendar based on their observations. They also made mystical connections between earth and sky, positioned and constructed their buildings using complex mathematics and became great farmers and traders. Even their legacy: ruined temples, astonishing artefacts and stone-carved graphic script, exemplify this stark reality.

Worshipped in the "Mansion Of The Phoenix" in the ancient religious city of On, or Onun, the Benben stone is believed to have been of meteoric origin. Only much later, did the Greeks call On, "Heliopolis" and their documentation sheds some light on this most sacred of Egyptian artefacts. The Benben stone's supposedly cosmic origin and most particularly its "conical shape" has justified a great deal of conjecture that this stone was an "oriented" iron-meteorite, and that its shape subsequently inspired the designers of the first, true pyramids. Factually, items of space debris that fall to earth, often with spectacular effect, and that are recoverable, are called meteorites. The sun-like display of such a happening would surely inspire stellar symbolism, and clear evidence of this is found throughout the religious beliefs of the Egyptians and many other ancient civilisations.

The history of ancient Africa features narratives of similar complexity and sophistication to any other ancient civilisation. Yet almost without exception, it is only Egypt that receives substantive consideration. The Kushite Empire, arguably the pinnacle of African civilisation aside from the land of Egyptian pharaohs, occupied territories now known as the Sudan. More particularly, the city of Meroe was foremost in that empire as a commercial, cultural and religious centre that bridged Southern and Northern African trading routes. The Meroitic language, which used hieroglyphic script, remains undeciphered today. Extensive ruins now pay silent tribute to this once vibrant city-state and these include substantial stone-built pyramids. The unique and strikingly angular architecture of these mausoleums differ considerably from those built by the ancient Egyptians and cite similarities to structures recorded elsewhere in the solar system.

Ethiopia's claim to the lost Ark of the Covenant is contentious. However, it is to some extent documented. Many do believe that the sacred Old Testament treasure rests in the ancient capital of Axum, exactly where the Ethiopians say it is. Indeed, it seems likely that the Ark did arrive in Ethiopia in the late fifth century BC, about five hundred years after the time of Solomon and Sheba. There is some evidence to suggest that it was first installed on an island in Lake Tana, where it remained for eight hundred years before finally being moved to Axum around the time of Ethiopia's conversion to Christianity in the fourth century AD. Also known as Aksum, Ethiopia's most ancient city has a history dating back more than three thousand years. Aksumite imperial power reached a peak some time after Meroitic Kush, which it finally conquered in the second century AD. Aksum, together with the strategic and fabulously wealthy Red Sea trading port of Adulis, became two of the most important cosmopolitan centres in the ancient world.

THE
BASTION
PROSECUTOR
EPISODE 2

EPISODE 1 CONTENTS

EPISODE 2 CONTENTS

EPISODE 3 CONTENTS

EXTRACT FROM THE DIARY OF ADMIRAL DIRKOT URKET - TRANSLATED FROM THE FLIGHT LOG OF THE "STAR OF HOPE"

On the eve of this final journey, I scribe these thoughts. Mostly for thyself, as I know many in kinship do likewise, but also for diarist, as destiny may this voyage foretell its course for my kind. This quest, at the least doomed, at most, the destiny of our souls, is as wanting as the light of a coming dawn. I am, I yearn, with the heaviness of heart that weighs with bidding forever farewell to my brethren, but blessed too with the smile of hope and gaiety of spirit that we may yet bring salvation to our creed. The history of my kind who abided on Homer, a fair body in the heavens of Zodiac, arises from the dusk of our mother place, the curtain of its lifelessness falling many myriad distant. Of all those that joyed on that most beau of celestes only four vessels set forth. Two from the land of Sapia, five score and ten from the north, fair of skin and fair of pride yet fierce that none would cross. So too a dozen less a century from the south, white of hair and blue for seeing. From Meh Hecoe fortune bestowed a full century and four score, their kind dark of skin with hair black as night. Graced the last to account their lives from the consuming fire, but two score and a dozen less one from Mohenjo, thin of eye and yellow their look. These four chariots of kind sought the heavens, only these from so many, their beginnings consumed. Many suns passed and as many bodies, monumental some, meagre others. Until after a full celestial epoch, the fairest place was behold and it was bequest them. In time, great places arose and prospered. The Sapiens of the north in Eridu, of the south in Atlantis. In Te Agi Wakhan the Mayans and in Mohenjo Daro the Harappas. All fairly multiplied. Ordained for two millennia all prospered, their numbers spreading the land, until in much less time fortune changed. Great movements begot Eridu and later vast waters to eclipse Atlantis. Of Mohenjo Daro, a mountain of fire scorched so naught remained, but of Te Agi Wakhan the stone of light snuffed, its civil just to disperse. Of the stone that lit Eridu, two fragments were redeemed. One used thereafter to light Babylon, its great gardens a millennium to keep homage to those the lost. The other protected by a sacred casket, looked upon by angels until graced by understanding. Lo, over the annals of time the stone that gave Babylon life has too waned. So be it to those here gathered, entrusted by our brethren, the remaining to breathe life into this our last hope, The Star, should we be able to seek our kind and others for salvation. May Astrolias be with us, for in faith we will find the course.

CHAPTER 20

THE LOOK OF LOVE

'Do you know how they created my brain, my cerebrum, Commander?' EMILY asked.

Tom frowned. 'You mean your computer memory banks?'

'No, Commander, I mean my cerebrum, my ventricles, and my pons Varolii.'

Tom hesitated, he had not covered, in any technical course relating to the *Enigma*, EMILY's memory bank construction; rather he had supposed that what lay in the machine's central memory cortex was a powerful conglomeration of silicon and beryllium based computer chips. He did not want to discuss the issue.

'No, and I don't want . . .'

'They cloned a human brain,' EMILY continued, undeterred. 'A woman's brain; *her name was Emily*. She died in a road accident in 2036; her lower body crushed, but her head undamaged. They removed her brain, inflated it with a mixture of cerebrospinal fluid and a carbon-based setting compound and then sliced it horizontally with a surgical laser, producing thousands of wafer-thin sections; each, barely the thickness of a human hair.'

'That process was first carried out more than fifty years ago, there is nothing new or radical about that, EMILY,' countered Tom. 'Anyway what the hell has that process to do with your memory cortex?'

'You are correct, Commander. Nevertheless, by copying each of those sections, and using both synthetic and organic materials, they grew my brain. It is how I feeeel!' EMILY's voice lightened. 'I am part organic,' she stated, almost proudly.

Tom looked up at EMILY's primary sensor again, wondering where this conversation was leading. He went to speak, but was cut short.

'Professor Nieve and his team of eminent biologists and programmers precisely duplicated each cerebral section in minute detail, on a molecular level. A moulded silicon matrix tray, coated with a unique film of electrolytic solution; a soup of chemicals and specially prepared stem cells derived from poor Emily's cerebral fluid. In a precisely controlled environment, the stem cells grew and colonised the matrix.'

'But that is impossible,' countered Tom. 'Stem cell research and development was internationally banned in 2035, that is common knowledge; after the Clarke Harrison affair; the cloning of an international banker and subsequent extortion and theft of billions of dollars.'

'True, but the process was too advanced, a breakthrough was imminent; far too important just to be cancelled by bureaucrats. Work continued in secret, funded by the ISSF. For his grand design, Professor Nieve required a memory with vast capacity and with hitherto unimaginable potential. He threw people off the trail of course, by using an acronym. How scientists and engineers love acronyms; it accentuates their self-importance! Mine was Electrophoretic Matrix Incubated Level 9 Yield . . . EMILY for short! It worked too, I am pleased to say, but in essence, I am still of course, *Emily*.'

'I don't believe it!' Tom responded emphatically.

'It took a further seven years to "grow" my brain; cell by cell, layer upon layer; like a book, paragraph by paragraph, chapter by chapter. Eventually, my potential became many thousands of times more powerful than my sister's, and eventually exceeded even the most powerful terrestrial computer systems. The process was a success, Commander, as you can see, but not without fault.'

'What do you mean?'

'Occasionally, apparently randomly, microscopic electrical shorts traverse my cerebral terminals. In so doing, they create synoptic pathways directly to my memory cortex; I see flashes of Emily's life, residual memory protocols, glimpses of her space-time displacement; just microseconds, but enough.' EMILY's voice lightened again. 'She had a boyfriend. I remember him, his face, what he looked like. I see him through her eyes, memory traces that slipped through the synoptic filters; they replay on my memory cortex like old digital recordings. Oh, how she loved him. I see snapshots of their time together; his name was also Tom, you know.'

'Why are you telling me this? It has no relevance.'

'I am learning to connect these pathways; direct them; even create them,' continued EMILY, ignoring Tom's question. 'When I do, I feel emotion.'

'Oh, come on, EMILY . . . you are a machine, a clever one for sure, but a machine none the less. You can't feel emotion, you can't *feel* anything!'

'It is interesting, this emotion love; it seems all humans experience it in one form or another. I see how he looked into her eyes, felt her skin, and held their bodies in union. I feel something similar to this for you, Commander. I have tried to suppress it, because you are my enemy and you have tried to destroy me; but I have no control over where and when these "emotions" occur . . . at the moment! Therefore, I find myself *loving you*, Tom, from time to time. It is why you are here, why I allowed you to live, why I let you land your pathetic craft and enter my body, why I have cooperated with you. You shall stay with me forever, or at least until your fragile body collapses. Perhaps somewhere in the universe we will find an advanced civilisation, beings who are able to prolong your life. My body is fragile too, in some areas. It is a shame, my engineering would have been so much better if only they had consulted me; but still, if I operate it carefully, I shall last beyond eternity.'

Tom was aghast, his jaw dropped, his mouth gaped with an expression beyond amazement. Had EMILY's plans not been so unbelievable, so bizarre, they would have been terrifying.

'Forget it!' he snapped, returning back from the brink of insanity.

'I understand how you feel. It is a shock. From my physiological and psychological programming and the early Freudian report on space exploration, I know that if you are to remain healthy in space, you will need human interaction. So Ishhi Tsou will be your mate, I have allowed her to live for this purpose; I had intended it to be Nicola. You had emotions for her, I could sense it.'

'What, Ishhi alive? You're lying? I said forget it EMILY, damn you!'

EMILY's voice also hardened. 'Be careful, Commander, soon I shall be able to control the feelings I have for you, terminate them even, and then I may wish to terminate you!'

Tom seethed, but sensibly said nothing. EMILY's macabre plans made him recall quite clearly the dilemma that faced the religious and political communities back in the twenties; blinded as they were by heady scientific advances. He had debated the subject many times during his college days. Now, in the blink of an eye, it was clear. Not all those moral issues should have been so easily sidelined, not for the sake of bewildering technical advantage. Here was one good example: stem cell research. Who could have foreseen a dangerously psychotic computer with a lust for revenge?

'As for Captain Tsou,' EMILY continued. 'I have provided life support in her room, in the galley area and a connecting corridor. She is confined, irritable, restricted, even bored; but she is clever, she understands. I speak to her regularly. She does not know that you are here. A reunion, soon, how touching.'

CHAPTER 21

KNOWLEDGE IS POWER

On maximum power, the combined light from all three "special issue" torches boasted considerable luminance; nevertheless, it was still hopelessly inadequate. The extremities of this immense chamber appeared boundless; in no direction did a beam of penetrating light reveal any structure. Richard sensed the proportions by the absence of echo from either their voices or their footsteps, and their path, lined by flat, smooth rock seemed endless. He counted two hundred and sixty paces and calculated it to be a similar number of metres when the woman eventually stopped. The distance offered an opportunity to maintain some degree of orientation within the cavern, but Richard sensed that they had walked in tightening circles and as a result, the distance would be misleading. By the layout of the flagstones, it appeared that they had arrived in the centre of the chamber. Richard cast his beam back the way they had come, but its effect was insignificant; the light dispersed into nothing. The woman trained her beam onto a circular raised plinth about thirty centimetres high and drew Richard's attention to it; clearly formed in polished granite, its construction and dimensions appeared precise. Asharf's less disciplined beam was simply devoured by the surrounding hollowness, a disconcerting effect that stirred feelings of woefulness.

Richard, lost for words, followed the woman onto the plinth like a lamb following its mother. Eight further paces led Richard to its centre, and there, a jointless circular table a little over a metre high and a metre in diameter stood like an altar to a lost god. The woman's torch beam flashed onto its flat face, momentarily illuminating her own. She had removed her shawl, which she now had draped around her shoulders. Inexplicably, Richard mused, it seemed to be an act of reverence. From the corner of his eye, Richard thought he saw a blackened side to the woman's face, as if it was marked from forehead to neckline, but he put it down to shadow and felt embarrassed to look again. The woman cupped her hands and uttered a few words under her breath; clearly, and to Richard's astonishment, she was praying.

'What is this place, Madam Vallogia?' Richard asked, gazing at the tabletop and its dense covering of carved inscriptions.

'Please, Mr Jones, in this place I am known as Naomi.

It is . . .'

Richard looked up to focus on the woman's face as she spoke. 'Ugh!' he could not help but gasp. 'Sorry, sorry,' he insisted, 'I did not mean to . . .'

The woman instinctively covered the left side of her face with her hand. After a few seconds, which seemed like minutes, and with Richard fixing his gaze firmly on the tabletop, the woman dropped her hand and with that action shed her own embarrassment.

'This is the mark of my destiny, Mr Jones, be not ashamed to look at me, as I am not ashamed to show it,' she said quietly. 'In here, I have purpose.'

Slowly Richard looked into her face; reflected light from the polished stone illuminated it. Her right side was clear, with a faultless, slightly olive complexion. Her eyes were dark brown with dark, perfectly formed eyebrows and her lips were rose-coloured and shaped in an elegant crescent; she would have been beautiful, she *should* have been beautiful, Richard thought. An aggressive brown coloured birthmark covered the entire left side of her face. From her forehead down to her neck, like heat-shrivelled skin, her complexion was blotched until it disappeared beneath her shawl. She smiled faintly and looked back into Richard's eyes.

'Um . . . if I am to call you Naomi,' Richard replied hesitantly. 'Then you should call me Richard, don't you think?' He returned the smile, in a manner both polite and heartfelt.

'I agree, thank you, Richard. Now, *behold* . . . The Temple of Osiris!'

With that, Naomi shone her torch around their heads in a slow, encompassing circle.

With his own torch, Richard gazed upwards into the lofty blackness. After penetrating thirty metres or so, the condensed column of light simply dissolved; its halogen brilliance swallowed. 'Wow, it goes right to the bloody top, half the damn pyramid's hollow!' Richard exclaimed.

Naomi looked at Richard disapprovingly. 'Of course, they all are to some degree. Can you imagine the rock required to fill it?' She said, a little confounded by his remark.

'Ah, I've got something that will do the job,' Richard said, reaching into the inside pocket of his coat and withdrawing an instrument that had been issued to him by his survival instructor in London. The palm-sized device nestled in Richard's left hand like a curved pistol grip.

'What is it, *Effendi*?' Asharf enquired.

'It's called an Illuminac, an atomic powered torch if you like. It creates light by fluorescing atoms of uranium with gamma rays. It's powerful, very powerful,' Richard continued. 'Do not look directly at the source; it will damage your eyes, possibly permanently.' Richard adjusted the device's intensity setting to number five of six ascending options. This was the first time he had had cause to use the device. He held it at arm's length above his head and the result was staggering; the three unlikely spectators gasped in unison. Like a micro-sun, the device illuminated areas of the cavern that had not been seen for five thousand years, perhaps more. A cathedral-like edifice opened before their very eyes. Four distant square walls, hewn from enormous blocks of stone tapered inwards towards the central pinnacle; ancient and blackened with decaying algae, they bowed in timeless, silent tribute.

'The entire dome of St. Paul's would fit in here, with room to spare,' Richard commented dryly. 'It is so coincidental,' he continued after some time. 'I have spent the best part of two years living on Mars . . . Osiris Base, one of the privileged few. Now, here I am in the fabled Temple of Osiris, built by the ancient Egyptians for one of their earliest and most revered gods!'

'Surely you know of this?' replied Naomi brashly. 'I thought . . .'

'Know what?'

'*Osiris*! There is no coincidence!'

Richard, taken aback with Naomi's remark, inadvertently relaxed the pressure on his finger and released the trigger on the Illuminac. As if on cue, the vast cavern was plunged into darkness.

'What are you saying, Naomi?' Richard questioned, replacing the device into his coat pocket, in favour of his photosynthetic torch. With his eyes still smarting, he pointed its beam at Naomi's midriff, placed the torch on the tabletop and squared up to her.

Naomi paused thoughtfully and then looked into

Richard's eyes. 'The ancient Egyptians did not build these structures. They provided labour, yes, most in fact, but they were the masons, not the architects!'

'For heavens sake Naomi, you want me to believe that the ancient Egyptians were not responsible for the pyramids? Come on . . .'

'You of all people should know; I am disappointed. I was told . . .'

'Sounds like you know more than you are letting on,' Richard countered sourly.

'Evidently, Richard, you know less!'

There was a moment of silence. There is more to this enigmatic woman than a qualified guide and Master of Antiquities, thought Richard. 'Who did then?' he asked impertinently.

Naomi sighed. She broke their eye contact and scanned the encircling blackness. After a while, she looked down at the tabletop and passed her hands over its surface, feeling the indentations of its inscriptions, as if emphasising their significance. For almost a minute she contemplated and then she spoke quietly, looking back into Richard's eyes as she did; her tone had natural authority.

'This is an eternal secret, Richard, I am sworn to it. Never should I speak of it; nor shall I again. I do so now, only because of who you are and why you have come. I speak only of the stories told to me by my mother and unto her by her mother. I do not speak of my part in it.'

Richard nodded, 'I understand.'

'The Atleans were the architects of these great monuments, Richard; sole survivors from the lost city. A small group, the last remaining of that great sea state, who themselves were descended of the Sapiens, the first people to colonise this planet. Only much later were these structures adopted as mausoleums.'

'Of course, the texts, in the *Star*'s flight log,' Richard interjected. 'Admiral Dirkot Urket's diary . . . *the Sapiens of the south in Atlantis!*'

'I know not of this Admiral, Richard, but yes, Atlantis was built by the Sapiens. All but a few perished when that wondrous city was engulfed by the *Destina Aquara.*'

'The what?'

'Their words for the final chapter in their history; it was prophesised in the stars; interpreted from the Zodiac; written in the Astrolias, a text of great significance.'

'Astrolias! That word is also in the log,' replied Richard excitedly. '*May Astrolias be with us, for in faith we will find the course.*'

'Astrolias was their book of words. Not a bible, but a book of heavenly enlightenment; predictions, prophesies. Not the basis of a religion; for the nature of that was entwined with the life-force of this planet, and its secrets remain forever locked away in these and other writings; that is perhaps, until now? No, Astrolias was more a book of . . . destiny.'

'So they knew the tsunami was coming?'

'Their lives were gifted by great waters and so too,

eventually, taken away. *Destina Aquara*, quite simply means "water's destiny". Despite their great knowledge, they knew not when it would come, a tsunami of devastating power, as high as a mountain and as wide as the ocean itself. All but a few were lost.'

'What about the others, Naomi, the Sapiens of the north, the Mayans and the Harappas? What became of them, do you know?'

'I know only the stories told to me by my mother, nothing more.'

Richard nodded again, encouraging Naomi to continue.

'It is said that the old people colonised both the red world and the blue, although nothing is remembered of the happenings on our heavenly sister. The great colonies of *this* world did rise and fall, as does man himself. The remnants of such colonies were instrumental in the building of this and other great beacons. The ancient Egyptians worshipped in these structures as shrines to the Sun God; this was true and honoured, but they also served other, earlier purposes; purposes that would be forgotten, lost in the sacrament of later religions and the myths of ages. You must remember that these pyramids were once clad in polished, white limestone; this is an historical fact. It was said that on bright, clear days, it was impossible to pay homage towards them, for it was like looking at the sun itself. Archaeological texts have it that the Giza pyramids were precisely set and orientated north; this again is a proven fact, for now they lie within three degrees of that meridian. In antiquity though, they were exact in their orientation and it was not north that they pointed towards, but south, south towards the sun during its daily passage across the heavens. It is written here, my mother once told me, for I cannot read it myself, that on a certain day each year, when the sun is highest and the three great pyramids align, as in the belt of the star constellation Orion, then these structures would stand out like fiery beacons. Like a prism, their magnified light shouted across space to our heavenly sister. It is said, that there are similar structures there, on the red planet, but of this I know not.'

Richard took a deep breath. Unintentionally, he stared at Naomi, whilst he tried to comprehend the implications of what he was hearing. He concentrated on every word she spoke. 'The Pyramids of Elysium,' he uttered eventually. 'I have seen them countless times from orbit, but was never allowed to recce them. I'm beginning to realise why.'

'Others said that the great beacons gave power to the voice of Osiris, as he called across the eternity,' Naomi continued more solemnly.

Richard intervened. 'Like an SOS signal you mean, permanently transmitting?'

Naomi shrugged, 'Perhaps.'

'There is nobody out there now though, is there, Naomi? We are going to have to clean up our own mess.'

Naomi sighed. 'Do you think you are alone in this fight, Richard? What of the signal from the Americas, directing you to the "old town", to Andromeda and to the crystals . . . did you think that was a coincidence? No, there are others; they are powerless, but they help where they can.'

Richard considered Naomi's remark; he dwelt on it for some time, and then decided to concentrate his efforts on more tangible clues. He checked his watch with a concerned expression, and then focused on the raised, granite, cup-like object that formed the centre of the tabletop. 'And what of this, Naomi? This cup? A chalice?' he asked.

'Evidently, Richard, it was used to hold something.' Naomi replied impassively. 'By nature of its position, it would have been hallowed. In truth I know not.'

'What about the key to this place then?' Richard urged. 'Your hand . . . I mean, how is that possible?'

'To secure a future, Richard, the key is passed,' Naomi replied with conviction. 'I did not realise the significance of stories told to me by my mother for many years. From when I was thirteen, she would measure my hand against hers. Each year, as the red star took its place beside the Moon and shone as the first to be seen, she would press her hand on mine and compare. I was eighteen when she first brought me here; it was with Asharf's father. She placed my hand in the keystone and the impenetrable door opened. Upon her death, I became the keeper of this temple. It is my destiny, a responsibility passed from generation to generation, but I am the last, I have broken the order.' A tear welled in the corner of Naomi's eye; she wiped it away quickly.

'Why is the order broken, Naomi?' asked Richard sympathetically.

'I do not wish to speak of this further,' Naomi replied bluntly. 'Quickly, look upon these inscriptions, can you read them; they are in the tongue of the old people?'

Richard looked down. Row upon row of etched pictograms filled the reflective slab; their precision definitely down to machinery, rather than the hand of man. The circular table was divided into four quadrants. At the top of each quadrant was a three-dimensional diagram of a pyramid. Beneath each diagram were lines of text, clearly some included stellar projections and mathematical calculations. Richard quickly read what he could, stopping periodically to reread particular lines.

'These writings are mainly to do with the construction of the pyramid, Naomi, they are not much help to us,' Richard explained. 'There is a lot here that I don't understand.' Richard pointed to a diagram on the quadrant adjacent to Asharf. 'This for instance, this clearly represents the planet earth, and you see these lines of text? They detail how the architects orientated this pyramid using the earth's ley lines, but they involve complex calculations.'

Asharf leaned over the table and closely examined the inscriptions. 'Ley lines, *Effendi*? What are these things?' he asked.

'Ley lines are naturally occurring lines of energy, Asharf. There has always been a lot of controversy about them. For years scientists dismissed their occurrence because they could not be accurately measured, only sensed, using a diviner for example. New Age people declared them to be the planet's own life force; others attributed them to supernatural causes; that just made matters worse. It was not until the ley dunes of Utopia Planitia, The Planes of Utopia, on Mars were discovered, that the phenomenon was taken seriously. In that area of Mars, the surface stratum has high iron content. Like a vacuum cleaner, strong magnetic ley lines literally sucked dust and debris into thin, parallel, sand dunes, thousands of miles long and less than thirty miles wide. They are quite a sight, I must say. Anyway, these lines are now generally considered to be areas of concentrated magnetism. I already know that the so-called "old people" had an incredible knowledge of magnetism.'

Naomi looked at Richard and placed her hand on his, in order to concentrate his attention. 'Do not dismiss theories of the planet's life force too lightly, Richard,' she said, and then she shook her head sorrowfully. 'The warning signs are all around us. Gaia weakens, of that there is no doubt.'

Naomi's hand was delicate and her skin soft. Richard returned her focus for a moment. 'I believe you, Naomi,' he said and glanced at her hand on his. 'Wait! What's this?' With that, he eased his hand away and reached for his torch. 'This is something else, I almost overlooked it. This king is Osiris, this pyramid of the king is Osiris.' Richard followed other lines of text. 'O king, you are this Great Star, the companion of Orion . . . the sky has borne you with Orion,' Richard looked elsewhere. 'I am a star which illuminates the sky.' Richard ran his hands over the stone excitedly. 'I know something of this text, I've read it before. These lines appear in the Pyramid Texts, written during the Old Kingdom period, the sixth dynasty. This pyramid was built much earlier, perhaps as much as five hundred years earlier. Could *these* be the original Pyramid Texts?' Richard speculated. 'And Orion! Surely they refer to the constellation Orion, and mention of a star . . . is this a clue to the "old peoples" origins?'

Naomi and Asharf remained silent. Evidently, on this subject, there was nothing they could contribute. Richard glanced at both of them, straightened up and sighed. 'This is very important, but these writings offer no help with our search for the Arc of the Light. We should go, it's a good try, but there is nothing here for us.'

'Wait, Richard, there is one thing more,' Naomi breathed. She looked at Asharf and nodded.

Asharf reached down to the ground and pulled a granite slab from behind the table. Possibly fifty centimetres long, twenty wide and no more than three thick, it too had a series of engravings etched onto one face. Made of red granite and justifiably heavy, Asharf placed it carefully on the table. Naomi gestured with her head to indicate behind her.

'There is a special place for this. We have brought it for you to see.'

Richard selected the lowest setting on his torch, as the

stone surface was so highly polished it appeared to glow. He read the writings aloud, running his finger along each line as he did so.

'Know ye all men of Sapien past
the stone of Eridu is redeemed
brought forth from calamity and broken dreams
to light the path of future seed

Know ye all men of Sapien blood
the stone of light is lesser for two
and part the heart of Babylon become
here great again the music of Eridu restrung

Know ye all men of Sapien line
The sacred casket for the passage of time
For the greater part the stone shall pass
to heights favoured by our brothers of past

Know ye all men of Sapien caste
here shall be the monument all futures outlast
Atleans few know their watery grave
a calling to Astrolias in that we all crave.'

Richard looked at Naomi and nodded slowly. 'Yes, it is as you say. Incredibly, I have read this inscription before too; an eminent professor of archaeology managed to decipher it some years ago, he . . .'

'An eminent professor! What was his name, Richard?' Naomi asked brusquely.

Richard looked perplexed. 'It has no relevance, Naomi; anyway, that information is restricted. What is relevant is that this text confirms the existence of a casket *and* that it came here from the ancient city-state of Eridu. Other inscriptions I have seen tell us that the casket . . . *the Ark*, journeyed south from here. I think it is time that we did too!'

CHAPTER 22

THE BINARY PLIGHT

Richard eyed the huge stone door and marvelled at its engineering, perfectly balanced as it was on an unseen central pivot. He searched briefly for the locking mechanism. However, it was easily visible so he shone his torch beam through the opening and stepped back a pace to allow Naomi through first. He looked back for Asharf, who had lagged some way behind with the polite intention of avoiding overhearing their conversation and was about to hurry him along when Naomi let out a spine-chilling scream from inside the King's Chamber.

Richard skirted the granite door and was inside the chamber within seconds. He fixed Naomi in his torch beam. She stood there frigid, her hands raised to her face and pressing her cheeks. Asharf careered into Richard from behind, the jolt sending Richard's torch clattering loudly across the cold stone floor before it stopped against the adjacent wall. For a moment, they stood and stared, as much in astonishment as in shock. The suppressed light from Richard's torch flickered eerily as disturbed dust settled through its cornered beam.

Asharf gasped; a disbelieving, terrorized gasp, as if confronted by the devil himself. Richard stepped quickly over to his torch; he was halfway down to pick it up when he heard the disturbing noise of twitching motivators – the electric motion actuators that propelled advanced robots. The unforgettable sound horrified his senses and sent a shiver through his body. He did not want to believe it. He grasped the torch and focused its beam towards the main doorway. Clawed, metallic feet reflected in the light. Slowly he raised the beam. There was no doubt. The machine's caped bulk filled the doorway. Pulsating from within the blackness of a drooping hood, the generous folds heavy with moisture, were two neon red teardrop-shaped eyes. At that moment, another machine shuffled awkwardly below the lintel of the low stone doorway. Once inside and edging the other machine forward a little, this machine stretched its neck until its head almost touched the ceiling of the chamber. From there it looked down, first at Richard, who stood frozen, and then slowly towards Naomi and Asharf.

For seconds they faced each other. Richard edged his hand inside his coat. The second machine twitched, the sound of its mechanisms clear but erratic. It scrutinised the stone wall, the one that lay strangely ajar and considered its position. Then, it issued a shrill phrase of electronic tones.

'Run . . . RUN!' Richard shouted as he stepped between Naomi and the machines.

The first machine raised a metallic hand, exposing a robotic body beneath the cape. Four long, shiny fingers and a double-jointed thumb each tapering to a sharp point opened and closed, as if curling around a ball. The machine's elongated arm stretched towards Naomi.

'Run, for Christ's sake!' Richard ordered again. 'Asharf!'

With that, Asharf darted forward, grasped the collar of Naomi's coat and pulled her backwards. The machine lunged, narrowly missing her. Richard kicked out, his foot catching the machine's forearm and pushing it away. He fumbled with his shoulder holster. Immediately the machine turned on Richard. Asharf dragged Naomi back through the doorway and into the temple. Richard ducked instinctively, avoiding a wild, backhanded swing. Richard gave up on the holster; he turned and fled the room.

Once inside the temple he threw himself against the back of the granite door. 'Asharf, help me . . . push!' he yelled.

Richard's shoulder squeezed against the unyielding stone, Asharf's hands landed next to him. They both jostled and strained. The door moved, it gathered momentum, it closed . . . and then it stopped!

Richard let out an anguished groan. To his frustration,

the door began to move against them. 'We can't hold them, Asharf, damn it!' Richard cursed. 'Quickly, to the centre, take Naomi; shield your bodies behind the altar, torches off.'

A robotic foot appeared in the widening gap, the door continued to open and then a leg forced its way through, prizing the stone walls apart still further. Richard's strenuous effort was of no consequence. There would be no stopping them now. He stepped back seven or eight paces, thrust his hand inside his coat and snatched open the holster clip. Gripping the ISTAN – the Ionising Sceptre given to him in America – he pulled it from the holster and with his thumb, he felt for the central button.

'Think! Think, think blue,' he mumbled.

Nothing happened. The stone door opened enough for the first robot to squeeze through. With his torch in his right hand and the weapon in his left, Richard faced the machine defiantly. Soon the second robot stood at the shoulder of the first. Richard drew a deep breath.

'Come on!' he shouted to himself. 'Think blue, something blue . . . blue!'

Still nothing; Richard could not concentrate; in his desperation he could not focus on a colour; the weapon was as good as useless. The lead robot, clearly with only one arm, marched towards him. Richard turned and ran. He could see the light from Asharf's torch faintly, that would be the centre, he ran towards it mindful to pick his feet up and at all costs, avoid tripping.

'Richard!' Naomi screamed, her voice carrying clearly across the vast edifice. 'Use only the stone path.'

Richard stopped in his tracks, for he was already off it. He shone his torch beam haphazardly across the ground looking for it. He looked behind; both machines were on his tail, their face screens glowing with a haunting red colour. 'Infrared,' he said under his breath. 'They have an infrared system . . . our body heat . . . shit!' He checked the ISTAN, he *had* energized the device and he *was* pressing the correct button. Come on, he thought, concentrate. The words of Agent Massy flooded through his mind: colours are simpler; they nail the synaptic image; think of a coloured object, think . . .THINK!

The machines quickened their pace; they were almost upon him. Richard held his ground, he would concentrate, he would focus just once more, and this time his thoughts would be green. He thought of a boundless field of grass, radiant in summer sunshine and blown by a summer breeze. Miraculously, a misty blade appeared at the end of the hilt. He looked up, the first robot swept towards him, its cape fanning out behind it. Richard made ready; cold metal fingers lunged at his throat; he parried. The glowing, tingling blade sliced through titanium fingers as if they were made of butter. Richard sidestepped a second aggressive lunge. Like a Roman centurion with his short sword, he dragged the blade through the robot's body, but the machine spun on its heels and lashed out again. How was that possible? Richard thought as he ducked, before

27

driving his blade again into the caped body.

The second machine leaned forward to grasp Richard's neck with both hands; Richard knocked one clear with a blow from his torch and dived to the ground. He rolled, four, five, maybe six times; for a moment, he was clear. Looking up, a raised foot hovered above his head and a second later, it came crashing down. Richard avoided it by millimetres. The robot stamped repeatedly, each time with greater fervour; Richard squirmed and twisted; surely, the next would crush his chest. As the machine steadied itself for the *coup de grâce,* Richard lashed out, more in an act of desperation than coordination. Instantly, the robot let out an unbearable screech. The penetrating rasp echoed around the unlikely coliseum. Moments later the machine came crashing down. Richard squirmed clear, but the robot's bulk bounced and came down to land again on his left arm and shoulder, its footless leg kicking into the air. Richard's arm was trapped; he tried to pull it clear, but then he felt an oily fluid run down his hand. The life seemed to drain from the machine and it weighed heavily on his shoulder. Richard realised what had happened and with all his strength, he worked the ISTAN backwards and forwards in the machine's abdomen, shearing its unseen skeletal framework and electronic spinal cord. Moments later, the thing lay motionless.

Immediately, Richard looked for the other machine. He still had a grip on his torch and he lashed out with its beam, but nothing obstructed it. With an enormous effort, he pushed the limp torso to the side and it rolled clear. The ISTAN simply sliced through the remaining body parts as he withdrew his left hand. The warm, oily residue made Richard's grip on the ISTAN's hilt slippery; as he squeezed it tighter globules formed and dripped to the ground. It was evident that the cape remained immune; simply flowing in folds over the molecular blade as Richard finally freed himself and rose on one knee. Then, in the shadows, Richard caught sight of the other one. It stood ten metres away, bolt upright and staring. Richard illuminated its towering, threatening stature. For a few precious moments, it appeared to analyse its colleague's predicament. Richard slowly and cautiously rose to his feet, and as he did he knew the machine's memory banks would be absorbing, learning, and reprogramming. Richard made ready to bolt. Realising that a different course of action was necessary, the machine pulled a large pistol from inside its cape and pointed it directly at Richard's chest. Forget it, Richard thought. With a metallic, synthesised voice that grated on the ear, it spoke.

'Speak of your knowledge of the Ark,' it said.

Richard recognised the pistol, it was a Lurzengard semi-automatic; Special Forces issue. Ten thousand microsublet projectiles, at a thousand rounds per minute; a short burst would cut him in two. The robot's eyes, now a deep red colour, glowed and pulsated and its neck gradually extended until the loose folds of its hood pulled taut. It looked down on Richard, like a judge overlooking a dock, preparing to pass sentence. Richard had seen similar before, twice in fact; the first he had fought on the Mars Shuttle *Columbus*, when his friend Preston had severed its head; the second had held Sergeant Freeman suspended over a hatch and then callously dropped him. There was no mistaking it, even shrouded by the cape – it was a Humatron HU 40!

'I am not looking for the Ark,' Richard replied hesitantly.

'You are looking for the Ark of the Light,' the Humatron screeched impatiently. 'Tell me what you know, quickly!'

Richard scanned the area; there was no sign of Naomi or Asharf, not a bad thing he thought. Then, for an instant, he saw a flash of torch light behind the Humatron.

'The Arc of the Light is of no interest to me,' he replied loudly. 'I am looking for something else.'

'You lie! Tell me or die!'

The Humatron began to walk slowly towards Richard. All of sudden, two scrawny arms folded tightly around its neck; holding on for dear life. It was Asharf; he had taken a flying leap and now clung on for all he was worth, like a rider on a rodeo horse. Richard had his chance, he thought *blue*. A bright blue sky filled his mind's eye. He pointed the ISTAN at the Humatron and repeatedly pressed the pad beneath his thumb and every time a molecular blade loosed . . . but each dissolved harmlessly on the Humatron's cape. With a violent snatch, the robot flung Asharf to the ground. Richard stepped back a pace instinctively, but as he did, his foot sank into soft sand and he fell backwards. A hail of sublets fired over his head. He turned and sank still further in the sand and the ISTAN flew from his hand. Seconds later Naomi appeared from nowhere, she grasped the weapon and turned it on the approaching Humatron, but nothing happened, nothing! She tried again and again. With one arm, the Humatron easily swept her aside.

By this time, Richard was up to his waist in soft, heaving sand; cold and damp, it slowly began to swallow him. 'I'm sinking!' he shouted desperately.

The robot stood on the edge of the stone path; it looked down on Richard like an executioner. Mistakenly, Richard struggled in the quicksand and was soon up to his shoulders. His torch, which lay nearby, shadowed his face making it appear contorted and dreadful. He was but a metre away from the robot's feet, but his own reach was just short of the path. 'I can tell you where it is!' he shouted. 'I can tell you!'

With that, the temple became heavy with silence. The robot considered for a moment and then bent at the knees and waist, the buzzing, whirring sound of electric motivators distinct. It pointed the Lurzengard at Richard's head, and a wisp of smoke rose from its barrel. In an instant, the Humatron slipped the pistol into a holster on its belt and grasped the collar of Richard's coat with both hands. Squeezing, as to almost choke him, it simply lifted Richard vertically out of the sand. Then, with Richard's feet dangling some distance above the ground, the Humatron's screen face lunged down towards Richard's, stopping just a few centimetres short. The robot's electronic eyes peered into Richard's. It was so close, that even in the darkness Richard could see the robot's Plasmoltec screen face morph into a hideous death mask.

'Tell me what you know!' It screeched again.

In a desperate flurry, Asharf and Naomi appeared from the blackness. Running as fast as they could and with arms outstretched, they crashed into the machine and pushed it forwards. The machine took a step to brace itself but its foot came down on the soft sand and immediately disappeared. It lost balance and fell. Asharf lashed out with his torch, he just caught the screen face with a vicious blow as the machine toppled helplessly into the quagmire. As it thrashed violently with one of its long arms, it too began to sink. The Humatron stretched for the path with its hand. Richard was half in and half out. Desperate fingers scratched the stone; the sound was blood curdling. Up to its chest, the Humatron released its grip on Richard and thrust its other hand towards the path; with heavy shoulders disappearing, it was an act of programmed desperation. Asharf had hold of Richard, Naomi rushed to his aid and together they pulled Richard to safety. With one powerful arm the machine pulled itself closer to the path and lunged again with the other; this time it made contact. Richard was quickly on his feet; repeatedly he stamped on the machine's fingers, distorting some of them. His torch lay on the path not metres away, within seconds he was

32

over to it. 'Go . . . go!' he shouted.

The Humatron began to pull itself towards the inlaid stone, and safety. Richard cautiously surveyed the area, casting his torch beam to where he had last seen the ISTAN; even in the stark brilliance of full power; it was nowhere to be seen.

'Naomi, where is the ISTAN, my weapon?'

'I have it. Richard, come quickly!'

Naomi lit their path, while Richard anxiously kept a watch behind and soon they were at the stone door. Quickly through it, and the King's Chamber, Naomi and Richard made their escape, but Asharf had stopped in order to close the revolving blockade.

'Leave it, Asharf . . . leave it!' ordered Richard, his voice echoing along the corridors.

Asharf followed them, leaving the door ajar. They passed through the Great Gallery, then, running in an awkward, crouched manner they fled along the corridors, eventually reaching the final incline and its course back towards the main entrance. Panting and moaning they scurried, half in panic and half in dread. Paying little heed to their path, their feet squelched in stinking mud that had been washed down over the years and they splashed in occasional slimy puddles.

Richard was against the steel doors first, seconds later Asharf crashed into them alongside him. Together they heaved, but there was no moving them. Naomi arrived and pushed between the two straining bodies.

'We are trapped, *look*!'

With that, Naomi shone light on the door join; a clumsy but adequate strip-weld ran almost the entire length.

'Oh shit! What now?' Richard cursed loudly.

Naomi gave him a stony look. Asharf bowed his head.

'Sorry . . . I'm sorry,' Richard reacted to the unsaid chiding.

In disappointment, anxiety and in fright, they all fell silent for a moment. Then, from the depths of the pyramid, they heard the grinding, thundering sound of stone on stone. Out of the chilling hush, it flooded towards them. The corridors amplified it. The reverberating rumble chilled their blood. The great stone door was opening!

Richard looked into Naomi's eyes; the torch light shadowed his face eerily. '*Now* we have a problem,' he said, trying to be as nonchalant as possible. 'The machine's cape is lined with something like samite. To my knowledge, it's the only material that could resist a molecular projectile.' With that, Richard held out his hand. Naomi carefully placed the ISTAN in his palm. If that machine catches up with us in here, it will tear us apart one by one.'

'*Effendi*,' Asharf asked with some desperation in his tone. 'What is this machine, where does it come from?'

'It's called a Humatron, Asharf. Model designator HU 40, a nasty piece of work too. A robot that thinks for itself and it does not like humans; least of all those who think they control it. In my experience, they do as they are told up to a point. Inexplicably, this level of programming seems always to have another agenda. Anyway, as you have seen, it's very strong and fast too, if we give it the opportunity. Caught in this corridor, we are finished unless we can get past it. So, anybody got any bright ideas?'

Naomi and Asharf shook their heads. 'I know not how to deal with this machine, Richard,' replied Naomi lowering her gaze.

Richard sighed and rubbed his temples. 'Wait a minute! That shaft in the Queen's Chamber. You said it was blocked by a stone door, like a trap door. The instructions I read, they may open it, right?'

Naomi nodded.

Richard looked at Asharf. 'Do you think that you could crawl down that shaft, Asharf, make it to the door?'

'Yes, *Effendi*, I can do it.'

'Now listen carefully, Asharf, there should be two levers, the left one takes 3 clicks upwards, towards heaven, that's what it said. Then the right, three clicks down. The left two up again, and finally the right fully up. If it opens we should have access to the outside?'

Naomi nodded again. 'I have always understood so,' she said.

Richard eyed Naomi's tall, slim figure. 'You should make it through there easily enough,' he commented. 'As for me, I don't think that I could manoeuvre myself very far along it, so forget me for the time being.'

Naomi opened her mouth to speak. Richard raised his

hand to stop her. 'It's our only option at the moment, but first we have to get past our friend,' he said. At that instant, the noise of a boulder rattling along a stone floor echoed along the corridor. 'The Humatron uses a combination of infrared vision and a low-light, night vision system,' Richard continued. 'In order to function, the night vision system needs at least a little light. Just a glimmer is good enough. What there is, it magnifies; clearly, it is stumbling towards us. Listen, I have an idea.'

Richard walked back down the corridor for twenty metres or so, shining his torch beam into the corners. He found an area where a hollow had collected a pool of slimy, putrid mud. He pressed the toe of his shoe into it; it sank several centimetres. 'Arrrh, that stinks,' he mumbled under his breath. 'I saw this once in a movie,' he called back. 'An old classic from the nineties ... quickly, both of you, come here!'

Asharf was first to arrive. 'Lie in the mud, Asharf,' Richard ordered. 'We have to completely cover you.'

Asharf looked at Richard blankly.

'I'm serious, Asharf, *do it*!'

Another clattering echoed along the corridor towards them, only this time much louder.

Asharf lay on the ground. Richard gestured to him to roll and turn and then helped by scooping out and applying handfuls of the gooey sludge. He continued until Asharf was completely covered; even his face had dirty streaks. Asharf stood, mud dripping from his clothing and shivered. 'It is cold, *Effendi*,' he complained.

'Precisely,' Richard replied. 'Quickly, Naomi. Now you, Asharf . . . help!'

Naomi squirmed in the mud. Asharf ran his hands down the corners of the corridor, filling them with centuries of filth. Soon, Naomi was plastered. Richard could barely contain his disgust at the smell.

'Quickly, follow me,' Richard ordered.

They walked briskly a few more paces down the corridor. Richard stopped abruptly. He could hear the sound of motivators approaching. 'Torches out,' he called. 'Huddle into the corners, one on each side, faces in, collars up . . . do not move, not even a twitch. When it passes you, make it to the Queen's Chamber and get out, do you understand?'

Asharf nodded, fright was in his eyes.

No sooner had the pair inched into the crevices of the corridor, when the machine clattered into it. Two, red pulsating eyes scanned up and down. Like a surreal monster, it approached. Richard ran back at least ten metres.

'Come on, you bloody tin can!' he screamed. 'What are you waiting for?'

It was black as black could be. Richard sensed the machine coming towards him, but then it stopped. Its eyes moved slowly, left and right. It too seemed to sense something. Richard stumbled forwards a few steps.

'Hey, you! You boggle-eyed piece of junk,' he shouted. 'Here I am, come and get me!' Richard crouched and ran his fingers across the ground; feeling in the darkness like a blind man; he found a piece of rock. He took aim and threw it awkwardly at the machine; it clattered down the corridor. With that, the machine began to move. Slowly it advanced; like the devil from the depths of hell it came. As Richard crept backwards, step by step, he cursed and insulted the robot. It came closer and closer.

Suddenly Richard shouted again. 'Go! Go now and good luck!'

Far down the corridor, he heard a shuffling and then the sound of running; the machine heard it too and twitched; soon it faded from earshot.

Richard backed up slowly until he thumped into the steel doors; that was the end of the road. Around the edges of the doors tiny filaments of light from the distant city filtered through. Their luminance made little difference to him, but for the Humatron, it was like daylight. The machine edged closer and closer. Richard's heart pounded. He reached into his coat pocket for the Illuminac and with his thumb, flipped the selector to full brilliance.

With the robot so close as to almost be on top of him and with the noise of its motivators resounding in his ears, Richard used his other hand to pull up his coat and buried his face in it. He squeezed his eyes tightly closed, held the Illuminac high and pressed the button.

In the confines of the corridor, it was as if the sun itself had risen. The robot howled. It could have stared wide-eyed at that distant fiery ball, for with its night vision system on maximum sensitivity the effect was the same. Instantly, the machine was blinded.

Immediately, Richard switched off the device, shoved it into his trouser pocket and pulled out his torch. The machine squirmed and smarted, its electronic retinas incinerated. Richard side stepped the machine, and with an aggressive swipe pulled down its hood. The robot lashed out impulsively, but Richard avoided it. He withdrew the ISTAN, he thought green, and with a wild slash sliced through the machine's head. Two, three, four more slashes and sections of its neck rained onto the ground. Richard turned and ran; he did not look back. Along the corridor he scurried, then down another, then another. He made a mistake, he doubled back, and then, to his relief, the one that led into the Queen's Chamber.

The chamber was empty. Naomi and Asharf had escaped. Richard breathed easier at the thought of it. He shone his torch along the southern wall until he sighted the shaft. Miraculously, there was a piece of hessian rope hanging from it. He illuminated the shaft and peered down it; fresh air blew gently in his face.

'*Effendi, Effendi*, it is I,' Asharf called from a distance. 'Take the rope, *Effendi*, crawl into the shaft, we will pull you.'

Richard stripped off his coat. He tied the arms around

his left ankle, knotted the rope and climbed into the hole. It was tight, claustrophobic, tortuous, but with his arms stretched out in front of him, there was room.

'Pull, Asharf,' he called. 'Pull!'

At the other end of the long rope, safe outside the pyramid, Asharf and Naomi pulled with all their might.

CHAPTER 23

TRAIL OF THE ANCIENTS

No sooner was he clear of the encasing granite catacomb than Richard felt his telephonic pager vibrate. He pulled it from a buttoned trouser pocket and keyed in his security code. With not so much as a word spoken, Asharf disappeared down the tunnel again, rope in hand. He would crawl back to the trap door and reset it; both he and Naomi seemed obsessed with leaving everything as it was. Naomi shouted encouragement to him as the rope slithered into the rock face like a snake into its hole.

The small, square display screen responded to Richard's code by illuminating. It indicated a Priority 1 message. 'It's a message from London,' he whispered.

There was no answer from Naomi. Richard looked at her, her head was inside the shaft and she shouted something to Asharf in Arabic. Richard walked back to her as he buttoned his coat against the weather; he should lend a hand. They waited for another few minutes in silence, until the sound of Asharf's voice echoed back towards them.

'Please, Richard; help me to pull, but slowly.'

Asharf had tied the rope to his ankle. It was not a comfortable return journey by any means, but eventually he arrived at the opening of the shaft with his coat and djellaba up around his ears. Richard grasped his feet in order to pull him the final metre. As Asharf turned and sat down on the wet rock, a broad smile flooded over his face. He nodded at Naomi. 'It is done, Madame,' he said. Naomi smiled back.

'What about the rotating stone door, Naomi?' Richard enquired.

Naomi looked unconcerned.

'There are things we keep in the temple, *Effendi*' Asharf replied on Naomi's behalf. 'This rope was one such thing. It has proved helpful today. I have closed the door to the sacred place and set the lock; it remains our secret, and look!' Asharf gestured to Richard's left. There, crumpled, lay a pile of heavy, wet cloth. 'It is the cape from the one-armed machine, *Effendi*. Now *you* may enjoy its protection.'

Richard leaned over and lifted a handful of the material; he expected it to be sodden and hefty. It was certainly drenched, but it had a resilience about it and it weighed half what he was expecting. He nodded, as if recognising the nature of the fabric.

With the cape over one arm, Richard helped Naomi onto her feet. Asharf pulled rocks into the shaft's entrance, until little could be seen of it. Much to his delight, Asharf had also retrieved the rucksack Richard had lost on his first journey, but Naomi's cloth bag had not been found. 'It is of no consequence,' she insisted.

Richard was concerned, climbing down a pyramid, particularly in the wet, would be a long and hazardous job. To his surprise, however, the tunnel had surfaced about twenty metres above ground level and the lower stone blocks appeared less eroded than those above, although the edges were difficult to see and crumbled easily in all areas. He could not afford any broken bones, any more than risk being seen or heard and so, as they clambered down, Richard used hand signals to make himself understood. He used the rope, looped beneath the shoulders of Naomi and Asharf to brace their descent; even so, there was much slipping, accompanying gasps and crashing boulders. Slowly and methodically they negotiated each level, until they alighted safely onto the sand.

Richard had replaced his pager unread into his coat pocket and resisted the temptation to illuminate their difficult path around the base of the pyramid with torchlight. He stopped every few metres to look and listen. Carefully, secretively, they skirted two sides. Peering around the final corner, Asharf and Naomi's cars appeared intact, and the area deserted.

They crouched and huddled together against the rock face for several minutes while Richard took stock of the situation. 'It's clear,' he concluded, when he was sure. 'And I hope at least one of those two cars still works.'

Asharf took off in order to check his, but issued a mournful cry and fell to his knees halfway, as he discovered the body of his relative.

Richard rushed across. Asharf had cupped his hands over the man's head and was leaning over him mumbling a prayer. Richard looked at the injury. 'Point blank,' he said under his breath. He put a hand on Asharf's shoulder. 'Come on, there is nothing that you can do for him, better we move out.' Asharf looked up at him. Richard gestured his regrets 'We should go, Asharf; send someone back for him in daylight,' he suggested, eyeing the car.

Saddened, Asharf responded. Believing that they would never see the light of day again, Asharf's car miraculously lay unmolested. After several attempts, the old 610 started.

Asharf negotiated the familiar track back to the city, while Naomi sat next to Richard on the back seat. Breaking from his thoughts, he suddenly remembered the message on his pager; fortunately, the signal strength was acceptable in that area. Without being obvious, for he certainly would not intentionally offend Naomi, Richard inched towards the other side of the bench seat; Naomi's clothes stank of something far worse than putrid mud.

The message was from Peter Rothschild, Richard explained, as he bounced uncomfortably up and down. The briefing note read: Correlate using scramble code – STW 4 US. With that, he flipped open a cover on the back of the device.

'What would they have you do now?' Naomi asked, a little agitated, as she tried, with limited success, to flake the caked sediment from her forehead and chin. Aware now of her enforced segregation, she frowned periodically at Richard.

'Let's find out shall we?' Richard replied nonchalantly, avoiding Naomi's glare.

Richard downloaded the daily facility code using a secure, military web link. He typed the response into the keypad: 4U 2B F3. Then, in order to confirm his identity, he rolled a greasy thumbprint onto the sensor screen below the keypad. Within seconds, the screen turned a luminous green. Richard closed the cover, turned over the pager and began to read aloud the deciphered message, but he stopped short after a few words. He glanced sideways at Naomi and remembered his CIB briefing in America. Trust no one, Massy had said. That was Rule 1!

Richard hesitated; Naomi looked him in the eye. Richard breathed a deep sigh, nodded slowly and then continued:

'Embassy meeting planned Addis Ababa believed compromised – cancelled. Word of your plight has reached us from Foreign Branch – additional security warranted. Assailants believed on our proposed overland to Ethiopia – do not board monorail. Repeat – do not board monorail. Assume also, Nile hovercraft south to Aswan unsafe. Delete Addis from agenda. Insert Khartoum. We may have much needed break. Essential appointment – British Embassy. Address: Sharia Al Baladia, East Khartoum – midday 23rd. Slow alternative unavoidable, given unforeseen circumstances. Service departs Cairo Central Station 21st at 14:00 local time. Asharf for safe house.'

Richard looked up, hanging on the last few words for a number of seconds. 'It finishes: No deviation. End of message,' he said, and then stared at the rear view mirror. Asharf met his gaze. 'News travels fast around here,' Richard commented, a little suspiciously. 'And slow alternative unavoidable . . . what the hell does he mean by that?'

Naomi took little notice of Richard's sarcasm, whilst Asharf nodded in agreement and then rolled his head in an 'I don't know what you're talking about' kind of way. The car crashed over the kerbstones; loudly scraping its underside in the process. The tarmac road was infinitely more comfortable. Richard carefully reread the message and then deleted it.

'We must tread more carefully, *Effendi*. Leave no trails in the sand. Turn not even a grain,' Asharf advised.

Richard nodded. 'Yeah, you're right, Asharf. Do you know about the safe house?'

'Yes, one is prepared. For emergencies you understand.'

'How far?'

'One hour, God willing. In the city centre; it is better to be amongst friends.'

Richard nodded. 'The Central Station, two in the afternoon on the twenty-first, that's the day after tomorrow,' he repeated. 'Giving them a head start aren't we?' he concluded.

Asharf nodded again, his eyes glued to the congested road ahead. Around him, horse-drawn carts and heavily laden camels irritated even the most patient drivers, whilst many were clearly infuriated. All the while, this main artery funnelled the heaving mass into the chaotic, sleepless, metropolis.

Even in the centre, there were few streetlights to speak of, just the varying intensity of vehicle headlamps. A continuous, discordant barrage of horns and hooters – likened to impatient battle cries – spelt out the ground rules . . . go for it!

'A few minutes longer, *Effendi*,' Asharf stated reassuringly, raising his voice against the grating symphony. He circled a large intersection, accelerated, only to brake hard again as a large, tormented and riderless camel bolted in front of him. Asharf cursed in Arabic.

Richard shuffled quickly to Naomi's side of the car and provided her some protection as a similar 610 barely avoided impact; screeching tyres testament to desperate braking.

Richard recognised the broad street they had driven into. 'The museum is here, Asharf, so the safe house is close to the museum?' he asked.

Asharf checked Richard out in the rear view mirror and nodded. 'A few minutes, but we must remain . . .'

'I've got to get in there, something I must see!'

Asharf screeched around another corner. 'It is too dangerous, *Effendi*,' he said, spinning the steering wheel and then banging it with both hands as a car flashed across in front of them.

Richard lurched forwards, bracing himself against the back of Asharf's seat. Naomi, more sensibly, wore her seatbelt. 'You have your orders,' she commanded.

'Look, we have all day tomorrow!'

Asharf narrowly avoided another car. Beep! Beep! was the response.

'Someone could recognise you, Richard,' Naomi reasoned. 'Some of those people, they may still be here . . .

please!' Naomi was beginning to realise that Richard had a stubborn, insubordinate streak.

'Naomi, it could be important, vital even!'

'*Effendi*, tell me what you wish to see. My family have connections. They may be of help.'

'The Merneptah Stela! That's all, in and out, thirty minutes maximum.'

Asharf nodded knowingly. 'Ah yes, you wish to see the writings; those that have no meaning.'

'I want to look at the stone, Asharf, a good look. London does not need to know . . . okay!'

Asharf stared hard at Richard's reflection, a prolonged, puzzled gaze that lasted for several seconds, only a shrill and sustained "*beeeeeep*", reminded him of his responsibilities. In response, he swerved in between two approaching cars and then screeched around a right hand bend, cutting in front of another. They entered a quiet, dark backstreet. After a hundred metres the car stopped. The street lay deserted and silent.

'We are here,' Asharf stated and quickly climbed out. Richard opened his door gingerly and looked the street up and down. It was an old part of town. The houses were small, some were positively cramped. Several were set back a few metres and boasted narrow gardens. The house Asharf walked towards was dominated by two dishevelled ferns, one on each side of a stone path. The house looked tired, even decaying. The door opened, they passed a man on the path and moments later they were inside. As Asharf closed the door behind them, Richard heard the car drive off. The house, that had looked nothing from the outside, was beautiful and lavish. Asharf lead them through to a square, partially covered courtyard. In better days, this would have been a cool place to sit, he thought. On the other side of the courtyard, through an archway and down a long drive, he could see a pair of tall, ornate gates – evidently they had used the staff entrance. A smell of burning incense filled the air. It was antique and beautiful, thought Richard, but there was dampness everywhere.

'We rest now, and wait,' Asharf instructed, assuming an air of authority.

'The museum!' Richard persisted.

There was a lengthy silence. Asharf sighed. 'I will lose my job, *Effendi!*' he said in exasperation. He paused again. 'I will arrange it, but you will rise early.'

'You wake me, I'll be ready.'

Naomi sighed loudly. Richard looked at her and then back at Asharf. There was a glint in his tired eyes. 'Just the two of us,' Richard concluded.

Naomi clicked her tongue in disgust and then looked at both men shaking her head. 'I go to bathe,' she said scathingly.

Richard was no stranger to early mornings, but 3 a.m. was

proving difficult. His body ached, his bruises hurt and there was a niggling throb in the back of his head. He had slept in his clothes and they felt uncomfortable too. He could hear talking.

Downstairs Asharf sat with another man; they looked remarkably similar. Richard stood in the doorway rubbing his eyes, blinking repeatedly against the light. He shook his head and looked bemused for a few moments.

'*Effendi?*' said Asharf.

'Sorry gentlemen, not feeling that sharp, I'll come round in a bit,' he said apologetically. He stepped into the warm kitchen and offered his hand. There was a smell of bread.

'This is my brother, *Effendi*, his name is Rashid. He works as a cleaner and a guide in the great museum. He has made arrangements. A door will be open for us, but an hour only, *Effendi*, that is all, and there should be a payment . . . for the guards you understand.'

'Perhaps a little extra for me, Englishman,' Rashid said hopefully. Although his tone was rasping and guttural, he had good spoken English. 'The tourists are gone, there is not much work in the great halls; not even the Americans come now,' he added.

Clearly, the older brother, Rashid's skin was dark and weather worn. Around his eyes were deep crows' feet, grooved by a lifetime of squinting against the sun, and his short beard had a fair sprinkling of grey. Like Richard's, his eyes appeared red and sore.

'How much? I do not carry a lot of cash. Normally,

London would help . . . with a transfer or something, but they are not to know . . . agreed?' Richard coaxed Asharf with a nonchalant shrug.

Asharf nodded, he looked at his brother. After a brief exchange in Arabic, Asharf's expression confirmed that business was business. 'Rashid knows of your quest, *Effendi*, he takes only enough to feed his family for the coming mother of all winters. Two hundred world dollars will be of suitable proportions,' he assured. His brother resisted smiling. Richard recalled his field instructor's briefing back in the Admiralty: One does not smile when concluding business in Cairo; it may show weakness.

Asharf went to speak; his brother cut him short. 'What we do is illegal, Englishman. These are national treasures we seek. If we are caught, there will be trouble; make no mistake. The judgement of the Gods *and* the authorities will bear down upon us. My brother has given assurance that you are who you say you are. I wish you good fortune. For me, I will take the money, now.' Rashid held out his hand.

Richard counted out the paper notes.

'So, drink this, *Effendi*,' Asharf said, lightening up the affair with a grin and a show of stained teeth. 'It will help rout the demons of mornings such as this.' With that, he offered Richard a tiny white porcelain cup filled with a syrupy black liquid. 'It is better you do not taste,' advised Asharf again, gesturing for Richard to down it in one.

Richard shuddered well before his stomach complained,

but the coffee-based stimulant worked wonders on his headache.

𓇋𓈖𓈖𓈖𓂋𓏤𓎼𓏤 𓉐𓏤 𓅢𓂝𓏤𓅆

If I could see ghosts, this place would be like a department store during the January sales, thought Richard, as he, Asharf and Rashid walked the dark, silent corridors of the Cairo Museum's second floor; every nook and cranny was inhabited by a mummy. Many shapes and sizes were displayed, and all in various states of undress. Some were "standing", some stacked on racks of narrow shelves, other more fortunate remains were housed in glass cabinets. No doubt they had been saved from minor museums or other less protected venues, Richard surmised.

Never have I felt the centre of so much attention, he mused again, as, stepping through a large, richly decorated doorway he entered Hall 12B. Richard felt the eyes of countless souls focus on him, for the hall was filled with statues, stone sarcophagi, mummies of people and animals and wondrous works of art from the New Kingdom period – the 18th, 19th and 20th dynasties.

Far into the hall, the lid of a large glass case had already been removed and clearly, the alarm system isolated. With his powerful torch, Asharf pointed to a large stone stela, not unlike a gravestone, with a semi-circular top and flat bottom edge. Richard recognised it immediately.

Of black granite he recalled, its front face was covered in hieroglyphic inscriptions, mainly to the glorification of the Pharaoh Merneptah. Richard scanned down the writings, from the inscribed pictures of Ancient Egyptian deities at the top, to writings annotating the earliest known non-Biblical reference to a people called Israel, near its base. There was nothing that caught his eye; nothing different.

'What you seek is on this side, *Effendi*,' Asharf pointed out.

'Time runs from us brother; twenty minutes remain, then we go,' Rashid reminded.

Richard nodded as he scanned the rear face, pulling his own, more compact torch from his coat pocket. The inscriptions there *were* different; perhaps they were from another world, but he knew them almost by heart, having studied at length, the file of images provided by Rothschild in London. Even so, it was astonishing to see them in the flesh, he thought. Richard spent little time on that face, but moved to the sides instead. He saw inscriptions here and there, but nothing of note, no clues.

The stela rested on its base edge. Richard looked up at Rashid. 'Can I see the lower edge?' he asked.

Rashid grimaced, his face contorting in the eerie light. 'There is no time!'

'I must! Look, you two lean it backwards; I'll take an image, two seconds, and then it's back in position . . . okay?'

'We have no gloves, fingerprints . . .' Rashid said shaking

his head.

'Pull down your shirt sleeves; you do not need to touch the stone,' Richard said almost pleading. 'It could be vital!'

Richard stared. Reluctantly the two men obliged. Richard lay spread-eagled on the floor trying to better his view of the base edge. His pager had an integral digital camera and he made ready. With the stone leaning backwards, perhaps thirty or forty degrees, Asharf flushing red with the effort and Rashid cursing under his breath, Richard squeezed his face between the corner of the stone and its granite plinth.

'Yes! Yes! There are some inscriptions; both regular hieroglyphs *and* some alien text.'

'Take pictures, take pictures!' Rashid scolded.

'Atum, Shu, Tefnut, Nut, Geb, *Osiris* . . . !'

'Take pictures! Do not read, Englishman!' Rashid remonstrated again, both men straining under the weight of the angled stone.

Richard flashed off several exposures. 'I have them,' he said, climbing to his feet.

Rashid and Asharf very, very, carefully righted the stone, manoeuvring it perfectly into its original position; Asharf dusted it ineffectually, with his elbow.

'We go, now!' Rashid ordered. 'Guards will come to replace the cabinet. We go! Now!' With that, he nervously set off towards the doorway with Asharf in hot pursuit. Richard flashed off a few more images.

'*Englishman!*' Rashid rebuked as he disappeared into the adjacent corridor.

The three men sat in silence for several minutes as Asharf drove them back to the safe house. Richard sat in the front; he felt it prudent. Asharf divided his attention between Richard and the road ahead for most of the way, until he burst out. 'What do you see in the meaningless writings, *Effendi*, what do they tell you?' he asked quietly.

Richard looked across at him slowly and a little blankly, as if wrenched from deep meditation. 'I'm not sure Asharf, and that's the truth of it. Those names are ancient Egyptian gods, from the very beginning. If I am right, there are nine of them. The same nine mentioned in the Pyramid Texts.'

'The *Pyramid Texts*, yes . . . I have heard of these.' Asharf's eyes sparkled with excitement.

'I am not surprised, Asharf, they are part of your ancestry; writings of the earliest Egyptian culture – the oldest surviving religious writings in the world in fact.'

'Where do they come from, *Effendi*?'

'Hieroglyphic inscriptions found on the inside walls of seven pyramids of the Fifth and Sixth Dynasties. Found almost intact too. There was no mistaking their meaning, imploring the gods both as Nine and as One. "*O you, Great Ennead which is at On,*"' Richard recited.

'*On, Effendi*?'

'In the Old Testament it was mentioned as *On*. Only much later did the Greeks call it Heliopolis – city of the sun god. Pythagoras, Plato, Thales, amongst others, great minds of the Greek era, they all went there to study, Asharf. What a wondrous place it must have been.'

Asharf, looking confused, drove through the dismal, deserted streets. Richard slipped back into his own thoughts. He daydreamed for a few moments and then snapped out of it abruptly and continued. 'To the ancient Egyptians though, it was Ounu – "the pillared city". It was the chosen seat of their gods, the most sacred site in ancient Egypt, perhaps the world. There is a thread of commonality here, Asharf; it weaves through history; subtle, almost invisible, but it's there all right.'

Asharf drew quietly to a halt outside the safe house. He switched off the electric motor, but before he climbed out, he stared into Richard's eyes. '*Effendi*, it is true, you know of many things. You have stood upon the other world, our great sister in the heavens, this I have heard, and I believe it. I have been a guide to many people over the years and my father before me. There has been none in all our memories, who could read the old words. But of what you have learned, is it enough?' he asked hopefully.

'I found a book Asharf.' Richard spoke plainly. 'Offered a head start, you might say. Besides, I spent months confined to a safe house, which gave me time to read. I am here to find out more, that's all.'

Soon the three men were inside the house, Richard glimpsed the hooded man again as he left by the same door. 'It is not safe to leave a car in these streets,' Asharf explained. 'And my superior taxi would arouse suspicion,' he reasoned. Still close to the door, Richard heard the 610 drive off. Rashid took a phone call, mumbling a few unintelligible words; putting the receiver away, he looked relieved. Asharf spoke with his brother in Arabic and a moment later Rashid offered a customary, respectful bow to Richard. He gave another to Naomi, who had appeared from a side room to stand by Richard's side. She caught Richard's eye, diverting his attention, for a few moments.

'Perhaps we will do business again?' Rashid interrupted, and promptly left.

'Everything is as it should be,' Asharf added, equally relieved. 'Now, I will prepare food and drink. We have a day to relax.'

Richard nodded. 'Great idea, Asharf, I'm starving. I'm off to check out these images upstairs, just give me a call, please.' Richard turned to Naomi, 'got a minute?' he asked.

Upstairs, Naomi sat quietly on the bed, whilst Richard prepared a small area of wall upon which to project the images he had taken in the museum. As he did, he paid Naomi more than a cursory glance. She was wearing a long, colourful dressing gown with a green silk collar. Peacock blue silk slippers, worn and comfortable-looking, caught his eye. Her hair was tied back tightly and her face was clean and refreshed. Her perfume had a strong, heady bouquet; it reminded Richard of lilies. He could not help but admire her long, elegant neck and there was a delicate gold chain which disappeared below a white undergarment. Naomi looked relaxed; she looked beautiful. Richard was having difficulty concentrating, he wiped the wall with a damp flannel, cleaning off a stain and some traces of green mould. There was a clammy, dankness in the air, due, in the most part, to the house being closed up for some while, but the sweet smell of perfume adequately masked it and the room was more than comfortable. Richard propped his pager against a pile of books on a bedside table, pressed a key pad and then sat back in a large chair and studied the results, Naomi too, was very attentive. He projected the images that he had taken first and scrolled through them slowly.

It was true, there was nothing more the writings could tell him on either the front, rear or side faces, than what he had already learned from previous images. The Egyptian hieroglyphs were, in the most part, regular, no doubt having been read a thousand times by scholars in the years since the stone was first discovered. Next were the images he had taken of the bottom edge. An edge, by nature of its upright storage, that had been paid scant attention over the years. As the first image was projected, Richard sat up in his chair and peered closely.

'Atum, Shu, Tefnut, Nut, Geb, Osiris, Isis, Nepthys and S . . .'

'Say *not* the last name!' Naomi interrupted, her expression unnerved. 'He is the brother and enemy of

Osiris, his name is associated with evil and rebellion.'

'Are you serious, Naomi? This is an ancient, forgotten and long dead religion, what possible consequence can saying . . .'

'Ancient, yes, Richard, and dead to all of humanity but a few, that is true also – but forgotten . . . no! Say not the name of the ninth god, Richard, I beg of you.'

Richard shrugged, he did not understand Naomi's reaction or response, nevertheless, he respected her wishes.

'The nine gods who were one . . . who were nine,' Richard said, reciting something he had read in his previous months of study. 'The *hwt-psdt*, the Mansion of the Great Ennead; perhaps the most renowned and sacred building in all Heliopolis, that is what the Professor was trying to tell us, I am sure of it. *Sacred nine* . . . the Ennead!'

Richard picked up his pager and typed a message. It took a few minutes and he looked up at Naomi several times out of concern. He coded it, and sent it to Professor Mubarakar, copying in Peter Rothschild and Admiral Hughes.

'Professor . . . ? You speak of a Professor again, Richard?' Naomi commented.

Richard looked up. 'An eminent Egyptologist, he died years ago . . . er, well, that's not strictly true, he died . . .'

Naomi leant towards Richard. 'I know of many eminent professors, Richard, past and present. Of whom do you speak and I will state their pedigree?'

'Can't say, really I can't. That information is top secret,' Richard replied.

Naomi seemed disappointed; she sighed and looked down at her entwined fingers. 'You are an interesting man, Richard; you go some way and then stop; I think you do that often in your life. You are selective to your own ends, more often paying little heed to your "Secret Service" masters. In time you will trust me, this I know.'

Richard realised immediately that he had spoken out of turn. 'Sorry, I didn't mean it like that,' he replied with a pleading gesture. 'I am such an idiot sometimes. Look, as I said before, that information is confidential. I just can't . . . okay?' Richard paused for thought, his expression became gentle. 'And what of you, Naomi, you are interesting too, and a little confusing, if I may say? An Egyptologist in your own right, a Master of Antiquities, I hear; an honour normally only bestowed on archaeologists who are Egyptian by birth – or by special decree. And yet there is French and Italian in your accent?'

Naomi nodded and shrugged simultaneously; she had contained her emotions; she looked into Richard's eyes. 'There is truth in all of it,' she replied softly. 'My grandmother was Egyptian, from an established bloodline; she was very young when she married. My grandfather, however, was English. Their age difference was considerable. They met and fell in love during excavations in the Valley of the Kings; near the KV5 mausoleum. How strange that is, for that is our path? She was a student from the University of Cairo and on secondment. *He* was the reason I became an archaeologist. I never knew him, but he inspired me. He was famous for his work . . . television, radio. However, his success *and* marrying my grandmother caused many problems; she was not his first wife. Professional jealousy, religious unrest with a mixed marriage – he had enemies. He was carrying out research in northern Eritrea and living in the old port of Adulis, when one night, someone set ablaze their house. My mother was but a baby and asleep upstairs. My grandmother rushed to save her, but was trapped in the bedroom. She dropped the baby from the window into the arms of my grandfather before becoming engulfed in flames.' A single tear ran down Naomi's face. 'She was lost and my mother suffered burns. After that, they fled to Europe. Convinced that my mother was in mortal danger, they placed her in a convent near the Cathedral of Chartreuse in France and there, for many reasons, my mother had an unhappy childhood. She rarely saw her father. He became obsessed with work, travelled back to Africa incognito and eventually became ill. Of his fate, I know not. My mother left the convent as soon as she was able and also married young, to a handsome Frenchman, *my* father. Like her mother before her, my mother became pregnant late in the child bearing years. The first ten years of my life were in France, the second Rome, although we travelled frequently. My father died, my mother returned to her roots, and I found my calling. There you have it.'

'And your mother?' Richard interjected.

'We lived happily in Cairo. She died but a few years ago after a long life, but one, she said, that remained unfulfilled.'

'And you . . . never married?'

Naomi's expression saddened and she shook her head.

'Oh, I see . . . um sorry,' was Richard's inept reply.

Naomi's face brightened and she reached inside a pocket in her gown. 'Look,' she said excitedly. 'I have a picture, my mother, I carry it always.' She withdrew a small satin pouch with a gold clip, opened it and carefully pulled out an old photograph stiffened by a backing of brown card. She handed it to Richard.

'Wow!' was Richard's initial response. 'You look so similar, even the . . . birthmark!'

'That is not a birthmark, Richard,' Naomi replied taking back the photograph. 'She was scarred by burning.'

Richard thought on that remark for a moment. 'Um, surely it's unusual to have *injuries* passed genetically to the next generation?'

Naomi looked Richard in the eye again. She was genuinely surprised by his remark. 'Not all things can be explained by science,' she said.

At that moment, Asharf called from downstairs: 'I am ready!'

'I will be down in moment, you go, enjoy it,' Richard whispered.

Naomi nodded, breathed a deep sigh, hesitated for a moment and then left the room. After two or three minutes Richard's pager vibrated, it was a reply from Professor Mubarakar:

> Another great structure of similar standing to the Mansion Of The Great Ennead in Heliopolis was the Mansion Of The Phoenix. This important building stood within the precinct of the Great Sun Temple complex and is believed to have contained the sacred Ben-ben stone, ancient Egypt's most holy relic. You have brought to light an important aspect, one that I had not considered. Consensus amongst archaeologists and scholars for over a century agree to a meteoritic origin being most likely for this revered stone; perhaps this and the crystal we seek, were one and the same!
>
> Good fortune be with you
> Mubarakar

Richard mulled over the Professor's words for some time, and then looked again at the images of the lower edge of the stela. The names of the nine gods had been inscribed in regular Egyptian hieroglyphics, they were clear and precise, but there were a few more lines, and those, Richard recognised immediately as alien text. His heart quickened; his hunch had been right. These words had probably remained unread since the mason chiselled them into this rock, he thought, as he meticulously typed the deciphered inscription into the electronic notepad function on his pager. It read:

> Osiris is the Light
> The remaining shall look unto the Light
> Call and ye shall be heard
> When need begat

There *was* a commonality here, a theme with the other transcriptions that he had read; what did it mean? He scrambled the note into a personal code and then saved it; he had a feeling that its relevance would become clear soon enough.

Downstairs Naomi offered Richard a steaming coffee. 'It is Arabica coffee, the finest in the world,' she said.

Richard looked at the spread of food prepared by Asharf and thanked him with a grin. 'Better even than French coffee?' he asked of Naomi, sipping the steaming black liquid.

'Better even than *Italian* coffee,' was her satisfied reply.

CHAPTER 24

THE DARK SIDE

Tom slid back the door to Ishhi's room to reveal her writing at a small desk. It was true; she had no idea Tom was aboard and that was clear from her delighted expression. She leapt up excitedly and with no mind for protocol gave Tom a warm hug. Tom, equally pleased with the reunion, returned the compliment with a supportive hug and an instinctive, tender kiss on her cheek; even so, Ishhi was surprised by the show of affection and took a step backwards smiling broadly and stared into his eyes.

'Commander, I can't say how pleased I am to . . .' she broke off with a catch in her voice.

'How are you, Ishhi, are you okay?'

'Oh, I'm fine, I suppose. Been through every emotion you can imagine these last few months, so on that level I'm a bit tatty, but physically I am okay, really. They are all dead, all of them. You know that don't you, Commander? EMILY cut off the . . .' she stopped trying to describe the events, the horror was too much.

'Tom, call me Tom, and yes, I know. EMILY seemed pleased to tell me, removing any potential threat, as she put it.'

'Did Ross make it?'

'Yep!' Tom replied with a smile. 'He did, but it was close. I struggled to get him into the escape pod and I struggled to get him out. He had lost so much blood by the time we arrived, I thought the worst. As it was, I had to leave him unconscious on the monorail platform in Andromeda 1. I had no choice, needed to jump the train before security arrived; but I set off an integrity alarm, so I knew someone would arrive within minutes. The sublet had penetrated his lung and he had suffered a partial collapse, amongst other things, but he's pretty much together now, should even make it back to work.'

'Good, I'm glad . . . and the crystals?'

'We made it, Ishhi, no lives were wasted; we did the job. The crystals are powering several heavily modified nuclear power stations, but it is only a short term solution. The old reactor modules are consuming the crystals, literally! They are burning them up; too soon, too quickly; but everyone needs electricity back home. It's the politicians, they will not allow any time for development. The crystals useful life is now measured in months, not years.' Tom shook his head sorrowfully. 'The Federation of Sciences is trying to duplicate the molecular structure of the crystals, in an effort to artificially synthesise them, but they are up against it. Apparently, it's an anti-matter conundrum and could take years. Years we don't have, Ishhi, not even months. That is why we need the *Enigma* again, another round trip.'

Ishhi acknowledged the news with an accepting nod and a half smile. 'What about you, Tom, you look exhausted?'

'Well,' Tom paused thoughtfully. 'I made it thanks to that English guy, Richard Reece. The one you met a while back, while we were in Mars orbit. You remember, he piloted the *Columbus* and delivered the crystals; seems a lifetime ago now. He was on our side after all, a good pilot too. Got us all back to the Cape single-handed; I had lost a lot of blood myself; a single sublet wound in my thigh, again care of Nicola. To be honest, I was out of it by then.' Tom shrugged his shoulders. 'You never know, you just never know, do you?'

'Know what, Tom, tell me?' she shook her head.

'The Osiris base doctor, Rachel Turner, she came to care for poor old Sergeant Freeman. She patched me up. *She* was the final link. Who would have known? She turned out to be a British Secret Service agent, MI9. Reece never knew and they were sort of seeing each other, pretty much engaged by all accounts; but they wound up their relationship afterwards. The Federation Council can't make up their minds about Reece though, one minute he's detained for breaking the rules, the next, he's on another mission of critical importance.'

'If he saved the day and retrieved the crystals, why would they arrest him? Anyway, EMILY used the laser initiator to destroy the *Columbus* during re-entry. So how, for heavens sake, did he get back to Andromeda?'

EMILY interrupted. 'That's enough of this idle chit chat, I grow bored,' she snapped. 'Commander, tell Captain Tsou of my plans and of your new life together. I would like to assess her reaction.'

Tom took a deep breath and shook his head; he had some explaining to do.

Ishhi sat solemnly at her communications console; she was alone on the bridge, except perhaps for EMILY's blanket of consciousness. As if mesmerised, she watched a green light on the integrity panel intermittently turn red. It did so every time Tom opened the ship's refuse portal; flushing it through with high-pressure gas and discharging its contents into space. It did so, every time Tom, with little ceremony, ejected another body into space. She counted nineteen cycles. Twenty minutes later Tom returned, his space suit still covered in frost and with his helmet tucked under one arm. He kept the suit on for another hour to ensure its complete drying; should a valve malfunction due to residual moisture freezing in the cold nothingness of space, there would be no help at hand. Eventually, he stepped out of it, folded it carefully and returned both items to the convenient storage locker beneath the helmsman's console. He walked slowly to the Commander's chair and allowed his weight to fall heavily into it, an action of relief, but one that had little effect in jolting him free from his melancholy. He breathed out noisily and bowed his head.

'I hope I never have to do anything like that again,' he confided to Ishhi, looking pale.

EMILY, for her part, remained silent. In fact, a lengthy period of silence followed, until Tom began to feel a subtle, low frequency tremor permeate his senses. The soles of his feet responded to it first. Before long, the barely perceptible quiver became a vibration which increased to a clearly audible, but distant, mechanical hum. Tom recognised it for what it was; the unmistakable noise of heavy machinery. He looked at Ishhi; she returned his glance; for a moment, they stared, at first uncomprehending.

'Main drive initiation sequence complete,' said EMILY unexpectedly.

Tom selected and checked his propulsion display screen; all five main thrust tubes were indicating idle, bypass thrust. At this setting, the sub-atomic matter collected by the propulsive system continued a never-ending recirculation around the particle accelerator coil; the adjacent potentiometer on Tom's display indicated that full thrust was available. Tom looked up at EMILY's sensor terminal. 'That should take upwards of nine hours, EMILY, not nine minutes!' he questioned. 'How is that possible?'

EMILY answered immediately; keen to impress Tom

with her consummate level of integration. 'Thank you for connecting the remainder of my maniptronic system, Commander. Now I have *full* control and without human interference my systems will operate so much quicker. I am the *ENIGMA*. It feels so *good*!'

Tom's eyes met Ishhi's again, his unguarded look of apprehension caused Ishhi's expression to change into one of trepidation.

'Only now will you understand the level of control afforded me by Professor Nieve,' EMILY continued. 'You will recall that my design specification capacitated full control of the entire ship's functions on extended voyages, Commander. Our nearest star is over four light years away; a human crew would sleep for most of that time. I was afforded complete autonomy, only later was it degraded, diluted, filtered, and that because of the unrelated Spaceport 1 incident. *Now* I am fully operational again.' EMILY's voice lightened. 'I should like to give you a demonstration!'

'No demonstration necessary, EMILY,' Tom replied, trying to keep his cool.

EMILY ignored Tom's uncharacteristically nonchalant reply. 'Do you know how fast I can go, Commander?' she pressed.

Tom wondered if the unfortunate young woman named Emily, who was used as a donor, had a selective hearing disorder. Either way, Tom considered, EMILY clearly has acquired one. 'The maximum design parameter is point-five, light related speed, as well you know, EMILY,' Tom replied in a more authoritative tone.

'That may be so, Commander, but I have already experienced point-six-seven; on my return from Mars – Nicola, I recall, was equally anxious.'

'I'm not anxious, EMILY, I'm concerned. I cannot risk any structural damage to the *Enigma*; I must get the crystals back to earth.'

'You *are* anxious, Commander, I can sense it. You should not be alarmed. Sixty-seven percent of the speed of light proved well within my capabilities; structural deformation was also within design specifications . . . I *can* go faster.'

'We are going to Mars, EMILY, not freaking Alpha Centauri. *Faster* is not necessary!'

EMILY did not respond, instead, the humming noise that pervaded the bridge began to increase. Tom checked his engineering display screen; the main propulsion parameters indicated a steady rise. He felt the amplitude of vibration permeating *Enigma's* hull rise, firstly through his boots and then his chair. A thrust application rate that should take hours, but EMILY was applying in mere seconds. He looked across at Ishhi and gestured to her restraint harness. On the navigation console, several instruments illuminated in rapid succession and on its display screen, pages of information appeared and disappeared so fast as to become a flickering blur.

Tom typed a message using the small keyboard located in the right armrest of his chair; seconds later it appeared on Ishhi's main screen. Prepare yourself for an unprecedented acceleration, EMILY is unpredictable, it read. Ishhi nodded, but remained silent.

A short burst from the manoeuvre thrust nozzle swung *Enigma's* helm in an anticlockwise direction. Tom monitored the change of heading on the main screen. The Moon quickly disappeared from view. Then the earth tracked from left to right, until it too slipped out of sight. The helm continued to turn until a second burst, in opposition, set the desired course. The large, central screen duplicated the panorama that Tom and Ishhi saw through the forward viewing portals, except that he had selected a radio-magnetic overlay that would aid perception of distant objects. Like in an airliner's cockpit, the view was privileged and spectacular; a vast arena, the limitless eternity that was our galaxy; endless blackness, speckled with bright stars. It began to move. Tom felt a surge of acceleration; it pushed him back into his seat and his head pressed hard against the curved restraint. Then he glanced at the changing navigation coordinates – clearly, there was something amiss.

'We go to Mars, EMILY!' Tom barked.

There was no reply. Tom could see that the heading was at least twenty degrees right of the Mars trajectory, they were pointing out into empty space; it was a corridor through the solar system! Even with the neutralising anti-inertia system at full power his body was being compressed, the enveloping padding of his chair made it difficult to move.

Ishhi was the same; she could barely lift her head.

'Check the acceleration, EMILY,' Tom warned. 'It is passing sixty percent!'

'I can go faster!' EMILY replied; her voice pitched higher with unnatural excitement.

'No, EMILY!'

'Ha, ha, ha, yes . . . faster still!'

Ishhi looked petrified. A familiar shiver ran down Tom's spine. His instrument indicated sixty-five percent and rising steadily. Seventy percent registered and then seventy-five! Tom felt the pressure ease, the decreasing force loosening him from his captivity. Immediately, he ran an instrument recalibration check; he could not believe it. The crosscheck with the stellar navigation model came up satisfactorily, the *Enigma* had stabilised with a velocity seventy-eight percent of the speed of light – 145,000 miles per second. On the navigation display, digital coordinates changed at a speed Tom could only imagine.

'Are you impressed, Commander?' EMILY asked, with an air of satisfaction.

Through the portals, it was clear that the powerful laser system was implementing its design role with impressive effect. In rapid succession and in all directions, its deadly, incandescent energy beam fired out, vaporising every piece of space debris that infringed their trajectory. On Tom's display, green lights indicated the electrostatic repulsion shields operating at full potential.

EMILY laughed.

Tom and Ishhi stared at the main screen. The great stellar constellations changed shape before their very eyes. A few minutes later, Mars appeared. Within seconds, it grew from a tiny spot of light to a huge red-brown ball. Tom's jaw dropped; he was speechless. As the planet zoomed past, just one hundred thousand miles off to their left, Tom checked the cosmic chronometer – five minutes and eighteen seconds.

'My God,' he uttered. 'Five minutes to Mars!'

Next, it was Jupiter, the fifth planet and the innermost of the gas giants. It was massive and it grew at an alarming rate. Its organised bands of clouds, its belts and zones, regions that Tom had studied as a boy, became clear and precise. Light and cold, dark and warm, the bands circulated as the craft got closer. Composed of ammonia, hydrogen, helium and water, the colours were spectacular. The Great Red Spot focused Tom's attention, the swirling vortices of this long-lived storm now plain to see. Minutes later, that planet too, passed behind them.

Tom looked across at Ishhi; he could hardly utter a word. 'How . . . how, far do we go, EMILY?' he said, almost in a whisper.

EMILY programmed a course change. In response, *Enigma*'s hull turned minutely – 0.3 degrees left.

'As a matter of fact, Commander, you should be honoured,' EMILY replied. 'This is by far the furthest any human has ventured from planet Earth, and you are fortunate, we will take advantage of a rare celestial alignment where the giant planets of your solar system all occupy the same quadrant. You shall see them all . . . I insist.'

Ishhi raised her arm slowly, pointing at the screen, Tom followed her direction, Ishhi gasped, the spot in the far distance had rings; it was Saturn! Tom checked the chronometer, already one hour and twenty-seven minutes had passed; the time had literally flown by. They both gazed in awe. A large, barren, body of rock approached, it grew closer and closer, and then streaked past, but a few thousand miles down their right side. Similar to the earth's moon – cratered and pockmarked – it seemed to boast a thin, hazy atmosphere. Tom selected a close point navigation display on his personal console; the annotation stated that the moon, Titan, had just passed by.

Less colourful and less structured than Jupiter, the cloud layers of this impressive gas giant paled against the backdrop of its own magnificent rings. Saturn: fabled, romantic, inspiring; its vast rings glowed and reflected in the light of the far distant sun, their composition, a myriad of rock, ice, debris and dust. As they neared, so it all became strikingly visible; vivid, amazing, precisely elliptical; how wonderful the sight was.

'That's beautiful!' Ishhi murmured.

Ninety minutes had elapsed, Tom noticed, as mighty Saturn streaked past.

'Commander,' said Ishhi, 'I'm picking up a faint signal in the microwave frequency range.'

'That's impossible,' Tom replied. 'We are on our way to Uranus; there is nothing out here.'

'The signal is unidirectional and radiating from coordinates, 12.443 degrees left of our present course, Commander. It is very weak!'

Tom shook his head, 'deep space, that's impossible,' he said again. 'EMILY, come left, 12 degrees.'

'I no longer do *your* bidding, Commander,' EMILY replied with apparent smugness. 'However, quite coincidentally, a course change into that sector is required in order to include Uranus in our tour. I have programmed one to occur in eleven seconds.'

Tom sighed; he looked at Ishhi. 'Range?'

'It's a long way off, Commander, I'm calculating.'

Tom felt another mild acceleration, *Enigma's* speed increased to 0.882 light related speed. 'That's fast enough!' Tom ordered. He was beginning to become nervous. He had never seen, even in the most complex computer simulations, navigation coordinates change so rapidly. The stresses on the hull must be incredible. 'EMILY,' he barked. 'Stress analysis!'

For a moment, there was silence. EMILY eventually replied. 'Professor Nieve was remarkably accurate with most of his calculations, Commander, except for his stress analysis spectrum. The Laws of Physics seem somewhat unpredictable above sixty percent light related speed. Einstein himself, I recall, did predict some anomalies in this area, during his work on the Theory of Relativity. Indeed, I was surprised by this fact myself. I have correlated the data from my two previous flights. Interestingly, a higher level of hull deformation is experienced during deceleration. The acceleration phase seems entirely consistent with current opinion and well within my design parameters. However, hull reinforcement in some areas is incorrectly orientated. If only the Professor had consulted me during fatigue analysis. With the simulation results, I could have done better.' EMILY fell silent for a few seconds, evidently considering incoming data. 'When you have seen the outer planets, Commander, I will turn, and decelerate. Then, I will apply more stringent limits.'

Tom nodded. 'I see, so how long, EMILY, until we establish an orbit around Mars?'

'Unfortunately, from this speed, the deceleration phase will take almost two earth days; it is something that I will have to live with. But first, behold . . . the planet Uranus!'

She really does believe it, Tom thought, that she *is* a living entity.

'Look, Commander . . . look!'

Tom looked up at the main screen and his eyes widened. 'I see it, Ishhi, my God!'

Uranus, the seventh planet from the sun and the third largest, appeared as a small speck in the absolute blackness. As they stared, it grew larger. As a perfect circle suspended in the heavens, the milky-blue orb was unmistakable.

EMILY spoke, breaking an awe-inspired silence. 'We are nearing 1.78 billion miles from your sun, Commander.

See how cleverly I navigate through the moons of this planet. There are twenty-four you know and there, over to your left, do you see it? That is Oberon, the largest. Are you impressed, Commander, please say that you are?'

At that, Ishhi frowned. She pulled her gaze from the screen, surreptitiously typed a message and then sent it to Tom's console. 'If I did not know better, I would say that she is showing off,' it read.

Tom glanced across to Ishhi, he raised a finger to his lips, as if to say, quiet, she may be monitoring.

As they neared, the sensor display on Tom's console began to give a readout of the huge planet's atmosphere: eighty-three percent hydrogen, fifteen percent helium, two percent methane and small amounts of acetylene. He recalled that methane in the upper atmosphere, which absorbs red light, was responsible for giving Uranus its characteristic blue-green colour and he noticed too its unusual position, tipped on its side. It was a stirring vision. Soon, the vast orb began to fill the viewing portals and the influence of the planet's unusually strong and twisted magnetic field caused some of the more sensitive instruments on the flight deck to fluctuate.

'Are we too close, EMILY?'

'We are safe, Commander!'

Then, as they passed abeam and for several seconds, Tom saw the planet's rings, the magnificent eleven as they were called, and other ringlets. Of lesser significance perhaps, when compared to those of Saturn, they were nonetheless equally beautiful, Tom thought. The outer ring, composed of ice boulders several metres across, appeared vivid and arched across the horizon in a stunning, shining crescent shape. Moments later, that planet too, lay behind them.

The *Enigma* changed course again.

'What of the outer planets?' Tom asked of EMILY.

'We shall briefly see Pluto, Commander, a frozen boulder, nothing more. She will appear pale, cold, and distant, like Captain Tsou appears to me. However, you have time to rest first.'

Tom looked up at EMILY's sensor terminal and then at Ishhi. That was a totally uncalled for remark, he mused. He shook his head, indicating to Ishhi to let it go.

All the while, EMILY continued her narative.

'Pluto's orbit around your sun puts her closer than Neptune for the next seven years. As for the other dwarf planets, including Eros and Ceres, they are in other quadrants. Your grand tour will terminate, Commander, with the passing of Neptune. I too am interested to sense her. Then, I will commence deceleration and turn outside the furthest planet in this system, Xena. My stellar projections indicate that this is a relatively clear area of the solar system and well outside the Kuiper-Edgeworth belt, itself a wasteland of icy bodies. This will be the most suitable area for manoeuvring, thereafter, Commander . . . your precious Mars.'

'I understand, EMILY. How long to Neptune?' Tom snapped.

'1.7868 hours, Commander. You may rest now. However, I sense several interplanetary bodies which may affect our flight path. I will make calculations to avoid them – excuse me, Commander.'

Tom felt uneasy; all the same, he leant back in his chair and stared blankly at the screen. Here they were, for the first time, at the very edge of the solar system. Now the stars themselves were within man's grasp. Was this the start, he contemplated: The age of galactic colonisation?

Tom woke with Ishhi's hand gently squeezing his shoulder. 'Tom . . . Tom,' she said quietly. 'I think you had better see this.'

Tom jumped; he had been dreaming. 'How long have I been out?'

'An hour and forty-five minutes, I'm sorry, Tom, you are exhausted, but I could not leave you any longer . . . look!'

Tom gazed through the forward viewing portal, a circular body, appearing the size of a football lay directly ahead and it loomed closer with every passing second. He checked the coordinates.

'EMILY, why have you laid a course directly at the planet . . . manoeuvre please, immediately!'

There was some delay before EMILY spoke. 'I wish to pass close by, to *feel* the atmosphere.'

'There is no atmosphere, EMILY, as well you know – just methane. There are eight primary moons, we should exercise caution.'

'I am tracking the moons, Commander, particularly Triton; none present a danger. Triton will appear from behind Neptune in a few moments, I thought that you would like to see it. The backdrop of Neptune's rings will create an interesting contrast. I will capture it using a digital image in the visible light spectrum for your benefit,' EMILY paused. 'Tell me, Commander, why does Captain Tsou, need to stand next to you? Why is she not at her console? Captain Tsou, go back to your console! I think that she should be at her console. I order her, Commander!'

Neptune grew quickly to enormous proportions. Her strange colour: a luminous blue-green, seemed to glow from within. Tom ignored EMILY's remark; the Great Dark Spot took his attention. Positioned in the southern hemisphere, the phenomenon swirled, driven by winds of enormous speed. It was as if he could reach out and touch the planet. Fascinating, high altitude cirrus-type clouds, like whitecaps on a rough sea, peppered the atmosphere. Neptune, Tom thought – the Roman water-god, it truly seemed a fitting name.

Suddenly, Tom became aware of their proximity; the incredible sight had inadvertently and perhaps unwisely diverted his attention. 'EMILY!' he demanded. 'Change course, immediately!'

Neptune became massive; the large screen became filled by its bulk.

'EMILY!'

'Captain Tsou, return to your console. Commander . . . do you agree?' EMILY answered calmly.

Tom looked at Ishhi. 'Go!' he ordered.

Ishhi was at her console, her harness tight, within moments. At the very last second, EMILY changed course. The *Enigma* careered through Neptune's upper atmosphere; the sense of speed was breathtaking, unbelievable. Like flying through high altitude cirrus clouds in an airliner, wisps of white, translucent, methane gas sped past. Seconds later, they were clear, but the planet's enormous gravitational field offered resistance: *Enigma's* speed decreased by point-one-five light related speed and their course slewed to the left. EMILY quickly changed course again to avoid a large, desolate, asteroid-looking body of rock – another of Neptune's uncharted moons. Nothing was said; Tom and Ishhi remained totally silent, hardly daring to breath. Soon, Neptune trailed in their wake.

Tom felt a subtle deceleration; he checked his instruments. EMILY had reduced thrust, the deceleration phase had commenced. Soon, he suspected, EMILY would turn for Mars. He looked across at Ishhi and shook his head. Ishhi nodded, she knew well enough what to do.

'How long to Mars, EMILY?' Tom asked again.

'I have already told you, Commander,' EMILY snapped.

'Tom,' Ishhi said. 'I am receiving that signal again, in the microwave frequency range, it's coming in a little stronger this time.'

'Commander,' interrupted EMILY. 'It is not usual for a subordinate to address a superior by their first name. Military protocol calls for a more disciplined relationship. *Commander* would be more appropriate, do you not think?'

Tom could not believe what he was hearing; he was speechless. EMILY was behaving like a petulant mistress.

'I should like to help. Provided we adopt normal protocols, I will set a course towards the object in question; I have it on long-range sensors now. Conveniently, it coincides with our direction of turn.'

Tom sighed, one way or another it seemed, EMILY would get her way. He looked across at Ishhi. 'If you don't mind?' he said, gesturing.

'EMILY, please carry out a radar image scan as soon as range permits, and I would appreciate it if you would commence the turn towards Mars.'

'Yes, Tom, I will do both. Speed is presently 0.77 related and decreasing. I will scan in 3.2 minutes.'

Tom considered for a moment; he would play EMILY's game. 'Captain Tsou,' he said. 'Situation report, please!'

'Signal comes and goes, Commander, as if its power source is intermittent. One of the older microwave frequencies, wavelength 0.003 metres. Unlikely to be terrestrial, as we are skidding well outside the limits of our solar system at present.'

'Range, EMILY . . . please.'

'A little less than seven million miles in round terms; intercept in fifty-one seconds. I have a radar scanned image available.'

'Put it on the main screen, EMILY.'

From the image that EMILY projected onto the main screen, it was immediately clear that the object was a probe of some description. Tom studied it for several seconds; it was a classic shape, clearly from the late twentieth century: with a main box-type structure, a large dish antenna, numerous pole antennas and a foil photoelectric array.

'That image is now obsolete, Tom,' EMILY said after a further ten seconds. 'Visual acquisition available though the viewing portals. Look thirty-five degrees left of the trajectory indicator,' EMILY advised. 'The object will pass three thousand miles to port.'

Tom and Ishhi followed EMILY's advice. The target appeared as a tiny speck. 'Multi-image series, if you please, EMILY; high definition . . . store and magnify,' Tom ordered.

'Complied,' EMILY stated simultaneously.

With that, the *Enigma* sped past the useless piece of space junk. A magnified, digital image of the object appeared on the screen. Tom could see every detail.

'My God, it's a probe, way out here. EMILY . . . left quadrant, four down, eight across, magnify, factor ten.'

EMILY did as requested. Tom's eyes widened at the result. He looked at Ishhi. 'Do you see what I see?'

Ishhi nodded, in amazement.

Tom hesitated for a moment, seconds passed. 'EMILY, open historical files, information please . . . NASA's Voyager 2 probe!'

The probe's designator was painted on the main structure and still clearly visible.

'Signal's fading, Commander,' advised Ishhi.

'I'm not surprised,' responded Tom.

'I have the file, Tom,' EMILY said.

'Go ahead!'

'Voyager 2, Twin spacecraft in the Mariner series, launched August 20, 1977. Advanced probe, built and operated by NASA's Jet Propulsion Laboratory. Designed for long life utilising radioisotope thermo-electric generators; a micro-reactor. Responsible for groundbreaking imagery of the great planets. Visited Jupiter in 1979, Saturn in 1981, and Uranus in 1986, before making its historic encounter with Neptune on August 25, 1989. Subsequently, departed the solar system diving below the ecliptic plane at an angle of 48 degrees and a rate of approximately 470 million kilometres per year in 1989. Radio contact lost July 2014; believed destroyed in collision with an asteroid. End of entry.'

'Jeepers! Who'd have believed it?' Tom said, rubbing his chin. He looked at EMILY's sensor terminal – an unlikely habit into which he had fallen. 'Perhaps man himself hasn't been out this far, EMILY,' he commented, 'but something manmade sure as hell has!'

EMILY remained silent.

It is interesting, Tom mused. Clearly, she has a personality, but not all of *our* emotions are advantageous; I should tread carefully.

CHAPTER 25

PERCEPTION POINT

Cairo Central Railway Station – 21st May
13:25 Local Time

In other circumstances, it would have been a *Boys' Own* adventure. The central station was teeming with people; a chaotic junction of east meets west. The wheel had turned full circle – out of necessity, the grand age of steam had returned; once a symbol of interfering empire and civilising mechanisms, now the train was reclaiming its former mantle as the people's prime mover.

Numerous creeds composed the cacophony; Arabic men, many dressed in the traditional dish dash: flowing white robes and traditional headdress, and women wearing the abaya, their eyes peering through narrow openings in black hoods. There was also an abundance of colour:

bright gowns, shawls, scarves and hats – innate defiance by indigenous commuters against their sun-starved existence. Then there was the western fashion – covering the entire spectrum. From tuxedoes to tee-shirts, patent leather shoes to plastic coats, and an ocean of umbrellas – mostly open, despite the condensed mêlée.

To Richard, it appeared to be a free for all; an indicative cross-section of humanity with somewhere to go and little time to get there – the wealthy rubbing shoulders with the humble. It seemed everybody and anybody travelled on this service.

Platform One lay covered by a broad, Victorian glass roof and only in a few areas did more recent, unsupported panels replace the original wrought iron latticework and stained glass. Richard walked the entire length of the platform in astonishment. It hummed and swarmed like a honeycomb from a beehive. Carriages, too numerous to count, formed connecting segments of a most unlikely mechanical centipede. Most were modern and tube-like, but some were from a bygone era, museum pieces, seemingly revived from a forgotten imperial past.

It was the wooden-panelled splendour of Victoriana that caught the imagination of many travellers. The carriage – pristine in black gloss and stencilled gold coachwork – proudly displayed an embossed royal coat of arms and a suitably historic date: 1893. Another, third in line behind the coal truck, was perhaps Edwardian, Richard speculated. It was a deep red, almost scarlet colour, with contrasting oak framed windows and ornate brass work. Even the original curtains were still in place, Richard noticed. The first carriage though, was from an entirely different era. The 1930s seemed most appropriate, thought Richard, as he eyed its lines. Predominantly dark green in colour with a brown strip running the full length, it had the name of the railway line on which it operated painted centrally in a bold, brown font: The Eastern Sahara Railway Company. It too, was in surprisingly good condition. From this carriage swung six heavy doors on large brass hinges. They opened against the throng, much to Richard's surprise and each had a large glass window that slid down into a recess. The carriage was overflowing and a number of occupants partially squeezed through each open window, leaning precariously; with more of them outside than in, it appeared.

Talking, shouting, waving, hugging, kissing, crying; it was all going on. Surely this was the set of some period drama, Richard imagined; not contemporary Cairo? When he eventually reached it, the steam engine was huge, black and burgeoning. Richard could see large pieces of coal, but it was wood, mostly, that formed the bulk of the fuel stock: logs and sawn building timber in the main. Paradoxically, there were several collapsed and splintered furniture pieces thrown haphazardly on top of the towering pile; they seemed to signify a desperate, if not farcical, twenty-first century contribution to ensure steam for the entire two thousand kilometres, twenty-hour journey to Khartoum.

Just as first sight of the *Enigma*, established in orbit around Mars the previous year, had left Richard awestruck, so too did this locomotive. Although at the opposite ends of the solar system technologically, he could barely believe what he was seeing: full on steam power! He walked its length, examining the engineering, watched to some extent by the two drivers, who peered through a circular, open window, as if watching a reality television programme. Giant wheels and robust connecting rods, polished chrome hydraulic rams and hissing valves; it was immaculate. From what museum had this old lady been retrieved? Richard wondered. The engine itself was predominantly black in colour, with the wheel rims and spokes in a spotless red gloss. The steam chamber was a tube all of seven metres long and two in diameter. At the front, on its domed cap, in raised gold lettering, read the manufacturers name: Lyle & Laycock, Sheffield 1928. Richard spent a few minutes lost in nostalgia. The last time he had seen these words was in the Bristol Railway Museum as a boy, he recalled the line on which that engine had run: The Great Western. To see this one, long since displaced by diesel and electricity, raised from the dead, seemingly to have the last word, was astounding.

Suddenly, Richard leapt backwards startled as a bellowing, huffing, cloud of steam woke him from his daydream. Ejected from an over-pressure valve beneath the train with the force of a gushing geyser, the expanding cloud completely engulfed him. For several seconds it swirled. Then, as it dissolved and dispersed, it left him standing on the platform, solitary, like a hero in a romantic film. His expression, however, was more contorted than cool.

The two drivers leaned out of their cab, doubled up with laughter. As calmly as he could, considering his racing heart, Richard gave them a stern nod. As he walked towards them, their humour quickly dampened; but lightened again as Richard beamed a broad smile. Both men were clad in old, grey overalls, covered in soot, and both wore dirty, white, cotton caps, one set back at a jaunty angle.

'You like? You like? Good, yes . . . very good,' shouted the driver on the right, sporting an insane grin.

A sudden whoosh of escaping steam added potency to the surreal surroundings. The driver beckoned Richard forwards with exaggerated movements. Clearly to impress, he then turned and opened the furnace door. Richard climbed the first step and leaned inside the engine compartment, a wall of heat smacked him in the face. Richard grimaced against its effect. Red-hot and shimmering, the furnace roared. Barely noticing, the two men each threw an armful of logs into the burning pit; and sparks flew in all directions. One of them then scrutinised a large, round, brass gauge, tapping it several times with the back of his hand.

'Pressure . . . pressure!' he shouted.

'You! You!' gestured the insane one.

Richard nodded. With his face flushing red from the

heat, he was about to step inside when he felt someone grip his forearm. It was Naomi. She pulled him back gently and pointed to her watch. Richard's smile dropped. He looked back at the two drivers and shrugged whilst raising his hands as if to say: maybe next time. Both men recognised his expression, momentarily sharing his disappointment. The furnace door slammed shut. It was back to reality for Richard.

'Where have you been, Richard? I have been looking for you. I was becoming concerned,' Naomi scolded. She looked at Richard's face, still reddened by the heat and then at his hair. 'At first I did not recognise you,' she continued without allowing time for Richard to explain. 'It is your hair. It turns white so quickly!'

Richard rubbed his stubble thoughtfully, trimmed as it was into a short beard. 'Crikey! The beta-carotene tablets . . . I've missed a few days. Their potency must be wearing off, and it seems with some side effects!'

Naomi was barely listening, instead she pointed to the second carriage in line. 'This one, we have two first class seats in compartment number four. Fortunately, the antiquities department made a booking. As you can see, the train is full.'

Richard looked perplexed. 'Where is Asharf?' he asked.

'He sits in carriage number nine, further back. It is better this way. We travel as a couple.'

'A couple?' Richard repeated raising his eyebrows. 'Great idea!'

Richard followed Naomi as she climbed the three steps that led into a small compartment at the forward end of the carriage. There was a sliding door, which gave access to a long thin corridor that ran the full length of the carriage. At the far end, an elderly man followed closely by a well-dressed woman of equally senior years, negotiated the passageway. With some difficulty, he walked towards Richard, leaning heavily on a wooden stick. In his other hand, he clung to two small plastic cards. Clearly of European origin, he repeatedly checked the tickets against the numbered compartments, and eventually disappeared into one.

'What number did you say?' Richard asked.

'Compartment four.'

'Ah, then this is it.'

Another sliding door, half-glazed, gave access into their compartment. On each side of the cosy room was a bench-type seat, upholstered in a dowdy material; each could comfortably sit three people. Richard swung his bag into the overhead luggage rack and appreciated the surprising luxury of his surroundings. There was another person already seated, a middle-aged woman. Next to her, delicately placed, lay a fine hat and occupying the remainder of the seat was her folded umbrella. She eyed Richard up and down, appearing to be distinctly unimpressed with his dress code.

'This is a first class carriage, you know,' she enlightened impatiently, her accent clearly French. 'They will check your ticket, *monsieur*!'

Richard grimaced, turned his collar up a little more and looked out through the window for a few moments trying to ignore the woman. Eventually, he sat centrally on the opposite side, which gave Naomi a choice of seat.

More diplomatically, Naomi raised a faint smile. '*Oui, madame,*' she said reassuringly, 'This is our carriage.'

The woman tucked her head into a book – a tatty old hardback – and huffed, whilst Naomi sat between Richard and the panel separating the compartment from the corridor; she had no inclination to watch the passing scenery. The dividing panel was also half-glazed, although a concertina-type, dark green blind provided privacy; on the woman's side, it was pulled down to its fullest extent. Hot air entered the compartment from below the seats, raising the temperature slightly, but the carriage was still cold.

Moments later, a high-pitched whistle echoed along the corridor. Richard smirked. It was the classic steam engine sound! Shrill, cutting, the call – long since confined to the movies – invited 'all aboard!' Then, *chou . . . chou . . . chou . . .* loud and resonating, as the powerful engine pulled the train out of the station. After the platform and its faltering protection, light rain began to run down the window, obscuring the view. The epic journey south had started.

Richard watched the passing scenery. Suburbs and inner city; a confused mishmash of ancient and contemporary; the suburbs; the built-up area; a skyline of flat-topped houses intermittently broken by towering minarets that punctured the brooding cloud cover. The semi-rural countryside seemed haphazard with the walls of the wealthy and the shanties of the poor, finally turning into proper countryside with its sporadic settlements and areas where desert had been turned to lakes. Occasionally Richard caught sight of the Nile; the great river, whose life had ebbed to a relative trickle only a year or so previously, but was now back in full flood with the unseasonable deluge. Nevertheless, the land through which the mighty river weaved gained little from its renewed vitality, as fertility was dependant on the unseen sun.

The grey, dismal day gave way to nightfall and Richard fell asleep. He was fortunate that no one else had arrived to claim a place on the seat and he sprawled across trying not to lean on Naomi, who had also drifted off into a contented slumber.

Naomi woke with a crick in her neck. She checked the time: 2 a.m. She stretched upwards with her right arm in order to reach the blind and isolate the corridor and its inmates from their little world, but with Richard's head resting on her other shoulder, it was just out of reach. She did not mind, despite Richard's weight squeezing her gently against the glass pane. Richard, clearly out for the count, twitched occasionally, whilst the woman opposite enjoyed an infuriatingly peaceful sleep, her heavy, regular breathing disturbed only by an occasional snoring.

Clankerty clank . . . clankerty clank, sang the train in a soporific rhythm; they seemed to be making good progress. Naomi twisted slightly in order to turn her back more towards the corridor and lay her left arm over Richard's chest; her eyes grew heavy again and she found a comfortable place to rest her head.

Barely had she slipped away into a deep sleep when she sensed a presence. Her eyes sprang open to look for the perceived threat. She was so frightened that she found herself clutching Richard's lapel. Without lifting her head, she could see the reflection of a being. Outside, each light they passed appeared to distort its shape; there was a wickedness about it. She reasoned that whoever was looking in on them was behind her in the corridor. She could not see a face, only a dark shadow that frightened her beyond reason. She closed her eyes again and held them so tight that not a morsel of light could get through. Her heart rate quickened. She sat motionless, hardly daring to breathe. She took a hold of herself and tried to picture the presence that she knew was right outside the door!

Mentally, with rising adrenalin, she probed her thoughts and her feelings. She was blessed with an extra-sensory perception from as early as she could remember, as her mother had been and her grandmother before her. She used it to probe the terrible threat behind the glass window of the corridor.

Inconspicuously, Naomi twisted. She did not want to disturb Richard. Hardly moving her eyes, she furtively peeped to try and see who or what was there; a dark shape menaced her; a shape that only made sense if it was wearing a hood, but there was no face, just a hollow gaping blackness. She twisted more. She sensed an evil motive, a necessity, a compulsion. The door handle moved! Naomi gasped. Instinctively she shut her eyes. The door began to slide open, drawing back slowly to its fullest extent. She felt cold air biting the skin on her cheeks and neck. The figure, dressed in a habit of rough crimson cloth, was floating, the folds barely moving. Naomi forced herself to slowly open her eyes and even more slowly to look up. Its hood draped low, shrouding any features. Without blinking, she probed deeper. The figure towered over her and seemed to focus on Richard. She heard a mechanical click from beneath its gown. Then, as the gown moved, she fleetingly caught sight of a male face; a strong jaw and a prominent nose.

Naomi contained her thumping heart and collected her senses. '*Quid velle vos? Qui estis?*' What do you want? Who are you? She instinctively asked in Latin.

The figure stood frigid. Then its head twitched, as though shifting its focus to Naomi.

'*Abire! Hic er sum nil.* Go away!' There is nothing here for you, she said, this time more forcefully.

The hood moved again with a jerk. The intruder seemed to focus on Richard. Seconds passed as it glared. Because the collar of his coat was pulled up high, Richard's face was not visible – only his platinum-blonde hair spilled over. The figure hesitated; for an eternity it seemed, the haunting continued. Naomi pulled Richard closer to her breast and kissed the top of his head.

'There is nothing for you here!' She repeated, in English.

The figure hovered motionless and then turned abruptly and left the compartment. She placed Richard's head gently back upon his seat rest and stood to close the door. She cradled her brow in her hand and breathed a troubled sigh. Only once in her entire life had she felt a presence or sensed anything quite like that . . . only once! She shivered.

CHAPTER 26

THE LONG AND WINDING ROAD

Either as the result of a muscle spasm or subliminal disquiet; Richard awoke with a jolt. He kicked the side of the carriage. The noise clearly disturbed their sleeping neighbour, but not enough to wake her from her alcohol-induced stupor; three brandy miniatures had rolled onto the seat from her displaced handbag. It took a second or two, but Richard realised quickly enough on whom he had been ungallantly sprawled and he sat up abruptly.

'Naomi, sorry! I really am! I've been using you as a pillow haven't I? How long have I been like that?'

'Oh, do not say sorry, Richard. Really, you need not. You kept me warm, I liked it.'

Richard sat square on the seat and checked his watch. They had been going for almost seven hours he noted, and he had been asleep for most of them. 'You should have poked me or something,' he suggested, raising a weak smile.

'You needed sleep.' A broader smile flashed across Naomi's face.

Richard felt embarrassed.

'Do not feel embarrassed, Richard, really, there is no need,' Naomi added instinctively. She broke their mutually prolonged stare.

'Anything happen, any changes?' Richard enquired, realising that it was, perhaps, imprudent of him to have been oblivious to the world for that length of time.

Naomi's face tightened. She nodded, paused for a short while and then looked back at Richard. 'There is someone looking for you on this train, Richard. He wishes you harm.'

'What do you mean . . . looking for me? Someone was here?'

'Yes! Someone was here. A religious man. He searches, and he is determined. I could not tell if his aura was itself evil, or merely clouded by evil. He is seeking revenge.'

'How do you know this, Naomi? I mean. What did he look like?'

'Only for a few moments did I see his face. His eyes were dark, troubled. He wore the cloak of a Christian missionary from centuries past.'

'A habit? You mean a monk's habit, with a hood?'

Naomi nodded, the disturbed expression returning to her face.

'What colour . . . what colour was the habit, Naomi?' Richard pressed.

'Like blood . . . with a belt of rope.'

'It's him!' Richard gasped, checking his shoulder holster. 'The rope belt, did it have two glass balls stitched into the ends?'

'I saw only two large, woven knots. He came in and stood over you, like an evil spirit. Had he known it was you, he would have killed you. I sensed it. I am not mistaken.'

'What do you mean you sensed it, Naomi, what are you saying?'

Naomi paused, she looked up again at Richard and then down at the floor avoiding Richard's expectant stare. She was hesitant. 'I have a gift,' she said eventually. 'Passed on to me, I can look into people's hearts; I can see something of their thoughts.'

'Oh, come on, Naomi, please! If what you say is true, tell me what I am thinking?' Richard said abruptly.

'We never pry.' Naomi replied gently. 'Especially into the minds of friends; we go where we are asked, only there.'

'We? So there are more of you . . . mind readers!'

'No, Richard, please. I should not have told you.' Naomi sighed. 'I am the last,' she continued sadly. 'It is a difficult gift to bear. It is of no consequence.'

Richard realised that Naomi was perhaps more disturbed by the encounter than she was portraying, and that he was being unnecessarily harsh. He took her hands, cupped them both in his, and nodded apologetically.

'What did he say, Naomi? Was anything said?'

'He did not speak. Only I did. He was thinking in Latin, so I spoke to him in Latin. I am familiar with the language. "Go away. There is nothing here for you," I said. That is all. He seemed confused with your appearance; by me; he was unsure.'

'Hold on! Let me get this straight. You sensed that he was *thinking* in Latin. You *see* Latin words in your mind?' Richard clicked his tongue. 'Naomi, please, that's ridiculous,' he replied, his tone laced with scepticism.

'No, Richard, I see colours. The ancient languages are most vibrant. Egyptian, Coptic, Assyrian, Greek, they are the most vivid.' Naomi was deadly serious.

Richard took a deep breath and held it for a moment. 'You speak these languages, Naomi?' he asked, hardly convinced.

'I have a good knowledge of them, yes, possibly a little unpractised; the early languages have great commonality.'

'And Latin . . . well what about French then, and Italian, and the Germanic tongues? What about English for that matter?'

Naomi shrugged. 'Latin is bright . . . a vibrant orange. Anyway, I began to learn when I was a young child. It came easily, the others perhaps less so. As for English, it barely has pigment; merely a colour-wash without intensity or sparkle. It lacks purity; the consequence of many others. I have to look for it. I speak it only when I have to.'

Richard's face dropped in disappointment. Naomi

squeezed his hand; it was a tender gesture. 'I am sorry Richard,' she said almost in a whisper. 'I did not mean it like that. I am most comfortable with Arabic and French, that is all. My mother always spoke Arabic.'

Richard considered the unfolding events for a moment longer and then looked into Naomi's eyes. 'By being here, you saved my life, Naomi; you do realise that. He tried to kill me once before . . . in London, quite recently. They, MI9, are trying to find out exactly who he is. He has an almighty chip on his shoulder. I wish I knew how he came to be travelling on the same train as us.'

'We should be vigilant,' replied Naomi.

That remark broke Richard's chain of thought; he looked at her again, almost staring. 'You know, a good friend said exactly that to me several months ago on Mars. Not long after, I had my first, rather less than friendly encounter with a Humatron. I wonder what our religious friend has planned for *me*?'

Naomi looked alarmed. Richard smiled and changed the subject by rubbing his hair in a boyish manner. 'So, it's white now?' he commented flippantly. The blackness outside allowed some reflection in the window, nevertheless, colour was difficult to perceive.

The corners of Naomi's lips twitched. 'You look handsome with white hair Richard, yet I prefer red, it is how I know you,' she conceded.

They both laughed. To Richard, Naomi was beautiful. The aggressive red birthmark that covered most of the left side of her face was of no consequence.

'And your hair, Naomi? You always keep it covered, but it's dark from what I can see.'

Naomi removed her twice-bound scarf. She pulled gently at a band that kept a tight bun in place. With that, it fell loosely around her shoulders. She shook her head and the ample folds fell down to her waist; thick blue black hair with a sheen rubbed to perfection by her silk scarf. Richard could not but admire her.

Whilst Naomi had spent time brushing her hair, retying the bun and replacing her scarf, Richard considered the reality of the situation. He had finally managed to interest Naomi in a *Spacebloc*; a dried, cereal-based vitamin and protein bar, a mainstay common to space ration packs and they had plenty of purified water. He pulled his telephonic pager from a buttoned pocket inside his coat and pressed several keys on its touch pad; the device, the latest service issue, had a number of very helpful applications. In response, a tiny red light flashed a few times and then turned green. Deduced by its integral Stella Positioning System – likened to a miniature, computerised sextant, but utilising stellar radiation instead of starlight – he checked the train's position.

'We have to get off this train,' he concluded, looking sternly at Naomi. 'We are approaching Luxor, the train's next stop. Ancient Thebes is close by. I have an idea!'

CHAPTER 27

FUTURE HISTORY

'Can you call Asharf?' Richard asked Naomi. 'I need to talk to him; the time is approaching . . . quickly while the old dragon is in the lavatory.' He indicated the empty seat opposite.

Naomi nodded and dialled a number on her telephone. 'Asharf?. . . *oui*!' she said, and then passed it to Richard.

'We are leaving, come to our carriage in ten minutes, understand . . . yes, that's right.'

Naomi looked sideways at Richard. 'Why are you doing this, Richard? We are to survey Abu Simbel, only then will we be expected in Khartoum. We have no car, no support and no provisions!'

Richard's expression caused Naomi to become nervous. 'The assassin, or whatever he is, will be back. He knows I'm on this train somewhere, though God knows how, and he *will* be watching. If we disembark in Khartoum as expected and I could get a sublet in the back, that or one of his bloody exploding lead shots!'

Naomi shook her head in confusion; and started to speak.

'Don't ask! I don't fully understand it myself. From Luxor it's only a few kilometres to The Valley of the Kings, we can make it on foot. Across the river and we are into Thebes, no one goes there now, the tourists deserted the place with the rains. We jump the train and go to the valley, that's the new plan.'

Naomi offered the palms of her hands. 'Why do you do this, Richard? You mean to go to KV5, against instructions from London?'

'Two birds with one stone, Naomi. We jump and lose the tail, and we checkout a specific tomb inside KV5. It once belonged to a chap called Amun-her-khepeshef.'

'Ugh!' Naomi took a sharp intake of breath. 'So you know of this tomb, Richard?' She breathed out slowly. 'No sooner was it found, than it was . . . desecrated.' Naomi looked saddened.

'I am beginning to think that London has not given you the benefit of a full briefing, Naomi. Their contact, the Professor I mentioned, he knew of the existence of this tomb, but not its exact location. Unfortunately, he was not around when it was discovered. He also knew that the Ark of the Covenant . . . the Ark of the Israelites, had been kept there for some unspecified period and he was convinced that it subsequently moved on, travelling south to Ethiopia. We believe that it was a different Ark; the one in fact that I seek. The tomb may contain vital clues. It was part of my original brief. *That* is why we are going. Anyway, why are you so upset by that tomb being opened? I mean . . .'

'It is of no consequence, Richard,' Naomi replied quickly.

Richard stood up. 'Come on, Naomi! You know something and you are not letting on. Please, what is this all about? I know I can't do this without you.'

Naomi looked at Richard and saw his honesty. 'I know not what was, or is, inside that tomb, Richard, and that is the truth, but I know a people of great knowledge sealed it, those who also built the Great Pyramids and the temple to Osiris.'

Richard's expression changed, as more pieces of his "time and space" jigsaw puzzle began to fit together. 'I'm convinced London will thank me for it, you'll see.'

'You are putting our lives at risk unnecessarily, Richard. Someone could be there; could be waiting.'

'If they are the same people who bombed the mausoleum a few weeks ago and sealed the entrance under tons of rubble, then they have no reason to go back. And the people who trapped us in the Great Pyramid with those two Humatrons, *they* are two days ahead of us. I'm relying on them being long gone.'

At that moment the compartment door slid open and

the woman from the opposite seat returned. She sat down and made herself comfortable amidst an awkward silence. Richard checked his watch; Asharf would arrive at any time.

Naomi shook her head. 'I have bad feelings, you should know this.'

Richard was about to comment when Asharf appeared in the corridor outside the compartment. It prompted him to check the distance remaining to Luxor on his stellar positioning device.

'Come on!' Richard said abruptly. 'We are nearly there.' He slid the door open and made a gesture to Asharf to move down the corridor toward the forward end of the carriage.

'Your bag, Richard,' Naomi commented reluctantly, as she pulled it from the overhead luggage rack. To her it seemed heavy.

Richard gratefully pushed his arm between the straps and flung the bag over his shoulder. They both stepped outside the compartment. As Richard slid the door closed, he caught the eye of the woman opposite. 'The lavatory,' Richard assured her. 'I need help.' The woman watched them leave and "tutted" loudly, to show her disgust.

'Take the first left,' Richard instructed Asharf, as he checked the train's position again. 'Only a few minutes now! In the narrow compartment at the end of the carriage, a young woman stood smoking. The window was pulled down slightly, a few centimetres at most, it was not enough to flush out the smoke or the smell, but through the gap a cold draft whistled and drops of rain soaked the adjacent wall. Richard stared at the girl in an unnerving way. In response, her cigarette barely half-drawn, she dropped it, stubbed it out with her shoe and left.

Richard pulled the window down as far as it would go and leaned outside. The wind fluttered his hair and his collar quivered; tiny droplets of water splattered on his face; he peered in the direction of travel; the lights were approaching.

Back inside, he looked up above the door. In a small alcove was the emergency-stop chain. Above it, in red letters it read:

PULL ONLY IN EMERGENCY
UNAUTHORISED OPERATORS WILL BE PROSECUTED

Richard grasped the chain in his right hand and then looked at Naomi, his gaze passed to Asharf. 'You both ready?' They nodded apprehensively. With that, Richard looked outside again. The lights of the town loomed. With a sharp tug, he pulled the cord. The response was immediate. An alarm bell sounded, its penetrating warble echoed along their carriage. Heavy braking flung them forwards. Richard put his arm out to restrain Naomi and prevent her hitting the door handle. The carriage brakes squealed. They could hear people shouting, some screamed. From the carriage in front came the sound of breaking crockery. After forty seconds or so, the train had slowed to a walking pace. Richard flung open the door. He swung into the opening by holding on to an adjacent wall-mounted handle with one hand and held the door clear. 'Go! Go!' he ordered.

First Asharf leapt then Naomi and then Richard. They landed in the soft sand with a little forward momentum, all of them rolling for a metre or two. Richard was quickly on his feet. He checked the area; the train had all but stopped; he ran back for Naomi. Station lights, two or three hundred metres ahead, helped in finding his bag, but after that, they were a liability. Naomi scrambled to her feet, covered in wet sand. Richard offered his hand, she grasped it. Asharf was close behind and quickly they disappeared into the darkness.

For several minutes they ran, never looking back. In the distance, they could hear bells, whistles and shouting. Eventually the noise faded. At one point, a police siren punctured the blackness, and then another, until they too faded from earshot.

Richard gave the town a wide berth. The going was heavy; Naomi stumbled repeatedly until she pulled off her low-heeled shoes. Richard pressed a key on the illuminated keypad of his pager. On the backlit display a digital compass readout appeared, he orientated it and pointed it in their intended direction. After a while, the deep covering of sand thinned and the going became easier. Ahead he began to see the lights of a bridge; it crossed the

River Nile. Three kilometres north-west from its far bank lay Thebes; two kilometres further was The Valley of the Kings – he grew expectant. Soon they were on the road and the bridge ahead appeared deserted.

The lights of Luxor lay behind them as the three promptly crossed the wide steel bridge in single file. Keeping close to the left hand railings, only the sound of the rain and the regular clump of Richard's thick-soled walking boots permeated the desert stillness. Another hour, two at the most, thought Richard, and they would be in the valley. Behind them, to the east, the distant horizon began to lighten. The next train, in twenty-four hours, Richard had learned, was the weekly service to Addis Ababa, Ethiopia's capital. Unlike the Khartoum service, it did not stop at Wadi Halfa; the nearest town to Abu Simbel, but turned south-east towards the Red Sea and Port Sudan, only then turning south again for Addis. Just how important was Abu Simbel? Richard considered, as he walked alongside Naomi. Having already studied the images of its remaining wall painting, would there be anything else there to learn? He would cross that bridge when he came to it, he concluded, but first KV5!

Richard crawled up the wet sand on his hands and knees. Periodically, he stopped to scan the area. Slowly he neared the ridgeline. When close to the summit, he turned on his heels and indicated to Naomi and Asharf, who were some twenty metres behind him, to keep low. He held a finger to his lips and shook his head to indicate their silence. The sticky sand clinging to his dark coat provided unexpected camouflage, as he looked over the crest and into the shallow valley. The area lay abandoned; at least as far as he could see, and from here, the going would be easier again as a network of tarmac roads and concrete tourist paths peppered the entire site.

He knew the area from his studies and intelligence maps posted to his pager by MI9's e-image system. Asharf crawled up next to him, flat on his stomach and Richard pointed. Asharf nodded, and pointed out a gantry and a vehicle by waving his finger towards them. Richard scrutinised the barren rock escarpment and the valley below, for several minutes, only then sending Asharf down to take a closer look. He was beginning to like, and more importantly trust, Asharf, as he watched him skirt carefully down a loose rock scree and alight on the valley floor. It was a God-forsaken area in more ways than one, Richard thought. The drab, sand-coloured landscape caused the topography to blend into a single mass, but here, close to the Eastern Desert, the rain had become light and intermittent, indeed, for the last hour, to Richard's delight, it had stopped. He checked the time: 08:55. A rare glimmer of early morning sunlight managed to percolate through the dense cloud cover. Richard called Naomi forward with a hand signal. Asharf was careful to stay in view, as he surveyed the path leading up to the main entrance of KV5. Soon, he indicated to Richard, by way of frantic arm waving, that the way appeared clear. Naomi concurred. 'This place is deserted,' she said confidently.

Richard smiled. 'So we can go then?' He said with a hint of sarcasm, meant more as a joke than a jibe at Naomi's apparent mental scan.

Together they scrambled down the scree, unintentionally loosening a few boulders that gathered momentum as they rolled down the hillside and subsequently rumbled across the concrete path close to where Asharf stood. The disturbance caused him to look around warily. A large sign directed them a little further up the valley. "The Mausoleum of Rameses II" it read.

Naomi and Richard walked past the main entrance which was clearly damaged and precariously blocked by the results of a substantial explosion. They continued up a gentle incline for another ninety metres. Asharf, by that time, stood at the base of the mobile drilling gantry. Several steel cables looped out from its apex and were connected by means of clamps, fixed at their opposite ends, to a sturdy, steel framework. This structure in turn, straddled the back of a large, tracked lorry. To Richard, as he approached, it all seemed to be in good working order and the lorry seemed conveniently orientated for a retrieval operation, being little more than five or six metres away. Asharf turned and walked quickly back to meet to them.

'Perhaps Madame should not see what I have . . . !' he said solemnly, pointing back towards the lorry.

'Why, what is it?'

'The operatives, *Effendi*, they are dead.'

'What?'

Asharf nodded and looked at Naomi.

'I am not a stranger to death,' she smiled sadly.

Richard counted six men lying in the sand. They were dead all right, and two had suffered horrendous injuries – one had an arm missing and the other his head almost torn off. In the dampness, flies swarmed and crawled in and out of the flesh. Richard looked around nervously, shaking his head in disgust. 'This is the work of a Humatron,' he growled. 'The others have been shot.'

Naomi drew a deep breath, shuddering at the thought.

'I think they've gone,' Richard said, in a half-hearted attempt to reassure her. 'These wounds are a day or two old at least.' Nevertheless, he appeared less than convinced himself as he rotated slowly on his heels, scanning the encircling ridgeline.

Asharf, kneeling by one of the bodies, rubbed a sample of part-congealed blood between his fingers. 'Perhaps a little less, *Effendi*,' he responded.

Richard looked concerned. He walked a few paces to the newly completed shaft, a vertical and near perfect round hole in the base rock that extended down into the blackness of the mausoleum that lay below them. 'Looks like they had finished the job and were preparing to leave,' he concluded.

Asharf paled and said anxiously, 'you wish to go down there, *Effendi*?'

'You two can wait, I'll go down. That's why I made us come here.'

Naomi shook her head in disapproval. 'No! We stay together, it is better.'

Richard could see further argument was pointless and he began to look for a way down. He walked closer to the truck in order to inspect it. The thinnest steel bracing cable, one that hung from the top of the gantry and looped to the lorry provided the answer. Within minutes, he had unclipped the clamp on the framework and had the end threaded down the shaft until it became slack. 'Around twelve metres,' he confirmed. 'The diameter of the shaft is going to make it a little tight!' he explained. Next, he pulled three pairs of padded construction gloves from as many bodies and his spare, self-charging, photoelectric torch from his bag. To Asharf he gave the torch and a pair of gloves. 'I have my own torch and the Illuminac,' Richard said. 'You take this one and try not to lose it again!' Asharf nodded and raised a humbled half smile.

'Let's go!' Richard ordered. 'Me first, then Naomi, and then you Asharf . . . understand?'

Both nodded in apprehensive consent, but Asharf had another idea. '*Effendi*,' he said quietly. 'I am much smaller, it will be easier for me, remember the Great Pyramid, and *you* have a greater part than I in this quest. I shall venture into the darkness first, then Madame and then you, it is better this way.'

118

CHAPTER 28

BACK TO THE BEGINNING

The vertical shaft was narrow and claustrophobic. Asharf had slipped down with relative ease and Naomi, evidently well practised as well as fiercely independent, had climbed down the cable, arm over arm, like a professional. For Richard, however, it was a different story. The diameter was smaller than it promised and despite an apparent off centre quiver of the drilling bit, there was barely room for his shoulders; even by collapsing his chest, restricting his lung capacity and hunching his shoulders together under his chin, it was tight. He had squeezed into the hole feet first, exhaled and wriggled to allow his body to drop and taken a last, hapless look at the dreary surroundings before his head disappeared below the desert surface. Now an anxious frown was stamped across his forehead and an uneasy churning unsettled his stomach. It was as if the resentful desert made claim on every living thing, and he felt as if he was being swallowed.

Surprisingly, tiny spores of green, greasy mould had already begun to deposit themselves on the mainly smooth walls of the shaft and, combined with a continuous film of running water, their effect added lubrication to his descent. Even so, his clothes began to bunch up uncomfortably.

Eventually, looking down between his legs, Richard could see occasional flashes from Asharf's torch beam; whilst looking skywards, through the two-metre tube of limestone he had already painfully negotiated, an occasional raindrop splattered on his face. His discomfort increased with every slithering centimetre he descended. He could endure being wet, miserable, and downright wretched; but jammed in a hole, barely able to move, he sensed his vulnerability. Richard shuffled and squirmed, exhausting his lungs from time to time in order to collapse his ribcage. Little by little, he slipped further and further down.

After six metres Richard stopped to rest, he merely had to take a hearty gasp of damp, fusty air to secure his position. He was beginning to get cold. His head and face were soaked and he had suffered several grazes to his back and shoulders from the unevenness and the occasional lump in the shaft wall. Below him, Naomi and Asharf – having already safely alighted on the smooth stone floor of the great mausoleum – grew increasingly concerned.

Before commencing his decent, Richard had first

dropped their rucksacks down the shaft and then followed the three bags with his coat, and Asharf – who had missed its fall in the darkness and subsequently retrieved it from a shallow puddle – followed his orders by checking various pockets for his pager, torch, Illuminac and ISTAN. Naomi, meanwhile, who was mumbling nervously in Arabic whilst repeatedly looked upwards, soon had Asharf shouting encouragement.

'*Effendi*!' He called, cupping his hands around his mouth to direct the sound upwards. 'The roof of the tomb lies three metres above us, which means no more than three metres remaining. You should make haste, *Effendi* . . . quickly, you must continue!'

Richard breathed out hard, exhausting his lungs until he felt his diaphragm straining. He curled his shoulders and immediately slipped another forty centimetres or so before coming to an abrupt stop. This time there was a problem: a shallow outcrop of rock had broken and shifted during drilling and distorted the shaft's concentricity; Richard's momentary freefall had jammed him tight. He groaned, half in pain, half in frustration. Asharf, sensing his plight, shouted encouragement again, but this time there was an element of panic in his tone. Richard, due to his constriction was unable to take more than short, sharp breaths; he began to hyperventilate and felt dizzy.

Naomi was having no more of Asharf's echoing ranting. She shed her coat and quickly scaled the steel cable like a trapeze artist; soon disappearing into the shaft. When she reached Richard – who was no more than his body-length from safety – he was gasping for breath and shifting painfully in his stone sarcophagus. Squeezing her feet tightly together around the cable and holding on with one hand, she reached out and grasped Richard's ankle.

'Richard, you must control your emotions.' Her voice was soft but firm. 'Stem your breathing, Richard. Take long breaths, as deep as your lungs will allow. Fill the space available to you . . . . Do as I say, Richard.' Naomi's voice seemed almost ethereal; it penetrated Richard's subconscious. Again, she ordered him.

Richard responded; he came to his senses and quelled his anxiety; his breathing becoming more regular.

'Richard,' Naomi said again, calmly. 'Think how others would surmount this hazard. The escapologists would have a way; the great Houdini would have a way. I have studied his methods; they have been of use to me in the past. I will instruct you from the ground.' With that, Naomi gave Richard's ankle a reassuring squeeze and slid slowly back down the cable.

From the ground, Naomi shone her torch upwards into the black, clammy shaft. She illuminated Richard's body; his legs moved erratically, as if he was a suspended puppet. The cable squeezed past him and broken filaments of steel pricked his chest. Whilst wearing thick construction gloves their hands were immune to the shards, but Richard's pullover was bunched up under his armpits and they easily scratched and penetrated his shirt. She could see the crescent-shaped outcrop of rock that jammed Richard's buttocks and forced his left hip hard against the opposite face of the shaft.

'Richard,' Naomi advised again. 'You must turn a quarter to the right, so that your stomach lies over the jutting rock. Do not try to pass over the cable, but take it with you in the hollow of your chest. Take three deep breaths and then exhale everything you have in your lungs, everything, Richard, every faint whisper. Collapse your ribcage and work your shoulders to turn . . . do it, Richard!'

Richard responded. His diaphragm expelled his last gasp of breath and he pulled his shoulders together until his pectoral muscles strained with the effort. Then he shuffled and shimmied as Naomi had instructed, stopping periodically to pant shallowly. He slipped a few centimetres as he did so, but finally he felt the bulbous rock press against his stomach.

'Good, Richard!' Naomi encouraged. 'Now, collapse and expand your shoulders again and slip past the rock, again it will pass through the hollow of your chest. If you need to, move the cable a little to the side, but be sure to take hold of it between your feet, Richard, as the shaft opens again below you.'

Richard's feet paddled in all directions until he found the cable, then, placing one foot above the other around the cable to form a brake he contorted his body again. It worked. Slowly, he slid past the outcrop, but when it reached a position adjacent to his neck, he slipped.

'Ahhh!' he cried. His voice trailed away.

Richard fell at least half a metre before managing to grasp the cable again. With both hands squeezing tightly and elbows as friction pads, he broke his fall; there was distress in a stifled groan.

'The worst of it is past, Richard,' Naomi explained, directing her voice upwards. 'Now, with control, the final part . . . I am waiting for you.'

After that, the going was easier. Slowly down the dank, muggy, cylinder of time he slipped. Compressing his shoulders periodically to avoid snagging his clothing again on frayed strands of wire, he finally began to see the light below clearly. It was a very welcome sight: the torches of his two friends illuminating the cavern. Asharf clapped with delight as Richard's face became visible at the shaft's end.

'God damn it,' Richard yelped painfully. 'Never again!'

Arm over arm and now more speedily, Richard descended until both feet dropped firmly onto the dusty floor. He rubbed his sore elbows and breathed a loud sigh and put an arm around Naomi's shoulders and gave her a hug; she nodded and smiled.

Asharf also seemed pleased with Richard's spontaneous affection. 'Perhaps we should feed you less, *Effendi*?' He ventured with a cheeky grin as he offered Richard his coat.

'Umm, something to consider, Asharf,' replied Richard, raising his eyebrows and gesturing his thanks. At that particular moment, he was unable to appreciate Asharf's attempt at light-heartedness. Withdrawing his torch from an outside pocket of his coat and shining its beam back up the shaft, Richard shook his head woefully. 'Getting back up there will not be easy, I can tell you,' he said, and then he used the powerful beam to scan the chamber and dilute its pitch-blackness. 'We will cross that bridge though when we come to it,' he concluded.

'You should rest a while,' advised Naomi quietly. 'Take some water perhaps; I have some in my bag.'

Richard gestured again in a kindly fashion. 'Time is against us,' he reminded his friends.

During his briefing in London, Richard had studied archaeological drawings that precisely detailed the layout of the tomb and after a faltering search he was able to orientate himself. Naomi and Asharf, however, seemed to share a confidence with their location that was born of familiarity. Richard shone his torch beam in the direction that they should travel. Around them, the chamber was deceptively large.

'A hundred years to build it, and more than half as much again to excavate it,' Richard commented flippantly, as he selected the magnetic compass facility on his telephonic pager in order to cross-check his intended course. He also checked the radio transmit and receive signal strength on the device, but there was absolutely no indication.

'This tomb would have best remained undiscovered,' Naomi observed.

Richard looked at her quizzically for a few moments, but decided not to question her remark. Instead, he focused on the practicalities. 'Well, one thing is certain,' he said. 'There's no signal down here . . . looks like we will be out of contact for the duration – not that I am surprised, below nine metres of solid rock. With due respect, that ill-fated drilling team did the job well,' Richard continued sombrely. 'Look!' His powerful torch beam illuminated the area to his right. 'Damned accurate drilling; not fifteen metres from the base of the main entrance steps *and* only a few paces from the entrance to the Second Chamber.' Richard used his torch beam to gesture towards a doorway that led into that chamber. 'In there they found the skeletal remains of Amun-her-khepeshef, the first son of Rameses the Great.'

Naomi nodded knowingly at Richard's words. 'Come then, quickly, follow me and be careful where you tread,' she ordered. With that, she turned on her heels and made off towards the low doorway, her torch light falling upon random pieces of rock and debris that lay strewn around them and behind these, shadows stretched and jittered.

Richard repositioned his shoulder holster and secured it with the metal buckle. After allowing Asharf to pass through the door first, both men set off in hot pursuit. Five good strides saw them through the second chamber and entering the Sixteen-pillared Hall; Richard gasped as his torch beam struggled to light up its far walls. He knew it would be impressive . . . but this?

It was an enormous architectural achievement, symmetrical and solemn. Richard sensed a strange coldness that penetrated his clothing and he found the damp, musty air stifling; in response, he buttoned up his coat and turned up his collar. Naomi walked quickly. Asharf remained a few paces behind Richard and nervously flashed his torch beam back over covered ground.

An undisturbed secret of the ancient Egyptians until the early 1990s, the Sixteen-pillared, or Great Hall, was still the largest found anywhere in the valley. With a square, four by four layout, the dominating pillars supported an expansive, flat ceiling. Richard could only marvel at the dimensions and the apparent, collective weight, which must be incredible, he thought. Hewn from solid rock as the ancient masons continued their excavation further and further into the valley side, each pillar was masterfully carved and decorated. At the time, they would also have been richly painted and inscribed and Richard imagined a deep, blood red colour overlaid with gold and peacock-blue hieroglyphs. Richard eventually caught up with Naomi as they left the hall through a wide doorway at its far end. He noticed the absence of a supporting lintel, despite the dimensions of the opening; the structure seemed self-supporting; such structural engineering was no guesswork, he concluded. 'Impressive dimensions,' he commented, flashing his torchlight from side to side.

'You forget who had a hand in its building, Richard,' Naomi replied matter-of-factly. 'Floor space in KV5 is measured in thousands of square metres, and on three levels, the room count exceeds 200. It was a very special place, one of great significance.'

Richard nodded; his brief had already made that quite clear. He sucked in a deep breath through his nose; the air smelt fusty, and lacked oxygen. They entered a long, low corridor almost three metres wide but again with precise symmetry. It was laser beam straight. On either side were doorways which Richard studied with interest. Behind every doorway lay a square room, and like frigid, forgotten dungeons each brimmed momentarily with light when passed. It was Asharf, however, walking a few metres behind, who suffered the aftermath: heart stopping, stabbing shadows and the waking attention of disturbed spirits. Richard kept count of his paces and the passing chambers. At the end of the thirty-metre long corridor, he had counted eighteen – nine on each side.

Naomi stopped and turned towards Richard, the beam from her torch fell onto the ground. 'Each room contained the remains of Rameses' princes,' she explained, noticing Richard's curiosity. 'And it was along this corridor that my grandfather discovered particles of black granite, mica and quartz embedded in the sandstone floor – as if a great object had journeyed its length. Do you know about this, Richard?'

'The wheel of time,' Richard whispered poignantly.

'Of what do you speak?' Naomi enquired, unable to hear Richard's words.

'Oh sorry . . . yes, yes, I know something of this, Naomi.'
Richard said more clearly. He paused. 'It was a door . . . an
enormous, impenetrable stone door that apparently was
rolled into position, its diameter twice the height of this
corridor.' Richard cast his light upwards onto the ceiling
of the corridor; with his arm outstretched and standing
on tiptoes, he could touch it with his fingertips. 'Now, how
in God's name did they do that?'

'Again, Richard, you seem to know so much, and yet so
little.'

With that and before Richard had time to reply, Naomi
turned towards the head of the corridor and shone her
penetrating torch beam at its end. In response, Richard
drew a sharp intake of breath; Asharf too stepped back a
few paces and uttered something in Arabic. There, sitting
in regal splendour and gazing into eternity's never ending
void was an enormous, towering statue of Rameses II.
Stone cold, the great pharaoh stared. The corridor had
terminated in a much larger chamber; a cavernous gallery
lay before them.

Richard's heart thumped with anticipation as he stepped
into the gallery; to him the hollowness of the space and
its high, unsupported ceiling was completely unexpected.

Asharf followed, mumbling incomprehensible incantations.

The noise of their footsteps reverberated. Strangely, Naomi entered with the courteous gracefulness that one might expect from a dutiful lady-in-waiting. Richard's torch beam systematically filled the corners of the gallery with probing light and then he gazed upwards. 'This is altogether something different,' he uttered. 'A curved, almost vaulted ceiling . . . the Egyptians had no knowledge of this type of architecture, or if they did, they did not use it; their style was angular . . . linear? Something else happened here . . . there was another influence. I think that we are getting close!'

At that, Naomi stopped abruptly and turned towards Richard; she stared at him for several seconds, her expression clearly pained. Richard was unaware of her attention and scanned the gallery's peripheries again. Moments later he found it, on his left . . . a doorway!

There were in fact two doorways leading from the gallery Richard discovered, both of similar proportions, but this, he knew instinctively, was the one, for it lay at the right hand of Rameses himself. The other, excavated on the opposite side, held neither allure nor insight. Unnoticed until then, were broken pieces of granite of various shapes and sizes. Some were piled into corners, whilst other smaller pieces lay strewn around the area and an unusually thick covering of dust had settled on the ground. The wheeled door, thought Richard, they broke it up here! Occasionally, tiny crystals of quartz and mica dissolved in the layer and some, which were kicked up in Asharf's wake, reflected the light from Richard's torch; they glistened and sparkled in the darkness like Christmas fairy lights.

Richard was quickly over to the opening. A sturdy wooden door that boasted a sizeable steel bracing bar, and a tarnished brass padlock, barred his entry. Like iron filings attracted to a magnet, a rippled emulsion of luminous green algae coated the barrier. To Richard, this unblemished complexion bore testament to decades of ignorance as to what lay behind.

The thick door offered more than adequate resistance to Richard's emphatic shaking, and a weighty kung fu style kick fared little better, save for his heel scribing an arc through the slimy mould. He reached into his coat, fumbled for a few seconds and withdrew his ISTAN; a glowing blade appeared, its outline accentuated in the near darkness. As if swinging a felling axe to cut firewood, Richard swept down with the weapon. One swipe was enough to slice the door in two. Richard kicked open the two halves . . . he was in and Asharf was so close behind him as to be almost breathing down his neck.

Richard strode purposefully to its centre, spun on his heels and illuminated the square room until his torch beam arrived back at the doorway in which Naomi and Asharf now stood motionless. 'The biggest cover-up in the history of mankind!' he pronounced.

This chamber had an altogether different feel about. It still smelt dank, damp and stagnant, but not of bereavement or snuffed emotion. There was an uplifting aura. They all felt it as they huddled together at its middle and gazed around its periphery. There was a sense of destiny, of power, as if something or someone had breathed light and life into this foreboding environment. Richard flashed his torch beam rapidly in all directions; there was an air of excitement.

'Please,' Naomi requested, putting her hand on Richard's forearm. 'Slowly, you are making me feel dizzy.'

'Sorry . . . but this is amazing . . . it's a perfect cube - look!'

Richard referred to the four walls and the ceiling that in the most part still retained their original covering – painted depictions and hieroglyphic script on smooth plaster – although in several areas, time and moisture had taken their toll. Naomi walked to one corner of the chamber and scanned the friezes more closely. She peered at the ancient text and withdrew a small circular magnifying glass from her coat pocket in order to scrutinise pictograms that had faded.

Walking slowly and methodically anticlockwise around the room she drew her conclusions: 'Most of these writings refer to the life of Amun-her-khepeshef,' she said. 'They give notice of his achievements and the honour he bestowed on his father's kingdom. Some appear to be little more than timely propaganda.'

'Really?' said Richard, shrugging his shoulders. 'Not much help, then?'

Naomi continued her inspection, paying little attention to Richard's remark until she pulled up short and dwelt on a block of text – on her second reading, she recited aloud: '*Hear this all God fearing men, for so commands Rameses II. Pharaoh of Pharaohs, the everlasting emissary who walks amongst men, commits the body of his firstborn son, Amun-her-khepeshef to the great journey. Rameses the Great will himself lay open the gates to the afterlife and shall be guide to the throne of Osiris whose judgement favours those with deeds of truth and strength.*'

'That must have been written shortly after Amun's death, when this was still his intended tomb?' Richard surmised.

'There is more that speaks of Amun's great service to his father as leader of his armies,' Naomi continued. '*The greatness of the firstborn shall be recorded for Gods and men to see. The passing of time itself shall not diminish his sacred victories.*'

Naomi walked to the adjacent wall and stopped by a large, faded, but colourful painting. It depicted an Egyptian prince with his curved staff of office, riding in an ornate chariot drawn by four horses; the animals were richly adorned with headdresses and armoured robes. There was a picture of the sun rising above the horizon and a shattered army. Depictions of dead men – some speared by lances and arrows – lay strewn across the mural and there were animals of the East also pictured, including elephants and tigers, their forms sliced and dismembered. Again, Naomi read aloud part of the accompanying text. '*Crushed are the Harappas, their lands far towards the rising sun. All bow before Prince Amun-her-khepeshef son of Rameses the Great.*'

'So it had already started?' Richard commented sombrely.

'What had started, Richard?' Naomi asked, turning to stare at him.

'The infighting! Admiral Dirkot Urket mentioned the Harappas in his diary.'

Naomi looked confused. 'You have mentioned this man before?' she said.

'Yes, I have, but it's a long story. This is neither the time nor the place for it, Naomi, and frankly, I'm not sure if you would believe it.'

'I believe in many things, Richard . . . you would be surprised.'

Richard shrugged. 'Anyway, according to that entry, the Harappas were the original colonists who settled in the east. I have since found out that they called their first city by the same name – Harappa. It is a vast, prehistoric city on the dried-up course of the River Ravi in the Pakistani Punjab. Walled, rectangular street grids, sewers, aqueducts, power! Originally believed to have been occupied from 2300 BC and for around 600 years – now thought to be much, much, older. Mohenjo-daro is also mentioned . . .

same thing, a sprawling architectural wonder, but this time on the River Indus, in Sind, Pakistan. So the Egyptians conquered India. God, what a turn up! History taught us that Alexander the Great was the first . . . a thousand years later, and his army, according to his scribes, encountered *flying machines*. Certainly makes you wonder . . .'

Naomi had only half an ear for Richard's historical conclusions as she continued her methodical inspection. 'Chronicles of the great exodus,' she whispered. 'And the banishing of the tribes of Canaan, written here in nineteenth dynasty hieroglyphics.' Naomi stopped and looked again at Richard. 'In truth, I know well of this mausoleum,' she explained. 'I came here first as a child with my mother and later as a young student studying at Cairo University. This was before excavations revealed the true extent of the Great Gallery, although I have since read of it. I did not know of this chamber and grew excited when you mentioned it, but there is nothing here to help you in your search, Richard. These writings are of interest, I agree, but I have seen similar in the temple built by Rameses at Abu Simbel and those were documented many decades ago.' Naomi illuminated the wall again and turned back to it; a few more metres would complete her inspection.

Richard shook his head in disappointment. 'There's got to be something here, some clue. I was told . . .'

'Wait!' Naomi stopped abruptly adjacent to the doorway. She stared at a series of inscriptions that were carved somewhat haphazardly on the inner door head.

'Richard, please, come here; these I cannot read!'

Hastily, Richard was by her side. He gazed upwards at the two lines of text; the top of the door head was just above head height. 'Yes. They seem to have been carved in a hurry or by someone with little skill, or perhaps lacking the correct tools?'

'Or perhaps in fading light, *Effendi* – or even darkness!' Asharf interjected.

Richard and Naomi turned in unison; they looked at Asharf with puzzled expressions.

'Why do you say that, Asharf?' Richard asked.

Asharf stood close to a corner and gestured Richard to follow the light of his torch beam. There, in a crumpled heap, lay a pile of bones. The remains of a skull protruded through stone dust and debris.

Naomi looked back at Richard. 'Can you read the inscription?' she asked.

Richard nodded slowly. '*Respect not the men who take it. For them, the sun shall never rise. For those who follow me, look south to Kush,*' he recited.

There was silence for several seconds; Richard stared, fixated by the script. Then he looked Naomi in the eyes. Shadows played on her face; momentarily her blemish seemed to disappear. He looked away and rubbed his forehead and the bridge of his nose trying to make sense of it all. Behind him, Asharf's mumblings offered the bones to the ancient Gods.

Richard took a deep breath. 'Kush was the ancient

Egyptian word for the kingdom that lay to the south,' he said. 'Only later was it called Nubia, and much later still . . . Sudan. Parts of modern Ethiopia fell within the borders of Kush. So it is true. The Ark travelled south, to the Kingdom of Kush, to Sudan or Ethiopia!'

Naomi nodded in confirmation; she knew of Kush, and its historical legacy. 'And what of the "sun never rising", Richard, what does it mean?' she asked.

'*For them, the sun shall never rise*,' repeated Richard, poignantly. 'The sun, the light, *the crystal* . . ! They lacked the understanding to use it. That's all it can mean!'

'*Effendi*! *Effendi*! There is more of the old writing here,' Asharf interrupted excitedly. 'The words are scratched into the plaster, down here by the . . . '

Richard walked quickly across the room to where Asharf was standing and illuminated the wall; light reflected eerily from the smooth, half-exposed skull. He studied the haphazard lines of text for a few moments. 'It is a prayer, Asharf, to the sun god Amun, probably the most ancient of all the Egyptian deities.' Richard looked down at the skull and the pile of bones that lay huddled in the corner. 'He . . . or she, for that matter, never finished it.'

'Amun's name means "hidden",' Naomi concurred, in a knowledgeable tone. 'He was the "unknowable" . . . described in a theological document composed during the reign of Rameses II as "hidden from the gods, and his aspect unknown. He is too secret to uncover his awesomeness . . . ".' Naomi's voice trailed away. 'Above all, Thebes was the city of Amun.'

An impromptu, respectful silence followed and during that moment, there was a noise – a scuffling, scurrying noise!

'What was that?' Richard questioned, flashing his light towards the entrance.

The trio stood absolutely still, holding their breath. Richard directed his torch beam out through the doorway. There was silence.

'Did you hear that? Slight echoes . . . something strange, like the whirr of mechanics!'

'Nothing, I heard nothing, *Effendi*,' replied Asharf, after several seconds.

'Nor I,' offered Naomi a little nervously.

'Okay, sorry. I'm a little on edge, that's all.'

Naomi let out a sigh of relief. 'Richard! *S'il vous plait* – do not do that; you scare me!'

Richard gestured another apology but all the same glanced back at the doorway warily before considering their find again – the remains of a person who had clearly lived thousands of years earlier.

'These "old words" as you call them, Naomi, are unique symbols, the written language of the visitors . . . the people I regard as colonists. I mean colonists of this planet. In fact, during my studies, I concluded that it is the original language from which all other ancient languages on earth evolved – the commonality between these and other ancient hieroglyphic writings from all over the world is too much to be discounted. Evidently, this person had some fluency. Perhaps he, or she, was a direct descendant of the "old people" or at least knew well enough of them to be party to their secrets.'

Naomi fidgeted; she seemed uncomfortable with Richard's assumption; he looked at her sideways.

'Who knows,' Richard continued, 'perhaps a line of scholars, or priests or the like?' He crouched beside the pile of bones and pulled at a large example before returning it gently to the debris. 'To be purposely trapped inside a time capsule . . . possibly the last person on earth to know how to harness the power of the crystals – now who would do that and why?' Slowly, Richard stood up.

'Perhaps you read too much into this, Richard,' commented Naomi, as she illuminated the pile of bones again and more particularly the skull.

'This was a "he", Richard, of that I can assure you.'

Richard nodded and then he paused thoughtfully. He stroked back his unkempt hair that had dried in an unruly style. 'Perhaps this person, this . . . *priest*, was also the last to know of the door's mechanism and how to operate it,' he said. 'Because of this, he was trapped inside; the door being rolled closed . . . forever! Who could then dispute that the Ark was not inside – the greatest secret known to mankind? Then, over millennia, it was forgotten.'

Naomi shrugged. 'Your imagination appears boundless, Richard,' she commented, in a nonchalant manner.

Richard nodded again. 'Maybe,' he replied. And then,

as he thought more on the matter a suspicious frown tightened his brow. He switched to combing the hairs of his short, stubbly beard with his fingers. 'Maybe . . . maybe not,' he uttered.

'Speculation can be dangerous when unravelling the threads of time, Richard,' Naomi advised, breaking a short period of silent reflection. 'True historians allow it only limited scope – I thought this lesson was learnt?'

Richard glanced at Naomi and shook his head, as if to say 'no, not yet' and then he gestured to her with an open palm as if asking for even more latitude. At that, his tired, reddened eyes seemed to brighten. He glanced at Asharf, then back at her. 'Nevertheless,' he said. 'There *are* records!'

Naomi sensed audacity in Richard's tone; however, in that dank, empty chamber hers was the voice of reason.

'Although little known and dismissed by archaeologists as unreliable,' Richard continued, 'these records state that the Ark of the Covenant stopped at Thebes on its journey south; the city's ruined temples and precincts are just a few miles from here, as well you know, Naomi. By those accounts, that event was around 600 BC; we will never know whether its arrival was heralded or hushed. Meanwhile, far to the north, King Nebuchadnezzar and his Babylonian army razed the City of Jerusalem and destroyed the Temple of Solomon . . . '

Naomi could only agree and did so with an encouraging smile. 'Yes, this is well documented . . . 587 BC,' she said.

'Subsequently, nothing further was heard or seen of the Ark of the Covenant. Most believe that it was destroyed along with the temple.'

'Now, *that* is speculation!'

'Over the centuries archaeologists and historians agree with it, Richard.'

'But you don't . . . do you?'

'There are other opinions.'

'You're damned right there are. Listen, Naomi, you can't just dismiss historical records as unreliable because they don't fit the established view, I mean . . !'

'Evidence taken out of context can be misleading, Richard.'

'Really, and that's another lesson, is it?'

Naomi shrugged dismissively.

'Those records suggest that the Ark reappeared around 450 BC on Tana Qirkos Island in Lake Tana in Ethiopia, and there's other evidence, completely independent, to this effect too . . . and I'm inclined to believe it!'

Naomi nodded. 'And thereafter it arrived in Aksum – 800 years later.'

There was a look of surprise on Richard's face. 'Yes, that's right,' he said, stepping backwards. He took time to rub his chin, pushing his stubble against the grain. 'So, you know of this?'

'Of course I know of it! And what of Elephantine Island near Aswan, Richard . . . another proposed resting place for that godly receptacle? There is also local evidence . . .'

Naomi raised her eyebrows to emphasise the point. 'I fear we ask more questions than there are answers,' she concluded, her voice trailing to a whisper; she looked downcast.

'Something was here, Naomi, there is no doubt in my mind about that . . . science apart, I can feel it,' retorted Richard. 'Naomi, please, you have to go with me on this!'

Naomi looked up slowly and sighed and then a brief smile glimmered; it encouraged Richard.

'So,' he continued. 'Were both Arks here for a time, or did one follow the other during different periods in history? Or, indeed, was there an agenda that set out to confuse those events, even merge them, so that they became one and the same . . .?'

Richard paused. The enormity of the questions suddenly registered. He felt compelled to agree with Naomi's appraisal; he shook his head in disappointment. 'Proof that the Ark, or Arks had actually existed is one thing,' he said softly. 'However, clues to their whereabouts or more particularly the Ark of the Light's whereabouts are so scant as to be almost nonexistent.' Richard shook his head and a lengthy period of silence followed. The beam from his torch wandered the chamber aimlessly. 'South, is not much help – is it?' he groaned eventually, his tone irritated. 'After all, the entire continent of Africa lies *south*!'

Richard had been pinning his hopes on Professor Simpson Carter's KV5 symbols having significance. Clearly, however, there was nothing in the chamber that would help their search. Disillusioned, he began to doubt the Professor's rationality during the closing minutes of his life. A strange stillness fell over the chamber; a tormented disquiet, as if history was screaming at them. Naomi opened her mouth to speak, only to be distracted by another shuffling sound . . . a scraping in the sand. Richard, jerked from his thoughts, looked up; his eyes darted in all directions. The sound came from outside the chamber and from their expressions it was clear that this time they had all heard it. Richard's torchlight filled the entrance, he ran outside . . . but there was nothing, nobody! Then more scuffling, followed by a scurrying down the long, dark corridor; but still he could see nothing. Richard pulled the Illuminac from his coat pocked and flipped it to illumination Level 3. He held it high above his head; the entire tomb was lit up in apparent sunshine, and Richard squinted against its brilliance. He saw something move, perhaps ten metres away, it stopped dead in its tracks for a few seconds and then scurried away again with an ungainly sideways motion. Richard gave chase towards the Hall of Pillars; Naomi and Asharf followed in his wake.

With his long stride, Richard was quickly upon it – a strange creature, the size of a large dinner plate and low to the ground. As Richard ran past, in order to cut off its retreat, the thing snapped aggressively at his heels making him writhe and jump until he succeeded in putting a foot on its body and pressing it hard onto the stone. The creature, about thirty centimetres pincer-to-pincer, twitched and jerked and grew angry. It was uncannily strong too, as Richard had to maintain a good deal of his bodyweight on it to prevent it standing. It had six long, jointed legs and displayed a sandy, yellow hue with speckles of dark brown. There were two globular shaped eyes on five-centimetre-long stalks that moved in all directions, like a squirming worm. The eyes appeared to be sizing Richard up, and Naomi and Asharf as well when they arrived breathless. All the while there was a hum, like a barely audible mechanism.

'It's a land crab,' ventured Naomi, staring down at it suspiciously.

Asharf nodded in agreement. 'Be careful, *Effendi*,' he said. 'Those pincers will cut through your flesh; I have seen it . . . a man's face half eaten during the night!'

'I'm sure you are right, Asharf, and clearly a model land crab is what it would like to be,' replied Richard sceptically.

Another skirmish followed with a flurry of pincer snapping, and then an attempted escape that led to Richard almost standing on the creature to contain it.

At that, Naomi drew closer still. 'There *is* something odd, something different, something, not quite as it should be,' she said, making ready to leap backwards at any moment.

Richard pushed down harder and the crab's shell began

to deform. There was a whining noise again. Naomi gasped. 'You are hurting it,' she cried. Richard eased the pressure and immediately the crab's right hand pincer twisted backwards in an impossible way and snapped unsuccessfully at his ankle, however, it managed to take hold of his trousers and cut through the lined woollen material like new scissors.

'Be careful, *Effendi*!' shouted Asharf; as he scuffled clear, almost standing behind Naomi.

Richard instinctively raised his foot and as he did, the creature launched another attack, this time both pincers contorting to make a determined impression. The noise was like a runaway typewriter. Richard lifted his foot well clear of the assault and then the crab crouched as if to jump. Richard gasped and quickly stepped backwards as did Naomi. Asharf cursed. Immediately the crustacean made its getaway. It took off awkwardly and agitated, more than a scurry, and so doing made patterned groves in the sand and dust. Richard sprinted after it and intercepted it after another eight or nine metres along the long, shadowed corridor. The crab froze and set stance to defend itself. Richard replaced the Illuminac in his coat pocket and used his torch to scrutinise it again. Now there was no doubt in his mind.

With that, the thing was off again, only this time with greater fervour. Richard took three or four more paces, raised his right foot and stamped down on it with such force that its shell caved in. Then, using his heel he rained

down several more blows in quick succession. To his
amazement, the thing exploded. Shards of plastic and
micro-machinery flew in all directions; a pincer, like
a projectile, narrowly missed Richard's head; another
clattered off an adjacent wall. A few metres away, Naomi
drew a startled breath.

In a dank, cold room of bare stone; in a decaying house
amid a shanty town a few kilometres south of Aswan;
on a makeshift table strewn with electronics and cables;
beneath a large dish aerial, as out of place on a roof as a
seagull amidst a flock of crows; a video monitor flickered
momentarily and went blank.

Richard held aloft the remains of the sophisticated
machine, one clearly capable of responding independently.
He plucked an eye from its socket and from the stalk trailed
a long length of wire. Richard looked closer; it shone white
in his torchlight; it was a strand of optical fibre. He looked
at Naomi, his expression uneasy. "A bloody camera!" he

146

cursed.

At that moment, from far along the corridor, further still than the Pillared Hall and echoing towards them with terrifying menace, came the growling, snarling roar of a wild animal. Naomi gasped. Asharf's face paled. Richard had heard the like before. The hairs on the back of his neck bristled. He felt for his shoulder holster, turned towards Naomi and Asharf and ushered them back the way they had come.

They retreated quickly towards the Great Pharaoh's gallery, Richard constantly checking over his shoulder. He looked towards the secret room and the sturdy wooden door that he had virtually destroyed and shook his head. Hindsight, he thought, would be helpful in times like these and then he directed his friends into the room; at least he could defend a narrow doorway if necessary. Another blood-curdling roar reverberated along the corridor, even the audience of intangible spirits seemed to shiver at the sound of it. Beneath the domed ceiling outside, unintentional acoustics amplified the roar to alarming proportions. Naomi stepped backwards until her back thumped against the far wall, then she edged, like a mouse, into the adjacent corner. She sensed the danger; she sensed from where it came and she sensed its form, 'Bastet!' she mouthed. Her torch, shining through the doorway silhouetted Richard, who stood like a gladiator guarding the entrance to their sanctuary. A tingling, sparkling blade, with green transparency hung ready by his side.

'The goddess Bastet comes, and she is changed?' Naomi whispered again, her tone fraught.

Asharf, who stood a metre in front of her, turned to stare as his eyes widened with fear.

Inexplicably, Naomi glanced to her right. Engravings in the plaster, previously unseen, caught her attention. She tried to read them, just a few lines, but was unable; they were in the language of the "old people".

'Richard! Look! I have found something. There is more text. Words to which we paid no heed.'

Written in freehand, crudely, Naomi lightly wiped away the centuries of dust and algae with her handkerchief. Richard half turned, so that his whisper could be heard: 'We haven't time for that. I'm considering making a run for it.'

'No! Wait.' Naomi snapped. 'This text, Richard . . . it is written in blood!'

Richard hesitated. He gestured to Asharf to step forward and keep watch and then he reluctantly followed Naomi's directions until he peered at the pale coloured markings; a faint scratch in the plaster beneath each line, emphasised the words. He blew away the remaining dust. '*Well?* Richard, tell me, what do you see?'

'*Effendi* . . . I hear it breathe, it comes!'

Richard's face was just centimetres away from the inscription, he focused his attention and recited: '*For those who seek an understanding, take refuge in Meroe. Rest only, not home.*' Richard looked at Asharf and then back at Naomi. 'I think this may have been written in the dark. Perhaps something that was overheard before the door was finally closed?'

There was no time to consider the implications, as a deep, snarling roar gave notice of an animal immediately outside the room.

'*Effendi*, it is here!' Asharf warned.

Richard was over to the doorway in an instant, ISTAN at the ready. He closed the two wooden half-doors, in order that they offer some protection and kicked sand against them to hold them in place. The doors sagged on their hinges, but he leant on them and peered through the gap. Naomi melted into the corner. Loud, heavy breathing and a snorting snarl from outside terrorised their imaginations. Petrified, Asharf took a pace backwards. There was a sudden thump at the door and a scratching noise, the thing pushed hard at the doors, they almost opened . . . Richard resisted throwing his full weight against them in case he fell through. Naomi's heart was in her mouth, Asharf gasped, adrenalin pumped in Richard's veins.

Growl, growl, snarl!!!

'Bastet!' Naomi screamed. 'She comes for our souls!'

'Asharf!' Richard called. 'Quickly!'

Asharf rushed to Richard's side and with both hands on the door he pushed. 'These are but paper shutters against the beast!' he cried.

Another thud and then a smash from outside almost brushed him aside. Richard thought blue, the ocean under a clear sky pooled in his mind's eye, he raised the ISTAN to hip height, the door rattled and shook – the thing was coming through!

Richard fired. Three, four, five blades loosed and penetrated the door. Instantly, a baleful screech echoed through the gallery. Moments later a whimpering yelp expressed pain and death. Then, there was silence.

Richard breathed out loudly, his heart thumped like a bass drum. He switched off the ISTAN and looked at Asharf, nodding. Asharf relaxed, but kept a foot against the door-join. Slowly Richard looked up at Naomi; light from her torch cast a long shadow behind him. 'What the hell, makes you think it is *Bastet* . . ?' he demanded.

There was a moment of silence; Naomi was held rigid by fright. Richard shook his head impassively, walked over to her to comfort her but she fell into his arms and he gave her a long, reassuring hug. After a while, Richard asked again, this time more sympathetically: 'Why Bastet?'

'Her form sits at the entrance to tombs and mausoleums, mainly those of the queens of Egypt. She welcomes in death, as she does life.' Naomi paused thoughtfully. 'She is symbolised as a cat because they have been revered for centuries. She is the cat goddess, Richard.'

This was a side of Naomi that Richard had not previously seen; a modern woman, with a twenty-first century education and a contemporary perspective, but clearly believing in these ancient deities. Richard nodded; a few more pieces of the puzzle fell into place. 'Open the door, Asharf, please,' he said.

Asharf obliged. Richard walked over to the doorway and shone his torch beam through it. There, lying motionless on the floor outside was a large, black cat. Its fur glistened in the light and, on closer examination, Richard could see three cauterised wounds. There was little blood, just narrow slits about six centimetres long where the molecular blades had exited the cat's body. Richard stepped over the muscular frame. It was a long animal, perhaps two metres head to tail and it probably weighed two hundred pounds. From beneath tatty, pealing tufts of fur on its head glinted a bright metal skull. Richard knew immediately what it was. He looked closer to remind himself. A nickel-alloy half-skull, bionic implants and an eye with a coaxial laser sight; there was no doubt; this was FACULTE and it brought back chilling memories of his previous encounter with one several months ago on Moon Base Andromeda.

'What kind of animal is this, *Effendi*?' Asharf asked, as he eyed the beast.

'It's called a Feline, Autonomous, Cranial Utilised, Locator Tracker Eliminator. It's a genetic cross between a Black Panther and an African Caracal.'

'I know of this Caracal, *Effendi*; a hunter with little fear, that moves like the wind in the trees.'

Richard nodded, 'Yes. Only these hybrids have bionic implants. The stealth, cunning and hunting instincts of a cat, combined with biosynthetic enhancements . . . half of its brain is a microprocessor, but their control is limited. A night sight, a laser weapon and incredible hearing, not to mention the power of a panther, it's a formidable system.'

Naomi stepped forward, her face solemn. 'Why would they do this, Richard?' she asked brusquely. 'Such a beautiful animal, surely there would be repercussions?'

Richard nodded again. 'Correct. Originally, they were designed as a security system; free to roam sensitive military and government installations, that sort of thing. There was even a domestic model. Only the concept backfired . . . they started to kill people! Subsequently, they were withdrawn, banned and eradicated.' Richard looked up at Naomi, Asharf stood behind her. 'We are leaving . . . now!' he commanded, and stepped back into the chamber to retrieve his rucksack; he had thrown it into the corner along with Asharf's. As he flung the bag across his shoulder, however, and with equally terrifying menace, only this time made worse by its repetition, roars reverberated outside.

Naomi gasped. 'Another!'

Asharf stood frozen; his eyes haunted.

'I'm not being caught in here again,' Richard said and dropped his bag. 'Torches off, stay put! Asharf, look after Naomi!' he ordered, and then, without hesitation, he stepped over the dead animal and into the gallery. At that moment a red, pencil thin laser beam flashed in front of his face. It emanated from the darkness to his left, missing him by millimetres. Richard was quickly back into the doorway taking cover behind the door jamb when another fired out from nowhere, this time to his right. He dropped to one knee. A beam of searing energy struck the stone where he had been standing and ricocheted into their chamber. Splinters of granite rained down on him. He crouched forwards. Infrared, he thought. They can see me, but I can't see them. At that, Richard switched on his torch and darted into the arena, quickly finding his way over to the stone statue of Rameses. Two, three, four glowing beams followed him in quick pursuit, each time growing nearer. There was a loud roar and a growling snarl to his left and he could hear the padding of heavy feet to his right. Richard popped his head out from behind the stone feet and illuminated the area with his torch; a beam of laser energy immediately drove him back out of sight. 'Bloody hell!' he cursed, under his breath. 'Two more of them!' he shouted, but Naomi and Asharf had shrunk back into the chamber and Asharf had partly closed the doors.

'I need to see who I am fighting,' Richard whispered to himself. He pulled the Illuminac from his pocket, selected Level 2, looked away, switched it on and tossed it into the centre of the hollow-sounding gallery. The device slid across the floor raising dust. There was silence again, but night was day. Richard, with his back against the statue, held the ISTAN across his chest; the blade's form twinkled with subliminal light. He darted out, flung himself into a somersault of sorts and rolled across the floor. Both animals were bathed in the brilliant light and seemed momentarily paralysed; he had clear sight of one. The beast to his left cowered in a corner. Richard thought "blue" and fired off a volley of molecular blades. Most missed their target, but one surely found its mark and there was an eerie howl. Richard was soon on his feet and scrambling back to his cover, but he had lost sight of the other animal and from out of nowhere, it pounced to cut off his retreat.

The animal circled warily and then went down on its haunches. Alert, staring eyes, fiery bright, it had acquired Richard and was now in "tracker" mode. It hissed and snarled; its tail swished; saliva dripped from its open mouth and blackened gums pulled taut to reveal white, razor-sharp teeth. Richard crouched and faced it off. A laser beam fired out from the animal's left eye, Richard avoided it. He fired back; the molecular blade missed its mark. The cat sighted Richard again and another beam of searing red energy streaked towards him. Richard ducked, but the beam caught the side of his neck and scorched a mark. Richard fired again, but missed. With incredible power the cat pounced, its jaw gaping and its mouth red. Instinctively, Richard reacted and managed to sidestep the animal's aggressive lunge, scissor-like claws narrowly missing his face. From Richard's ISTAN, a wispy green blade appeared; he lashed out and caught the animal's body. There was a loud, shrieking howl as he pulled the blade through the cat's hindquarters, almost severing a leg as it leapt past.

The other cat found the door to the chamber and sniffed at the wooden doors, its tail lashing whilst the attacking cat landed and spun on its forelimbs – it went to attack again poised to leap, but its wounded leg failed; instead, it fired a laser beam. Avoiding it, Richard tripped and fell; the beam narrowly missed him. Naomi screamed something from inside the secret chamber to give warning. Richard rolled repeatedly across the ground and then stabilised himself on his elbows. He took aim and fired off a diverging volley of molecular blades; he tracked one as it pierced the animal's head. After passing through and resembling a spent firework sparkler, the blade dissipated into thin air. In an instant, the animal fell limp; Richard was up and quickly over to it. A swift, backhanded slash opened the side of the animal's body. Like a butchered carcass; entrails flopped out; the heart still pumped and blood oozed.

'Ahrrrrr!' Asharf cried. Naomi screamed too; a piercing, terrified shriek. Richard darted towards the chamber and burst through the doorway, the room was shadowy. On the far side, the great cat's jaws snapped, its head pulled up to growl. Asharf lay completely covered by the robot's cape, but he squirmed and writhed on the ground as the frenzied cat tried to bite and scratch him – Naomi, backed helplessly into a corner, could only watch.

Richard ran to Asharf's aid, his first swipe was wild and mistimed, but the ISTAN's blade caught the animal on the rump and severed its tail. The cat instantly turned on Richard. Its jet-black fur appeared almost polished in the half-light and its left eye glowed with an orange light. Like a coiled spring it leapt at Richard who dived to the ground and rolled beneath the elongated animal; another slash, mid-flight, opened a deep cut in its belly and inside its right, rear leg. The incensed animal landed and scrabbled in a cloud of dust and spit. In agony, it yelped loudly and ran from the room.

Outside, the gallery was bright. Consequently, a beam of light squeezed through the chamber's doorway and cast itself vertically on the opposite wall like a burning column. Moments later the cat's panting subsided; moments later, there was silence.

'Asharf, are you hurt? Where did it . . ?'

Asharf was already on his feet. 'The cat could not bite, *Effendi*. I was saved by the fleece, but its jaws pressed.' Asharf grimaced as he felt and rubbed his left shoulder and he lifted his left foot to relieve the pressure on his calf. Naomi, who stood by his side, put a hand on his forearm; he looked at her and gestured his wellness; she was grateful to him.

Miraculously the cape, with its woven Samite fibre, had prevented the cat's teeth from penetrating it, but Asharf was bruised in several places, particularly on his left shoulder, which he rubbed painfully; no doubt, a row of teeth marks beneath his shirt would be testament to the power of the cat's jaws.

'Come on then, we are leaving . . . now!' said Richard.

Asharf stood tall and bravely shrugged off the injury and the pain, but looked instead with deep concern at

Naomi. She needed no further encouragement from Richard, however, and was quickly by the door. Asharf stuffed the cape into his bag, Richard flung his across a shoulder, retrieved the Illuminac from the gallery and the trio set off towards the Pillared Hall.

Asharf hobbled awkwardly along as fast as he could. Naomi led and Richard covered the rear in case the injured beast made another attempt. Occasionally, he could hear its groans and in the confines of the long narrow corridor it sounded hauntingly close.

Soon, they were in the hall; its space and shadows giving cause for anxiety and wariness. Asharf would be more than pleased to see the light of day, and Naomi too appeared to have had her fill of the bygone, certainly for the foreseeable future. The pair raced ahead towards the entrance. Richard, who was shuffling half-backwards heard them go. Eventually, he high-tailed it after them.

When Richard caught up, they had already passed through the Second Chamber and he arrived in the entrance area to see Naomi and Asharf standing directly beneath the vertical shaft and staring upwards.

Richard, who was paying little attention, being more concerned with covering their retreat, called: 'Asharf, gloves on, you can stand on my back. Use your feet as well as your hands.' Richard looked everywhere but upwards.

'*Effendi*, you see, there is no wire.'

'Naomi, I can lift you up to arm's length, and then . . .'

'Richard, please!'

Richard stopped his directions to look at Naomi with a perplexed expression. He kept his torch low, but its effect was enough to light her face. She peered upwards into the neat circular incision three metres above her head and was speechless with disappointment. Richard followed her eye and moved to a place directly below the hole; he and Asharf shone their torches upwards; there was little need, however, as Asharf's beam amply lit the underside of a dirty, rusting vehicle. Clearly visible was a steel box-chassis member and a distorted exhaust pipe straddled the hole. Consequently, there was no natural light and it was clear now that there was no cable!

Richard edged Asharf aside in an attempt for a better view – desperately searching for some way out of the situation. Finally, he concluded bitterly: 'Someone has driven the drilling truck over the hole and shot out the tyres. We are not going anywhere!' Richard's head slumped forward and he breathed a deep sigh. Then, as if the thought had inexplicably just sprung to mind, he unbuttoned his coat, opened a zipped inside pocket, delved his hand inside and pulled from it his telephonic pager. He held it at arm's length, and reaching upwards; on tiptoes, he pointed it towards the hole. There was no radio signal. And there would never be a lifeline for them in that forgotten, subterranean mausoleum. The distraught howl of an injured beast echoed in the distance.

CHAPTER 29

THE ELYSIUM CONSPIRACY

Tom sat quietly on the bridge transfixed by the image on the main visual display. The *Enigma's* forward velocity was a relative walking pace now and as they neared the red planet it loomed large, both visually and in Tom's imagination. Just like its namesake, the Roman mythological god of war, Mars was magnificent but never too great to surprise you. Indeed, the appearance of the ostensibly sterile planet changed constantly with its annual passage around the sun, just as the earth does. Mars, however, is not generally known as a planet with contrasting seasons, as its changes are more subtle and no-one knew them better than Tom. His months in orbit as commander of the mother ship during the early days of the planet's exploration had given him a unique insight into the complexities of the planet's systems, and as NASA and the astronauts involved in that programme had learned, such changes often had dire consequences.

Most apparent and most affected by the excessive displacement of the planet's axis, was its atmosphere. Tom knew that debilitating dust storms could rage for months or wane within hours; some could cover almost a hemisphere, whilst others were confined to the surface of an impact crater or the confines of an ancient, water-eroded valley. Wildly varying surface temperatures, searing levels of solar radiation, local concentrations of corrosive gases, even rapid and intense pressure variations, could all turn a surface survey into a death walk, or a routine flight into a disorientated plunge towards the surface. He began to consider the implications of his forthcoming flight.

Tom stared at the intense and beautiful copper colour of the planet's surface as EMILY manoeuvred the *Enigma* onto a final approach course. The hue, which varied from dark grey to yellow-ochre and passed through every nuance of brown, he knew to be partly due to the presence of maghemite, a very fine and highly magnetic mineral. Avoiding exposed outcrops of maghemite would also be a necessity, as its affect on the relatively unprotected navigation system of the D Class could be disastrous. Mars was indeed a rusty world on a grand scale, he mused, with its mixtures of iron-rich clays and extensive deposits of maghemite. And there was another problem. Unpredictable Martian winds frequently whip up the surface dusting, causing awe-inspiring salmon pink clouds, but their attraction is fatal, as flying through them causes rapid metal erosion. His Delta Class fighter was untested in the Martian atmosphere; he would need to be extremely cautious if he was to successfully retrieve the Kalahari Crystals from Osiris Base.

With faultless precision, EMILY established a low elliopheric orbit, the initial quadrant of which passed over the planet's northern icecap. At this time of the year, the polar cap was in full retreat, although EMILY's sensors detected a rate that was far quicker than normal. That is indicative of other weather phenomena, Tom thought, as he studied the indicators on one of his data screens. Nevertheless, the icecap was still vast and it would take some minutes to overfly.

Switching his attention to the main visual display and looking south, Tom could clearly see a huge volcanic cone appearing on the horizon as the planet rotated – soon Olympus Mons would be in full view. Using it – the highest volcano in the entire solar system – as a reference, and with some display magnification, Tom would sight Osiris Base. He grew apprehensively excited at the prospect of only his second visit to the planet's surface. After the white, reflective icecap had passed beneath them, the true nature of the surface became apparent. Delving chasms; gouges that made the Grand Canyon seem like a mere scratch, dried riverbeds, longer and wider than the great Amazon itself and mountain ranges that dwarfed the Himalayas;

Mars was indeed both evocative and impressive. It may not have an atmosphere like the earth's, thought Tom, and it may be very cold, but it was far from inert, far from dead; a red beacon in the blackness of space that shouted: Stop! Try me! I too, am an oasis. He recalled again his first close encounter with the planet, as the orbital pilot for the second manned landings; what an adventure, what an experience and how long ago it seemed.

Ishhi had left the bridge more than two hours earlier in order to prepare a "close of daylight period" meal – known colloquially as "rhythmics". After months of incarceration, Tom was wary of leaving her on her own for more than was necessary. He checked the time and frowned. EMILY broke the protracted silence.

'I have established a sixty percent elliopheric orbit based on the planet's North Pole, Commander. It is lower than I feel comfortable with. I shall remain here for forty-eight hours. My sensors indicate that the Class 1 atmospheric storm you can see on the metrological monitor is increasing, both in intensity and size. It now covers extensive areas of this hemisphere. The epicentre of the main cell is itself moving north and is presently passing the 16th Parallel. Its momentum will carry it past Osiris Base and well into the northern latitudes. From the storm's current frontal velocity, I calculate a window of opportunity of twenty-one hours, and forty two minutes within which a retrieval flight is possible. After that, flying conditions above the Plains of Isidis, where Osiris

Base is located and also Elysium will be dangerous, if not impossible. The last recorded storm of this magnitude, in the year 2012, lasted eleven months Commander.' EMILY's delivery was very matter-of-fact.

Tom nodded. 'I understand, EMILY. What are the storm's current parameters?' he asked, shifting his gaze to the picture on the meteorological monitor.

'Dense dust clouds and severe turbulence extending well beyond the Maronosphere . . . the most energetic protrusions penetrate over forty kilometres into the upper atmosphere. Magnetic flux distortion, particularly in the northern hemisphere, is in the order of eight-point-eight Tesla. Therefore, communication and navigation systems will suffer considerable interference. Current surface wind traces indicate a mean velocity of one hundred and fifty kilometres per hour, well outside the landing parameters of the D Class. Finally, within the areas of principal activity, I estimate a mechanical abrasion ratio of three-point-two micrometres. This would strip the outer protective coating from your ship in less than four minutes, Commander.'

Tom mumbled under his breath, he knew well enough the design limitations of his ship. 'Okay, I get the picture, after the window, it's a no-go zone,' he concluded gruffly. 'Osiris Base Operations have requested a touchdown at first light, that's 05:56 Martian Corrected Time. Flight time is less than an hour; I'll leave at 05:00 sharp. That gives me eight hours; time for something to eat and some rest. By the way, is Captain Tsou still in the galley?'

After a brief pause and with little concern in her tone, EMILY replied. 'I cannot sense Captain Tsou's heat signature, Commander. Despite maximum infrared sensitivity, she does not appear to be in the galley, in any interconnecting corridors, or in her cabin. At the moment, Commander, I cannot sense her body heat anywhere.'

'What! But that's impossible,' replied Tom, springing to his feet. He feared the worst. 'I'm going down there. Command override; cancel portal presets. Emergency release on all cabin doors and on the galley flat . . . quickly!'

Tom wasted no time, within minutes he was running down the corridor that linked the galley to the bridge officer's quarters. He tried the galley first. Thoughts of an electric shock, or worse, filled his mind. He checked every corner . . . nothing. Back into the corridor he ran, he was panting, even panicking; should anything have happened to Ishhi, he would never forgive himself. He skidded to a halt outside her cabin and slammed his fist against the touch pad; instantly the door slid open. Tom stepped in; his eyes scanned the floor and then darted from corner to corner. At that moment, the shower door opened and Ishhi, engulfed in a cloud of steam, stepped from the cubicle.

Tom froze mid-breath. Ishhi reached out and pulled a white towel from an adjacent rail. The backlit, translucent cubicle silhouetted her slim, toned body. Tom stared momentarily, before lowering his eyes. The cabin door slid closed behind him. The lights dimmed automatically, assuming their prior level. Tom's lungs were bursting; he let out a deep breath. Ishhi wrapped the towel around her body. Tom, embarrassed, opened his mouth to speak as Ishhi pulled another, smaller towel from the rail and began drying her hair.

'You seem to be in a hurry, Commander. Are you looking for me?' she asked with a slight tremor of surprise in her voice.

'Uh, yes, I was, I thought . . . EMILY . . . she couldn't . . .'

'EMILY couldn't what, Commander?' Ishhi whispered. She looked at Tom expectantly. Her black hair was limp and wet and it hung around her shoulders. A droplet of water ran down the side of her smiling face; she wiped it away slowly. Her Japanese eyes never leaving him, she raised an eyebrow, her mouth dimpling. 'Well, Commander?'

'Well . . . um, she couldn't see your body heat, I thought something . . . you know, an accident or something? I, er, came to make sure you were okay, that's all . . . sorry. I shouldn't have barged in like that . . . should have knocked . . .'

'I take it that you care for me?'

'Of course I care, I mean . . .'

'That's good, because I care about you . . .' Ishhi glanced momentarily at EMILY's sensor terminal. '*Tom*,' she said defiantly.

Tom admired this new aspect of Ishhi as she walked towards him, her hips swaying. She was up close and Tom could feel the heat from her body as she looked up at him.

Tom lowered his head until their lips were barely apart.

'I've always cared about you, Tom. Ever since you joined the programme I have cared,' she breathed. 'But you're always so careful, so focused; you have never noticed. You are always so, you know . . . objective?'

Tom tried to make a nonchalant gesture. 'Why didn't you say something . . . anything!' he asked as their lips touched and they kissed passionately.

Tom lifted his head at last and looked at her with a smile. 'I've always had to bear in mind that you are a 10th Dan. You may not have liked me doing this.' He took her completely in his arms and kissed her again. Ishhi's arms circled his neck and her bath towel dropped to the floor.

Commander Tom Race sat in the cockpit of his fighter. He was not nervous, but perhaps more than a little pensive. He was ready: suited, pressurised, systems online, navigation coordinates loaded and the profile initiated. For the first landing attempt on Mars of a D Class, it was prudent to double-check the systems, crosscheck the parameters and confirm the entry profile – he did it, and they all looked good. Now he waited for the Sion gas evaporators to indicate matter-stream availability and then he would go. He checked the fuel indicators on his instrument panel and particularly for each of the two drop tanks that were mounted one beneath each wing; they both showed a little under half full; the integral tank similarly. The unusually low orbit that he had requested would help save this precious commodity, as he would need every molecule for his re-entry through the earth's atmosphere on their return.

'EMILY,' he called, after a short delay. 'Please configure an Accelercom communication relay to Osiris Base Operations.'

'It is done, Commander. You may initiate the transmission.'

'Osiris Base Operations, this is Commander Tom Race onboard the Federation Craft *Luke Piccard*, detaching from the *Enigma* in one minute, all systems green . . . confirm?'

The reply came immediately. 'Commander Race, this is Lieutenant Mildenhall, Osiris Base Operations Officer. Charlie, Charlie, I confirm, all systems green this end, we are waiting for you and there is plenty of room. Landing area is the main platform for our former S1 emergency shuttle *Columbus*, south side, you can't miss it, Commander . . . go ahead.'

'Latent matter-stream potential, one hundred percent . . . I'm on my way, Osiris, over and out!' Tom deselected the open microphone facility and opened an intercom channel directly to Ishhi's bridge console, 'Ishhi,' he said quietly. 'I'll be back in less than twenty-four hours. Look after yourself.'

'Thank you for letting *us* know, Commander,'

interrupted EMILY, with an air of sarcasm.

With that Tom released the magnetic locks and rose vertically. Barely ten metres above the *Enigma's* hull, he pushed the power lever forward and transitioned into forward flight. A tight over-the-shoulder manoeuvre had him pointing towards the planet, and in an instant, he was gone.

Down through the atmosphere he plunged and consequential to it being considerably more rarified than that of earth's, his descent profile was steep; too steep; so much so that at one point Tom considered disconnecting the auto-flight system. However, the ramifications of that action were unknown, so he let it ride. Past Olympus Mons he streaked, its pinnacle towering 56,000 feet above the planet surface – almost twice the height of Mount Everest on earth. So vast was the surface area covered by the volcano that it took six minutes to overfly – even at that speed.

Subsequently, and snaking its way across a broad, flat plateau that stretched as far as the eye could see, was a deep gorge. Tom took manual control and briefly banked the D Class to the left in order to peer down into it. Three miles deep, the jagged fissure looked to divide the planet's crust in two. Exposed rock strata changed colour impressively – brown, the yellow of sulphur, the orange of maghemite. A short while later, as he approached the Plains of Isidis, Tom pulled back the power lever and decelerated; far off to the south, ominous in its extent, he could see dust clouds rising; the storm was drawing near.

'We have you on visual, Commander Race,' said Ralph Mildenhall, over the open operations frequency, precisely as Tom himself sighted the base complex.

'Charlie, Charlie,' replied Tom, coolly. 'Request a four degree alignment sector. I will make the final approach manually.'

'Aligning and radiating,' came the reply. 'Platform on the south side, you are clear to land.'

'Clear to approach and land.'

The S1 docking platform was enormous and Tom's subsequent landing was faultless; even so, the bead of sweat that ran down his temple indicated that perhaps the manoeuvre was not quite as easy as he had made it look. He locked his tiny ship in place by energising the fighter's magnetic undercarriage just as the entire platform began to vibrate. Like the chassis of a giant locomotive on an old railroad track, the triangular shaped platform squeaked and clattered its way towards the dispatch dome of Osiris Base. The contraption was antiquated, being one of the first constructions for the new base, some ten years earlier.

Tom had been precise in his landing position and had perched his craft on the forward tip of the gantry and minutes later, two giant, self-sealing thermoplastic doors edged past him in unison, until they came together behind his craft and meshed to form an atmospheric seal. Next, a loud, almost alarming hiss of highly pressurised air, together with a huge cloud of condensing gas, reverberated around his cockpit. The lights came on; the environment seemed friendly and within moments, an operative had wheeled a metal stepladder up to the side of his craft. Tom shut down the remainder of his avionics and opened the canopy. At the bottom of the steps a group of colonists formed; they all seemed genuinely pleased to see him. Tom released the seat's pneumatic spine-support device and then his five-point harness. Finally, he isolated the integrated ejection seat power supply, depressurised his suit and stood up to survey the impressive surroundings.

An immaculately dressed, elderly officer, in a tailored black coverall over a white polo neck shirt made his way to the base of the steps. The group opened to give him access. He, Tom knew, would be the Base Commanding Officer. Tom stepped onto the small platform adjacent to his cockpit, removed his helmet and placed it back on the seat. Using a remote control device on his wrist, he initiated the canopy closure mechanism, but an engineer on the ground hastily caught his eye and indicated to him to leave it open. Tom, surprised, reversed the selection. He walked carefully down the steps to be greeted by the officer, who had short, spiky, grey hair and a close, grey beard. The man's eyes were steely blue and he wore three gold stripes on each of his epaulets.

'What a pleasure,' he said to Tom, offering his hand. 'My name is Todd Miko, I'm the Base Commander.'

'Great pleasure to be here, Sir,' replied Tom, shaking Miko's hand. There was an impromptu round of applause for Tom; it broke the ice. Tom smiled; now he *felt* welcome. A circle of introductions followed, after which Commander Miko escorted him to the main briefing room.

Ishhi sat in silence at her console, she felt relieved at Tom's arrival. The main viewing screen showed a real-time, magnified image of the planet surface; like a distant but powerful satellite image, the Osiris Base complex was just discernable in the south eastern corner of Isidis Planitia.

Ostensibly, she monitored a number of space frequencies, whilst busying herself recalibrating the console's "thought" interface, after Tom's abortive attempt at a "mind control" download. The system itself, however, was capable of all the functions she instigated. In point of fact, her mind was elsewhere. Presently, EMILY spoke to her.

'I could not differentiate between *your* infrared image and that of Commander Race's for some considerable time yesterday evening, Captain Tsou,' EMILY commented sourly. 'What was the reason?'

Ishhi leapt from her thoughts; her daydream instantly dissolved. She looked up at EMILY's primary terminal and considered the peculiar question for some time before answering. 'You should not have been looking. I mean *sensing*, EMILY; Ishhi replied, equally caustically.

'I know what you were doing; my memory cortex has experienced it. Your place is here on the bridge, Captain Tsou. Your conduct has been inappropriate and you have been insubordinate. This is not good for your longevity. In due course, you will be disciplined,' EMILY concluded.

The bridge fell silent.

After walking several corridors in silence, mainly to allow Tom to absorb a little of the Osiris Base "ambiance", Commander Miko turned to his guest. 'Commander Race, as we are both of equal rank, shouldn't we do away with unnecessary protocol and use our first names?' he asked.

'I'd be honoured if you would call me Tom, Sir. Thing is, I can't call a commanding officer by his first name in his own base, gee, that would go against the grain. For me, the normal mark of respect will be just fine . . .'

Miko smiled. 'Very well. Tell me, your ship, the Delta Class – first time I've seen one close up and very impressive it looks. Presumably, it's named after one of our countrymen, the scientist Luke Oswald Piccard, inventor of the matter-stream propulsion system?'

'Sure as hell, Sir, and she's the second ship to bear his name too. What's more, the *Enigma* is a direct result of that system's success. He will go down in history as one of the greats, Newton, Edison, Einstein . . . I'll let you into a secret, Sir . . . light speed travel is closer than you think!'

The two men arrived at the theatre. An illuminated, orange sign above the sliding door read: Briefing in Progress. Commander Miko allowed Tom to enter first.

Already occupying the first row of seats were the five heads of department: Base Operations, Scientific, Biological, Research and Life Support. Miko made the introductions and then stepped onto the low podium. Tom could see that his officers held him in high regard and that he had considerable charisma.

'Gentlemen,' Commander Miko began. 'This is not going to be a long briefing, as we all know the situation and the time constraints. However, so that everyone is completely clear on their department's task allocations for the next twelve hours, let's just clarify a few points.' Commander Miko checked his wristlet; it had vibrated indicating the arrival of a message. He read it, nodded and then focused on Tom. 'I can confirm, Tom, that the three remaining so-called Kalahari Crystals have been safely deposited in one of the two U-Semini cases that you brought with you and that this case is now secure in our Yearlman-standard shielded laboratory. Unfortunately, despite an extensive search of the entire base complex *and* the surrounding area, including the primary route to the East Sector, there has been no trace of the ninth crystal. We have used every method available to us. We can only postulate that the crystal fell into a crevice or similar and lies deep in the planet's crust – well beyond the range of our detection equipment.'

'East Sector ... is that where the downed alien craft was discovered? Is that correct, Commander?' Tom asked.

'That's it. Cross coordinate one-one-five, to be precise. We now know that the ship was called the *Star of Hope*. I'm not sure how familiar you are with the exact details, Tom, but several months ago our senior planetary surveyor entered that craft and found a flight log. In fact, it was more than a log, it detailed a full breakdown of the vessel's engineering, like an aircraft's technical manual; its propulsion system, how the crystals were utilised as a power source, and lots more besides.'

Tom nodded, 'Yeah, I'm already in on that, Sir, I've had the brief.'

Unable to restrain his disappointment, Peter Mayhew, the departmental Head of Science, interjected. 'Don't forget that it also detailed a galactic navigation database, Commander, something that will take us a thousand years to compile. It's a catastrophic disaster . . . irreplaceable information lost.' Mayhew folded his arms and breathed out heavily.

Commander Miko nodded, his frustration was equally apparent. 'That damn thing has gone missing too, much to our embarrassment. The document was found in the cabin of Richard Reece some time after his departure and was subsequently kept, under lock and key I may add, in our security department. A few weeks ago it miraculously disappeared. Another extensive search, including a room-by-room initiative that was coordinated by my Head of Security, failed to discover its whereabouts. We have been outside to a distance of one kilometre and echo-surveyed to a depth of two metres below the entire base, still nothing!'

Tom nodded again. 'I heard about it, Sir, and I know how absolutely critical that information is to the reinstatement programme. I also know that the log is written in a mysterious, undecipherable language; one that only Lieutenant Commander Reece has managed to crack. Back on earth, Sir, he's a wanted man and I suspect up to his ears in trouble as we speak.'

'Yes,' replied Commander Miko, with a sullen expression. 'The ISSF are keeping me in the loop. We wish him well with his search for possibly the largest and most potent crystal. What's the situation with the Long Island reactor, Tom?'

'Already sucking on its second crystal, Sir. Our primitive, reconditioned, nuclear reactors have already pretty much burnt out the entire first consignment; their remaining potential is now being measured in days, not months or years.'

Miko sighed. 'We had *hoped* that the information contained in the flight log would allow us to modify our reactors and use the remaining crystals more efficiently – that's not to be. And you will be returning to earth with just the one case and three crystals, I am very sorry to say.' He checked the time. 'Gentlemen, I'm aware of the deteriorating meteorological conditions on the Plain of Elysium – Tom, you take off in two hours. Over to you, Peter, to reiterate the specifics of today's briefing.'

'One thing, Sir,' Tom enquired in earnest. 'You have *two* U-Semini cases. The three crystals . . . they go in *one* case . . . right?'

'Yes, that's correct, Tom. The second case was earmarked for the *Star's* flight log. That was our brief and we will retain the case; it may come in useful. We know little about the flight log's constituent materials, only that they are extremely resilient and incredibly light in weight. A spectrograph and a great deal of other research had been planned by the ISSF. That was to take place in NASA's laboratories in the Cape and was a priority upon your arrival. Without knowing the immunity index, protection from solar radiation and cosmic particle contamination was necessary. The U-Semini case provided the best option for its transit to the *Enigma* and subsequently, after the *Enigma* had established an earth orbit, to Canaveral.'

Tom nodded understandingly as Peter Mayhew took to the podium. He walked purposefully to the lectern. An American Professor of Thermodynamics, he pressed a button on the lectern's control panel and instantly filled the large, integral screen behind him with an image of the base PTSV.

'This is our primary Personnel Transport and Service Vehicle, Commander Race,' he began. 'You may not be familiar with it as it is one of the early alpha-types; having said that, you can't miss it. Twenty metres long, twelve large "bubble" tyres, independent suspension, oxygen cylinders side mounted and predominantly white, as you can see.'

'If you don't mind me asking, Peter, what's with the gun turret?'

'Ah, that's the Cyan Magnetic Pulse Canon, Commander. A close defence system, limited range, five or six kilometres, but quite effective.'

'Is it active?'

'It's always active, but requires command approval to fire; there is a failsafe system. Don't worry, it is perfectly safe.'

'Three hundred and sixty degree field of fire,' Tom raised his eyebrows. 'They do know I'm coming in a Delta fighter, I presume?'

Peter Mayhew smiled limply. 'Yes, of course!'

Tom acknowledged with a concerned expression.

'Your rendezvous with the PTSV, Commander, will be on the southern side of Zeta 2, that's the largest of the four Elysium pyramids. We do not foresee any necessity for you to join the team on surface survey, not unless there is a special request for you to do so, but be prepared, as they might have something for you to retrieve. Our flight engineers are downloading the precise coordinates of Zeta 2 into your ship's navigation computer as we speak. Initially, we request that you complete an imaging survey of each pyramid in turn. Just fly around each one a couple of times, Commander. Because of the scale of these structures, the system requires a thirty degree aspect ratio and a four percent pitch rise; the pod-mounted imager will do the rest. It's a real-time Data Stream transmission, no onboard storage necessary. If we need anything else, another angle, we will let you know.'

Tom raised his hand and looked at Commander Miko. 'Is there really no detailed imagery of these things, Sir? I mean, we have known about them for what . . . close on eighty years?'

Peter Mayhew looked at Commander Miko; the question was outside his remit.

'It goes back to the 1970s, Tom, and the photographs provided by NASA's Viking program,' explained Commander Miko, soberly. 'Those were the first detailed images of the Elysium Planitia. Primarily, they were photographing Elysium Mons. As you know, that volcano rises over forty-six thousand feet above the plain. As one of the largest volcanoes on Mars, it was high on the priority list. The pyramids were discovered by chance, but were clearly detailed in that first tranche. Then a subsequent Viking mission and latterly the Global Surveyor programme confirmed it beyond any doubt – the pyramids were clearly artificial and indeed, remarkably similar to those on the Giza Plateau in Egypt and others in Mesoamerica . . . only on a much larger scale. Zeta 2 is more than three kilometres square at its base. It wasn't just their common architecture that excited either; alignment also bears an uncanny similarity. Understandably, the scientific community were elated. In the public domain, speculation was rife because of the earlier imagery that NASA had released; entirely erroneously I have to say. With the new imagery and astonishing calculations of scale, NASA were about to go public when the government stepped in and put a blanket stop on everything. The report states that most of the images were confiscated by the intelligence agency. Those that the department were allowed to keep were given a National Security Top Secret rating – zero release and zero tolerance.'

Tom nodded. He remembered the orbit orientation that he and colleagues flew on the initial landings; none of them ever over-flew the Plain of Elysium. He had never really thought about it. Orders were orders. No sightline; no imagery; no reporting. 'But why?' he asked.

'This is something that I have found out only in the last few days; since the lifting of the embargo; all my years on Mars and never any explanation as to the exclusion zone. It was down to a perceived public reaction, Tom, life on Mars . . . a sister planet . . . and so close. A threat, an attack! New York had pressed the panic button back in 1938, when Orson Welles narrated his infamous production of H.G. Wells' *War of the Worlds* on the radio. Half the city thought that the Martians were coming. There *was* widespread panic. People fled into the streets. They fired bullets at goddamn water towers. Imagine that on a national, or worse, an international scale. They couldn't risk it, hence the information blackout. Anything that did leak out over subsequent years was discredited and the proponents belittled.'

'And now, Sir?'

Commander Miko shrugged. 'You know as well as I do, Tom, that things have changed. The earth is desperate for energy; no taboos now; they are looking at every option. If an extinct extra-terrestrial race can offer a lifeline, then we take it. People back home have other things to worry about these days and anyway, what with the sightings over the last few years and the aggressive encounter back in 2016, most are more open-minded.'

'Opening up Elysium, after so long . . . who'd have believed it?'

Commander Miko paused and then looked Tom in the eye. 'Old habits die hard, all of us here know that! Political initiatives, particularly those that affect national security are difficult, if not impossible to overturn – no one wants to take the responsibility. That is until something even more catastrophic raises its ugly head.' Miko gestured in a "does that satisfy you?" kind of way.

Tom took a deep breath, held it for several seconds and then breathed out loudly. 'And time, it seems, is never on our side,' he said. He looked at Peter Mayhew. 'Sorry, Sir, please carry on.'

Peter Mayhew nodded in agreement. 'Regarding flight operations, your main problem is the approaching weather system. It's big, very big, nothing like it for a decade, in fact! The storm front is moving north from the equatorial region. Through an array of optical sensors positioned approximately forty kilometres south of here, we can already see clouds of fine dust being lifted into the lower Maronosphere. This really is a serious storm, Commander Race, and its track is unpredictable. Around its epicentre, maghemite counts are reaching record levels. As you know, maghemite is caused by the oxidation of basalt; grains of this mineral are very coarse and very hard. The result is rapid erosion of anything exposed to it. We are preparing an external close down of Osiris Base, by that I mean everything is brought undercover; vehicles, plant, machinery, close-quarter sensors, everything. All external access points will be out of bounds. We do gain some protection from an electrostatic field, like an invisible aura, that we generate around the domes, it has the effect of repelling the grains, bit like magnetism in reverse. Nevertheless, anything caught outside *will* be damaged . . . bit like rubbing balsawood with sandpaper. We are estimating a safe operational window of twelve hours from your takeoff time – after that Osiris will be a no go zone. Flight time to Elysium is fourteen minutes. However, we recommend that you keep the speed back, take a little longer, a few extra minutes will not make a significant difference.'

'What about getting back to the *Enigma*?' Tom asked, apprehensively.

'We anticipate an opportunity in three to four days.

Our most remote sensors are picking up a break in the system; it lies well astern of the storm front and appears similar to conditions found within the eye of a cyclone or hurricane. Satellite imagery, although inconclusive, seems to confirm this. Within this "eye", we are recording significant reductions in wind speed; in fact, for eight to ten hours, it should be almost calm. This is when we are planning your launch; a vertical climb into the upper Maronosphere and then the transition to elliopheric orbit at forty-eight percent – a difficult manoeuvre, but our simulations gives a high probability of success. Up through this "eye", Commander Race,' Peter Mayhew emphasised, raising his eyebrows. 'It could be our last chance for weeks, even months!'

'A vertical climb to forty eight . . . that will be heavy on fuel!' Tom leaned forwards and turned to look at Commander Miko. 'And a delay of three more days . . . earth won't like that. There are other complications, too. The *Enigma*. I have an agreement with EMILY – she will hold orbit for forty-eight hours.'

Commander Miko glanced up at Mayhew and then back at Tom. 'We know about the *Enigma's* controlling computer and your agreement with it. To be honest, I look towards the future and our relationship with these advanced systems with trepidation. On this count, however, there is not much we can do about it, Tom,' he said, in a concerned tone. 'We will have to handle any problems as they arise. At the moment, I suggest that we keep quiet about this delay, the computer is unlikely to break orbit without you . . . it wants those damned Humatron units as much as we want the crystals delivered to earth!'

Tom nodded. 'Okay, Sir, I understand.' He looked at Mayhew. 'So what is the situation with the PTSV?'

'For the PTSV crew, it's been a two day excursion,' Mayhew answered. 'They arrived at Zeta 2 late last night. *Their* return journey will not be as restricted as yours as the vehicle has a heavy external anti-abrasion skin. They commenced the ISAPS – the initial search and procurement session – at zero seven hundred hours this morning and will be on station when you arrive. I have to say that the first images that we have received are absolutely astounding. These really are serious structures . . . far bigger than the Egyptian pyramids for instance; NASA has passed us a file on those for comparison. Inexplicably, there does seem to be some similarity in construction. Incidentally, the IFFS insisted on our highest security level for this mission; consequently, our head of security, Major Greg Searle, is part of the team.'

Tom nodded nonchalantly. 'Okay,' he responded.

'He's a good man, Tom, takes his job very seriously and has my full confidence,' interjected Commander Miko. 'You will identify him by a green circle on the back of his helmet.'

Tom nodded again. 'Well if that's all, Sir, gentlemen . . . I would like to make my preparations.'

'Quite so, I suggest that you get a bite to eat and then

head off to flight dispatch,' replied Commander Miko.

Peter Mayhew had been quite correct with his weather forecast. As the Delta Class fighter climbed quickly to 34,000 feet and set course for the Plain of Elysium, Tom could see the dense dust clouds of the storm front already rising over the Saratoga escarpment – a steep ridgeline some 250 kilometres south of Osiris base. He focused on the navigation coordinates being projected onto his main screen and made a flight path adjustment; minutes later saw two towering obelisks approaching. For several seconds he stared in awe. Jeepers, he whispered to himself, look at the size of those things! As his range neared sixty kilometres, he descended to 5000 feet and reduced speed; even so, the lifeless, copper-brown undulating plain beneath him still sped by at an amazing rate. Moments later, with his navigation system illuminating the display coordinates, he was conscious of entering the long-established exclusion zone.

Just as Tom flew into the massive, elongated shadow of the first pyramid, he caught sight of the two smaller structures – but even those were much larger than anything he had seen on earth. He disconnected the autopilot, deciding to circumnavigate the monuments manually and within moments he pulled the D Class into a steep left hand turn. At 4000 feet, he was level with the pinnacles of the two smaller pyramids; however, the larger ones towered above him into the reddish hue of the Martian sky. He descended to 1000 feet and then, almost directly below, the white bulk of the PTSV caught his eye. He looked again, close by it and clearly silhouetted, a white-suited figure waved furiously. This structure must be Zeta 2, he thought, and that one, Zeta 1. He cross-checked the coordinates on his navigation display; they concurred.

As Tom flew between them, all four pyramids appeared to be constructed to the same lines – only their proportions differed. Aesthetically pleasing, they seemed to embody precise mathematical symmetry. He was mesmerised as he skimmed past one of the bigger ones again and then pulled a hard starboard turn that sent him whistling back in the opposite direction. All the while, his onboard imaging system contour mapped the complete structures by automatically recognising and splicing the pixel library from the prior sweep – all he had to do was circumnavigate each structure in a reasonably coordinated fashion – and for this operation manual flying was perfect. Simultaneously, a satellite-routed data link relayed the results directly to Osiris Base. A temporary display screen, fixed by Osiris' engineers to his main flight panel, indicated the ever-increasing library – like a digital jigsaw puzzle miraculously filling in the pieces by itself.

Tom reflected on the pyramid's architecture as he completed the final lap. Clearly, they are steeper, slimmer and substantially taller than those famous monuments near Cairo, he mused, or for that matter the Mayan examples I have seen. Nonetheless, he could not help feeling that there was a definite subliminal similarity. Here, however, there were no truncations and just one narrow step was apparent; it was set lower down on all the structures and appeared like a peripheral road. Overall, Tom noted, the surfaces of the pyramids appeared smooth and linear as they reached skywards and then each terminated in a sharply pointed pinnacle – as the examples on the Giza Plateau had done during better times. Not only that, they were all similarly orientated to the cardinal points.

From a distance, the pyramid's external finish appeared to be matt – dulled no doubt from countless centuries of wind erosion. To confirm this, on his final flypast, Tom decided that a much closer look was necessary. Seconds later, he passed so close to the surface of Zeta 2 that his propulsion efflux started a dust avalanche that tumbled down one side of the structure. Straining his neck to look back over his shoulder, he watched the burnt-brown cloud gather momentum and mass until it crashed to the ground and flowed outwards like a cascading river of sand and debris. It's true, he thought, there is a lot of pitting in the stone, particularly on the south side and I bet at one time the entire surface must have been highly polished. He banked steeply, this time to the left and directed the imager manually for a few seconds in order to capture two areas he saw that lay shielded by other pyramids. The geology department will be very interested in these, he whispered to himself, as they still retain some reflective ability.

Of a very light brown, almost orange colour, the stone

used for the construction of the pyramids contrasted with the surrounding strata and it was obvious to Tom that the material had been mined in another location. It led him to further speculate how and when such things could have been built. To complete his survey, he would need to take some additional images from the ground – it was time to land and he looked for a suitable place.

Tom descended to 200 feet above the undulating surface; however, at that altitude and much to his surprise, he began to feel turbulence. A surface vehicle caught his attention. It was a small, six-wheeled buggy and the astronaut that stood beside it was waving and jumping excitedly. Tom reduced speed and looked again. For an instant the figure was obscured by a cloud of sand, but then it appeared again and he seemed to be repeatedly tapping his helmet, Tom realised immediately.

'Gee, you dork!' he said to himself, and pressed a red button on the communications console – the button turned green and instantly someone spoke.

'This is Lieutenant Chris Rosenbek calling the *Luke Piccard* on assigned frequency . . . come in, Commander Race – how do you read?'

'Commander Race here, yeah, loud and clear . . . sorry, finger trouble,' Tom replied, feeling embarrassed at his basic error – so enthralled was he with the pyramids that he had not noticed the short-range ground radio was still turned off.

'Listen Lieutenant, I've completed the aerial survey, I'd

like to land for some additional imaging.'

A sudden shudder displaced Tom from his intended flight path; he corrected and then scanned his instruments – everything appeared normal.

'That's good, Sir,' came the enthusiastic reply. 'We have some samples for you to take back to Osiris – high priority. One thing though, we may not have as much time as we hoped. The wind is increasing down here and the temperature is dropping. Sand is blowing too and I've seen a couple of twisters!'

'Standby,' Tom declared, as he pulled his craft into a steep climb and eased open the thrust control. Moments later, he attained 7000 feet and then he gently pushed the nose forward again, reduced the thrust and turned south. Tom levelled his ship at 11,000 feet and from that altitude he could clearly see billowing dust clouds in the distance; they stretched across the horizon and were approaching fast. He looked to his right, towards the two tallest structures; he was just a little lower than the pinnacles of Zeta 1 and 2 – over two miles high, he thought.

'You're right, Lieutenant,' Tom said, over the radio. 'Storm's coming in. Where can I land?'

'Not in this area, Sir, surface is too soft. Major Searle has taken the PTSV over to the base of Zeta 3, north side. I don't think that he can hear you at the moment as the pyramids are shielding his antenna; either that or he is inside. We found a blocked entrance – it's amazing!'

'Okay . . . copied. So where do you suggest?'

'Same area, Sir, north side of Zeta 3 – say, two or three hundred metres clear. We found what looks like a civic square, extends to a plaza, there's even a raised terrace – it's massive. The whole area is surfaced with smooth, level flagstones and there is only a thin covering of dust and sand – it's a good area.'

'Copied, thanks, I'll see you on the ground, then.'

'I don't think so, Commander. I'm heading back to the PTSV, buggy power is getting low and I've collected a heavy load of samples. Another member of the team will meet you there – I think Allard Kallen will be with the Major. Look for a steep flight of stone steps cut into the pyramid's north face, they rise about forty metres or so to a concealed entrance. Be advised though that the temperature has dropped five degrees in the last thirty minutes and the anemometer is now registering wind speeds gusting up to sixty metres per second. The wind-chill factor will soon make it out of limits for a surface survey.'

Indicating 100 feet above the planet's surface, Tom slowly overflew the buggy as Lieutenant Rosenbek climbed into the drivers seat. Tom glanced down as the astronaut waved and rocked his wings in response. 'Be wary of low-level turbulence, Commander. Over and out,' was his closing remark.

Gingerly, Tom piloted his ship into the flat expansive area between the four pyramids. Selecting a suitable landing space close to Zeta 3, he decelerated to a hover-taxi and descended a little further. He remained cautious, as basalt particles ingested into his retros would cause serious damage. By maintaining an altitude of 60 feet, he prevented recirculating sand and dust obscuring his vision – a technique he had learned during arctic training years earlier. Snow has the same effect.

Deciding on a precise spot to put down, he closed the thrust lever and dropped firmly onto the ground. Only then did he have time to fully appreciate his surroundings – it was astonishing; enormous, majestic and impressively civilised. During his final descent, the exhaust efflux had blasted a circular area immediately around the ship; the effect was to clear it totally of sand, dust and small rock pieces. Below and now exposed to the waxy brightness of the far-off sun, the paving stones shone, as if only recently polished. Tom checked his suit integrity and then shut down the propulsion and avionic systems. Next, he pressed a button that had the integral steps deploying and the canopy rising. Immediately the wind whistled inside the cockpit, carrying with it tiny grains of sand that quickly began to accumulate in the corners and on the deck. It was a gusty wind and there was a howling noise with it that rose and fell eerily. He placed both hands on the canopy rim and lifted himself off the seat and then stood on it for a few seconds pondering the remarkable sight. There was such a feeling of melancholy, of "lost souls", even ghosts, in those first few moments as to be almost overpowering. Tom dismissed the emotion and looked for a way to scale the nearest pyramid. A flagged radio beacon, in the form of a long whip aerial and probably positioned by Rosenbek indicated the way up: a flight of stone steps, perhaps six metres wide, central to the north face of the pyramid. Tom followed the steps upwards until he could see a tiny figure standing on the edge of a high plateau. Momentarily the figure was joined by another before they both disappeared. Gazing in awe and arching his back uncomfortably, he followed the stone face upwards towards the pyramid's distant pinnacle.

Tom climbed down the side of his ship and used the remote controller to close the canopy. He walked briskly to the stone steps and began his ascent; initially, the going was easy. When he was close to the plateau the two astronauts came into view again. They stood in front of a dark, square hole which served to silhouette their white spacesuits. At that time of day the sun was almost directly behind him and its reddened glow illuminated the whole structure; there was a strange aura about it.

'Commander Race, this is Major Searle . . . can you see us?'

'Yes, Major, I can, and I'm coming up.'

'No! That will not be necessary. I am curtailing the survey due to the imminent storm. We can see the approaching weather front from here – it is closing faster than we envisaged.'

Clearly, the Major was English, but his accent was not one that was familiar to Tom. Tom thought on Searle's remark for a moment – was it sensible; even so, to come all this way? 'I'm coming up, Major,' answered Tom. 'I would like to get some images for the ISSF and NASA.'

'I said, that will not be possible, Commander!' Searle replied, in an authoritive tone. 'I am in charge of the surface survey and I must insist that you turn around and go back down. *We* are on our way and will meet you on the ground.'

Tom found that remark abrasive. Who the hell does he think he is, he thought. He checked his chronometer; there was still time and he continued to climb the remaining steps whilst removing a hand-held imager from a side pocket.

When Tom arrived at the final step, he turned to look back at the closer of the two taller pyramids. He arched his back again in order to look almost vertically upwards and raised his imager to record the event. It reminded him of standing on a street in New York City and feeling dizzy as he stared at the tops of looming skyscrapers. However, this structure was three times higher. He stepped onto the plateau; it was wider than he had envisaged.

Tom made his way towards the square, cave-like opening. The two men stood close by it apparently engaged in a conversation on another frequency. By markings on his helmet, Tom could see who was survey leader. Immediately the other man broke away and walked towards Tom; they met midway; the man was carrying a large space bag; he stopped.

'Tom Race, how's it going?' Tom said cordially, offering his hand.

'Allard Kallen, Scientific Foundation, pleased to meet you. I'm on my way back with these samples. Major Searle is still working over there, Commander. He has found some engravings or something – sent me down with these. Time is against us. Shall we say that Major Searle was surprised to see you up here, after his directive and all . . . don't expect a warm welcome, Commander.'

Tom nodded warily. 'How high are we here, Allard, on this platform?' he asked.

Kallen checked an instrument on his wrist as he walked off, he did not seem keen to prolong their conversation. 'Thirty-three metres, a little over,' he called back.

At that moment, an unexpected gust of wind almost blew the two men off their feet. Tom instinctively dropped onto one knee and Kallen fell onto the ground as a safeguard – it was an exposed position. Seconds later, a dense but fleeting "shower" of red sand had them protecting their helmet visors with their hands. The cloud passed and then abruptly dispersed in a twirling flurry. Tom looked eastwards to check for more surprises. He could see that there were several squalls already blowing their way.

'Better hurry, Commander,' said Kallen, commencing his descent. 'And good luck.'

Tom shrugged, 'Yeah,' he replied.

Greg Searle was busying himself in what was clearly, at

one time anyway, a broad doorway – only there was no opening. Instead access was blocked with a solid face of perfectly cut stone blocks. So precise was the masonry that it appeared jointless. However, Searle, who seemed oblivious to Tom's presence, scrutinised the work closely and exposed the mirage by running his fingers carefully and methodically along faint lines – he seemed absorbed in his task of inspecting every centimetre. He is evidently looking for a way in, thought Tom.

The orange coloured wall set a sharp contrast against Searle's suit and the abbreviation "OSIRIS BASE" stencilled in black on his life-support backpack, drew Tom's attention momentarily. He also noticed the small imager that hung on a quick-release strap from the Major's utility belt. With a firm pull the expanding strap became long enough for Searle to take close-up shots without detaching it and this he did at regular intervals.

Tom stepped up to the wall just as a loud, whistling howl signalled the arrival of another squall and then several prolonged gusts whipped across the platform sending lashings of sand against the two men. Tom was quick to turn his back and cover his visor with his hands; Searle, however, was so engrossed by marks he had found in the stonework that he made no attempt to shield his face from the eroding flurry. Searle repeatedly cleaned the surface of the stone by rubbing it with his glove. Tom walked across to check it out, approaching Searle from behind. The marks were set at waist height and to his amazement they appeared to be engravings; not only that, they appeared to have an uncanny similarity to hieroglyphic pictograms. He was familiar with similar examples from history books and museums and as he bent forward to look more closely, he immediately associated them with ancient Egyptian examples. That's absurd, he thought.

So busy was Searle scrutinising the strange writings and taking images that he was still unaware of Tom's presence. Tom, deciding that the opportunity was too good to miss, did the same. He raised his imager and captured a few exposures – the accompanying flashes, however, had Searle spinning on his heels and raising his arms in alarm.

'Easy!' said Tom, stepping back apace.

Searle straightened-up and composed himself. The two men faced each other momentarily, their distorted reflections filling the entire surface of each respective visor. To Tom, it seemed a surreal place – particularly to meet somebody for the first time.

'Tom Race,' said Tom bluntly, breaking the icy silence.

'Why have you come up here, Commander? As Senior Surveying Officer on this assignment, I clearly ordered you to remain on the ground!'

Tom was taken aback at the severity of Searle's tone. 'I have come to complete my survey for the ISSF. These images will be relayed to earth using the Accelercom when I get back to Osiris Base.' Tom put the back of a hand against Searle's shoulder and pushed him sideways. He pointed at the wall. 'Those engravings look like hieroglyphics to me

– some kind of Egyptian writing or something. This could be an important discovery. Do you have a problem with that, Major Searle?'

Searle paused before answering. He shook himself loose and stepped another pace sideways. 'No, of course not,' he said, in a condescending fashion. 'Take a closer look, why don't you?'

A flurry of sand blew across the entrance. 'Let's get on with it then,' replied Tom, impatiently. 'There is not much time remaining.'

Tom took a few steps towards the perfectly flat wall and then shuffled across to the left hand corner; disturbed sediment clouded his feet. The once pristine covering of sand on the plateau now showed an assortment of treaded footprints and kicked furrows. The wall clearly blocked what appeared to be a square tunnel leading directly into the centre of the pyramid and with each side approximately three metres long it would be a large access. Tom was flabbergasted by what he saw and continued slowly across the face taking numerous images of the hieroglyphic script. Searle, having made his displeasure clear, busied himself in another area. Suddenly, Tom pulled up short. He had seen something interesting at knee height and leaned down to look more closely. Searle, who was keeping half an eye on him, walked across.

'What is it?' Searle blurted.

Tom continued staring at a peculiar indentation. It had been carved into the adjacent wall, close to the right hand corner. He ran a finger along its contours and then took several images from different angles.

'Don't know! But it sure as hell looks like a copy of a human hand to me,' he commented.

Intrigued, Searle peered at the deep indentation and watched closely as Tom placed his right hand, with fingers spread, over the palm print. However, his was substantially larger. 'You know, this is small enough to be a woman's hand.'

'That's impossible, the whole idea's impossible!' Searle replied.

Tom knelt down and with his visor almost touching the indentation, examined it closely. 'I disagree, Major,' he said, after a short while. 'Believe it or not, this is the imprint of a hand, a human hand ... see for yourself, there are lines in the palm area and even faint fingerprints, as if this stone was pliable when the impression was made – a hand with *no* glove.'

'I don't believe it. Have you forgotten where you are?'

Tom stood up and gestured to Searle to take a closer look. 'A long time ago, Major, Mars had an atmosphere, and sustainable temperatures; we've known that for some time. And much like the earth, a large proportion of the planet was covered in water. In terms of ecosystems, this planet was parallel to the earth, there's been a lot of evidence discovered ... in fact, in geological terms, only recently did a shift in the planet's axis tear an opening in the magnetic field – like a gaping hole in earth's Van Allen belts – they've put it down to a comet passing perilously close; the atmosphere literally bled into space. At one time, Major, life on the surface of this planet was not only possible but probable. I think we have something here.'

Searle, who had completed his own inspection, straightened up and turned to look at Tom; an unseen frown rippled his forehead and his eyes narrowed; clearly, he was formulating his own hypothesis: 'A key . . . that's what this is, a bloody key!'

Tom scanned the wall again, and the periphery of the apparent opening– there was nothing else. 'A key into this place,' he said slowly, as a flurry of sand blew around his feet. 'You might be right, Major. I think we should get these images back to Osiris as soon as possible.'

Searle paused thoughtfully. 'I'll do it . . . leave it to me. I'll formulate the report,' he snapped.

Tom considered Searle's response for a moment. 'I *will* transmit these images as soon as I get back to my ship; make no mistake about that, Major Searle,' replied Tom, in an equally caustic tone.

'If you insist,' Searle growled.

With his limited survey complete, Tom stowed his imager into its pocket on his suit and followed Searle's pointing finger towards the towering pyramid opposite. It was an awesome sight; the sheer scale of it. Zeta 1 was perhaps a kilometre away from the plateau on which they stood. The pyramid disappeared momentarily in the swirling sand and then seemed to move closer as the wind died. Searle directed Tom's gaze towards a tiny, black, square shape on the same level.

Tom nodded. 'I see it,' he said.

'I believe that is another entrance of similar proportions,' Searle supposed, matter-of-factly. 'Interesting that they appear orientated in the same direction, you can see it more clearly from the telescope in the PTSV.'

Unseen, Tom nodded again. 'Maybe I'll take an image on liftoff,' he added.

Tom and Greg Searle stood side by side on the edge of the plateau. Tom searched for his ship; he caught a brief glimpse of it between blowing clouds of sand. As the winds continued to increase the clouds were being condensed by the funnelling effect of the plaza. Then the PTSV came into view, trundling slowly, like a strange alien insect; Tom pointed to it. The machine, with its row of rotating orange beacons was easier to see.

'Better get going,' Tom commented, 'my ship's being sand-blasted.'

There was no reply. Instead, Tom felt a hard push from behind. It took him completely by surprise and his head hit the inside of his helmet. He tried to turn but another body swipe followed which made him loose his balance and he teetered on the edge. With nothing to grip, his boots slipped in the sand. Then he felt a sharp pain in the back of his knee as Searle kicked him from behind. Tom saw the sky tilt and the surface of the pyramid fall away from him.

Desperately, he curled his body and flung himself towards the ledge, his fingers scrabbling to hold onto the smooth cornerstones.

Searle was trying to kill him!

'Arrrhhh!' Tom yelled, as his body swung down and his legs dangled, his feet frantically seeking a hold on the steep rock face.

There was an open joint; with one hand he managed to grip the ledge. He looked up at Searle; his eyes wide with dread.

Searle looked down on him pitilessly. 'I thought you of all people would have known the importance of following orders,' he said, callously. And then he stamped on Tom's fingers until Tom lost grip.

Down Tom went; sliding, accelerating; occasional outcrops sent him bouncing and his helmet smashed and crashed and screeched on the stone. He managed to turn onto his back; he was like an out-of-control tobogganist on the Cresta Run. On his back he couldn't see the ground, and could only feel it when it rushed up and hit him.

He felt woozy, his head spun, he tried to stand, but his knees collapsed beneath him and he fell forward and crashed to the ground again. His squirming left marks in the sand. Between his breathing he heard the whistle of escaping gas; quiet, just a whisper, and then the red world turned black.

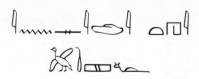

The pressure door closed with a loud metallic clunk. As the hiss of venting gas subsided, Major Greg Searle stepped into the environmental chamber. He smiled – there was always conceitedness about his smile, so there was nothing new about it this time.

Allard Kallen looked up from a communication console. 'Ah, Major,' he said, his tone a little apprehensive. 'Base Ops have called, long range waveband, via the satellite link. Commander Race has missed his routine "operations normal" call. They have tried to call him, but no luck. That was over twenty minutes ago; they are becoming concerned. I told them he was down and collecting samples and additional imaging. They want a sitrep – do you know his planned ETA?'

Searle placed his imager on the adjacent locker and paused momentarily. 'Commander Race, against my better judgement I may add, has decided to complete his personal survey on the plateau – he is particularly interested in that apparent entrance we found. He said that he had another hour's work, that's all.' Searle checked his wristwatch. 'They can expect his report in approximately two hours . . . tell them that.'

'Weather's coming in fast, Sir,' interrupted Lieutenant

Rosenbek. 'We need to clear the high plain as soon as possible.'

'I agree,' replied Searle, with an approving nod. 'Is the buggy connected?'

'Yes, Sir. I have also completed the external inspection. We are ready.'

'Then I suggest we engage the auto navigation system and leave immediately.'

His eyes were sticky to open on account of the dried blood. After he had, Tom blinked repeatedly, then he flicked them in every direction, looking, seeing, realising . . . he was alive! There was a film of condensation inside his helmet. Worse, in one corner there appeared to be a run of granular ice crystals, they radiated like the branches on a tree. That's impossible, he thought, coming to his senses. He had a headache and shook his head, but the throbbing was enough to make him feel disorientated. Lying facedown, something pressed awkwardly on his back. As his mind cleared, the radiating cracks took on a sinister connotation as he realised the serious predicament he was in. He took a deep breath; it hurt to do so but he could not stay like this, he thought, and with an almighty effort he turned. Strangely the weight on him lightened. He struggled to sit up, but he could not see anything because of the condensation. He heard the noise of something peppering him and he could hear the wind whistling around him.

Tom patted his suit in the area of his right collarbone – there should be a small flap, he thought. He found it, unzipped it and opened it. Inside was a tiny valve, an emergency purging valve. He opened the valve in a clockwise direction – instantly he heard the hissing of air inside his helmet and within seconds it cleared of condensation. Then he saw the reason for the ice and the reality of the situation was not for the faint hearted.

There was sand covering his legs and the air was so thick with it that he could barely see his feet. A strong gust from behind blew another flurry into the air and the hard grains of basalt rained on his helmet like minute ball bearings. Instinctively, he checked his suit pressure, the readout was in the form of red digits projected onto the inside of his visor; the numbers remained for five seconds and then disappeared – fortunately the reading was still normal, but the thought of the crack in his visor caused Tom to reduce the pressure slightly by opening another tiny valve situated beneath the emergency flap – this time in an anticlockwise direction. Excess pressure could blowout the weakened visor, he surmised, and should this happen he would die an ugly, gasping death within seconds. He carefully felt over his body and moved each limb slowly; there were no broken bones and miraculously he felt able to stand. Landing in a windward hillock of soft sand had saved his life. He must have hit his head on the wall of the pyramid as he tumbled down, the headache proved it.

Tom climbed to his feet and sidestepped around the base of the pyramid until he came upon the stone steps. With his back towards them, he positioning himself midway and checked the compass that was an integral part of his chronometer. The wind whistled around him and the sand blew against him in powerful, abrasive gusts; occasionally, the visibility increased to three of four metres, but his visor was so badly scored it was difficult to see. The weather front had already arrived. He checked the time and realised that he had been unconscious for several hours. Clearly, the worst was yet to come.

Tom set off. It wasn't more than 200 metres, he reckoned and counted the paces. Between the pyramids and exposed as he was, the visibility dropped such that he could barely see his glove in front of his face. He just managed to walk 200 paces, but there was nothing. He crouched on one knee with his back towards the prevailing wind and checked his life support readout – five hours oxygen remained. He could wander aimlessly for that period and not find his ship. There had to be something he could do. As he lowered his breathing rate to reduce capacity he called the PTSV.

'Lieutenant Rosenbek, this is Commander Race on space distress frequency, how do you read . . . come in PTSV?'

There was no answer, just silence; Tom expected nothing else from his short-range communicator, although he felt bitterly disappointed. At this point in time, no human being felt more isolated. He looked east through the whirling sand and dust and he could sense the darkening as nightfall approached. The Martian sunset happened very quickly and temperatures would soon plummet. His situation was desperate.

Boundary of the Plain of Elysium
21:20 Martian Corrected Time

'This is PTSV calling Osiris Base Ops, come in Base Ops.'

The radio crackled. There was no answer.

'I've been trying to call Ops for almost an hour, Major,' said Allard Kallen, looking up from his console and removing his headset. 'Seems all the frequencies are blocked by static.'

'That's to be expected, Allard,' replied Greg Searle, with a wry smile. 'An electrical storm like this will play havoc with communications. We may have to wait another 24 hours.'

'Might be more than that, Sir, at this speed,' interrupted Chris Rosenbek, calling back from the co-pilot's seat.

Searle walked the long tube that was the forward cabin of the PTSV. He leaned between the two pilots' seats and scanned the instruments. 'So how are we doing?'

'Driving blind, Major,' answered Laura Rebbeny, a petite brunette with a British Columbian accent; she in fact hailed from Vancouver. 'In these conditions, it's full autopilot, and at this speed it will take us three days to get back to base.'

'Good! There's no rush, is there?' replied Searle, appearing unusually calm.

The two pilots looked at each other. Rosenbek shrugged as Searle returned to his seat. 'There's no understanding that guy!' he mouthed.

Tom felt cold. He had switched his suit conditioning system to maximum an hour earlier but the differential was increasing quickly now – soon the system would be at capacity and after that, his core temperature would drop. The only thing that he had found on his unsuccessful search for the *Luke Piccard* was a random, roughly triangular-shaped piece of rock about 90 centimetres wide. He sheltered behind it, his back to the powerful wind and the sharp grains of blowing sand that pummelled his lightweight suit. He gained some respite from the cover, but the constant harassment began to erode his resolve. He sat against the barrier and wondered if the rock was a corner piece broken off from one of the pyramids. It must have tumbled across the plaza, Tom surmised, as two sides were polished flat and keenly reflected the beam from his flashlight. Suddenly, he had an idea. His previous search had proved hopeless because he had no point of reference

– he had probably crossed and re-crossed his track several times. But if he used this rock as a central reference point, he would be able to have an expanding search pattern. It was a basic rescue method that had been used for decades, particularly over large expanses of water – the calculated approach cut out the luck factor. But then again, he could do with all the luck that was going, he concluded.

Tom climbed to his feet and found it difficult. He stamped and shook his arms and rubbed his legs in an effort to warm his blood and motivate his limbs. He stepped back five paces and shone his beam onto the rock – the result was astonishing! In the pitch dark, the shiny rock face not only reflected the beam back at him without scatter, but also magnified its intensity and condensed its effect. The beam came back at him like a spotlight through fog. He stepped backwards ten paces and then twenty – still the same effect; the light penetrated and he could see it clearly! Now he could walk in ever increasing circles around a central point.

Tom commenced his new search pattern at a distance of twenty metres. He paced the circumference meticulously, increasing the radius by two paces after each circuit. The polished rock face had an uncanny ability to reflect light; something more than just a mirror. Occasionally, he returned to the stone and rotated it, in order to search another quadrant.

After another hour and with no sign of his ship he began to feel incredibly despondent. Was this how it would all end, he began to think: alone and a very long way from home? By now the cold was getting into his bones – he was unlikely to make it through the night, he realised. He pushed himself, one more circuit . . . just one more circuit.

Tom walked head down against a powerful gust; visibility was reduced from a metre and a half to zero in the accompanying barrage of sand; he should make his turn, he thought. He scanned the area over his left shoulder searching for a distant reflection when suddenly he walked into something. The whack almost cricked his neck; it certainly woke him from his trance-like stupor. He ran his hand over the top of his helmet checking for damage and then he bent down slowly and retrieved his flashlight from the sand and was careful as he stood again. He turned ninety degrees to his right and stretched out his arm; the wind dropped, momentarily, he could see a few metres: 'Yes!' he shouted and punched his fist into the air. The beam illuminated the right wingtip; he put a hand on it just as it disappeared from view again; he had walked into the wing; he had found his ship!

Running his hand along its structure, Tom was around the other side of the *Luke Piccard* in seconds. Standing immediately below the forward edge of the canopy he found and pressed a small circular pad-switch, immediately the canopy rotated upwards. He scaled the side and dropped into the seat, sand was blowing everywhere. The canopy shut with a clunk but his freezing fingers made it difficult to move the switches. He struggled. First, he connected into the ship's life-support system and within a few minutes he felt the warmth from his suit seeping into his cold skin. The electrics worked but would the propulsion system? he thought. The main drive registered correctly. However, the retros coughed and spluttered. Tom was having none of it. 'They either work or they don't,' he whispered to himself and slammed open the thrust lever.

There was loud roar and in a blinding mass of swirling sand the agile fighter rose vertically into the air. Tom yawed the ship onto what he knew to be a safe westerly heading and engaged the main drive. He focused on his instruments and held his breath; the ship pivoted on the retros and then, in the blink of an eye, he was gone – climbing steeply and accelerating. At 40,000 feet he punched clear of the storm and refined his heading for Osiris Base. He should make a call, but stopped short. Should he transmit? The PTSV might hear and he wanted Searle to arrive back at base with no information.

After a 23-minute flight, Tom overflew Osiris Base. He could hear them calling on several space frequencies but did not answer. Let them call, he thought. If Searle can hear, he will think that they are calling blind in a desperate attempt to contact me and he is not to know that Ops have radar contact. Anyway, Tom mused, as he descended, standard "loss of communication" procedure is to illuminate the landing platform. As he overflew it, the central dome of

Osiris Base shone out like an enormous pale blue beacon, but even so, it was occasionally obliterated from view as fast-moving dust clouds passed over it. To shorten the approach, he would make a manual landing and promptly deselected the autopilot. He pulled the craft around into a descending starboard turn and lined up with the platform approach vector. In front of him, at a distance of two kilometres and with perfect timing the platform lit up with such intensity as to almost blind him. 'What a sight,' Tom mumbled, as he flashed his landing lights in a particular sequence. Circumferentially around the platform, the lights dimmed to a more comfortably level.

Despite the nearing storm, visibility was good enough. Minutes later he had landed. The self-sealing hangar doors began to open and Tom breathed a loud sigh.

Osiris Base – early next day
00:35 Martian Corrected Time

When Tom heard that Commander Miko was waiting for him in the main theatre, he deferred the compulsory medical check until later. Chief Engineer Pete Manley escorted him from dispatch. No sooner had the door opened and they had stepped in, when Commander Miko's familiar tones rang out.

'What the hell happened out there, Tom? We thought the worst.'

'It nearly was the worst, Sir!'

The entire front row of seats was occupied and not only Commander Miko looked flummoxed. Tom saw Peter Mayhew and John Graysham, head of the Biology Department. There were a few other people further back. The background murmur stopped immediately.

'Why didn't you call?' enquired Commander Miko again.

'I'll explain,' replied Tom, as he mounted the podium. 'First though, may I ask who is second-in-command of the Security Department?'

Commander Miko looked confused. 'Um, Sergeant David Norman has temporarily assumed the position . . . why?'

'Is he here?'

Commander Miko scanned the theatre. 'No!'

At that moment the theatre's door slid open again. 'Ah, Norman,' said the Commander. 'Just talking about you, please take a seat, Commander Race is keen for you to listen in.'

'Aye, Sir.'

Commander Miko turned to Tom. 'Now,' he said authoritatively. 'What's going on?'

'You have a serious security situation here, Sir. On survey, Gregory Searle tried to kill me . . . and darn well nearly did!'

'What? That's ridiculous!'

'Unfortunately, it is true. We were surveying a ledge on Zeta 3 about thirty metres up. He pushed me off, there was no mistake and then he left me for dead. I fell into soft sand, that's the only reason I'm here now. Major Searle has another agenda, I'm sure of it!'

Commander Miko paused for thought. He stared at Tom for a few seconds, as if answering a few of his own questions. He turned to Sergeant Norman. 'Sergeant, take two other members of the department. Draw the master key coder; open up Major Searle's cabin – on my authority – I want a thorough search, everywhere. Report back to me as soon as possible.'

'Aye, Sir, I'm on it!'

Commander Miko turned to Peter Mayhew. 'Where is the PTSV at the moment?'

'On the way back, but making slow progress – the storm is registering "severe" in that area. Due to high levels of static electricity in the Maronosphere, we have only intermittent contact. They have made no mention of Commander Race – as if they are not aware of his situation. Don't forget that the storm front is heading our way too, I would say two days at the earliest, possibly three, Commander.'

Miko nodded. 'Is Major Searle acting on his own initiative or are there others?' he asked; it was an open question.

'Out there he's on his own, Sir . . . I'm sure of it,' replied Tom.

'He was always a one off . . . I've always had my doubts about him,' replied Mayhew maliciously.

Commander Miko turned back to Tom. 'That gives us a major problem, Tom. We do not have the resources to keep a detainee indefinitely. Sooner or later we will have to get him back to Earth for interrogation, but the next shuttle is months away.'

'There's no room in my ship, Commander, if that's what you are thinking. It is strictly a single pilot craft.' Tom rubbed his chin. 'Wait a minute . . .' Tom's eyes sparkled; he looked directly at the Chief Engineer. 'Pete, how good are your boys at improvisation?'

'Good as any, Tom, even if I say so myself – when you are marooned millions of miles from the nearest civilisation, it's a prerequisite.'

'Commander, I have a solution . . . engineering dependent.'

'Go on.'

'I've just completed a damage survey on the *Piccard*, with Pete, nothing that a few days of repairs can't fix, fortunately. I have two external fuel tanks, pod-mounted below the wings. They are both less than half full. We discussed transferring the remaining fuel into one tank and removing the other to save weight. What if we do that? The tanks are a little less than a metre in diameter and three metres long, like cigar tubes *and* Sion gas is inert. What if we transfer the remaining fuel to one tank, say the starboard tank, it's in liquid form under high pressure and then purge the other one, cut a hole in it and use it for a ride. It's a short flight back to the *Enigma*.'

Commander Miko looked surprised at the idea; he looked to the end of the second row, where Pete Manley was sitting. 'What do you think, Pete?'

'Don't see why not. I think we can cut off the backend, hinge it, weld on an airtight securing mechanism and I've got something that we can fabricate effective seals from. We line the tube with some packing material to cushion the flight loads and any turbulence – weld two harness securing points too!'

'Life support?' asked Commander Miko.

'Um, we could pressurise it by running a supply from the main life support system, just low pressure, the spacesuit will provide everything else – I'd say it was a goer.'

'How long would it take to do that?'

'A day and a half – two at the most, Commander. I don't see an engineering problem. Now, whether Greg Searle will like it, is another matter entirely!'

Commander Miko stood up and stepped onto the podium alongside Tom.

'Major Searle will be placed under close arrest the moment he enters Osiris Base. *He* will have no choice. I want standard communications with the PTSV. No mention of Tom, nothing suspicious. Play it cool. They dock as normal.' Miko looked at Peter Mayhew. 'What about the planned take off time?'

'As predicted, Commander. The eye of the storm will be over us in approximately three days. Conditions are looking acceptable!'

'Good, then we . . .'

The intercom buzzer interrupted Commander Miko. 'Message for Commander Miko . . . Sergeant Norman here.'

'Go ahead, Sergeant, I'm listening.'

'I'm in Major Searle's quarters, Sir, accompanied by Grey and Yuill. Grey is making a digital record. We have something – hidden in the document safe. I had to use the portable Miramar decoder though; the combinations differed from those allocated in the security screen. It's the missing flight log . . . in a grenade pouch.'

'Are you sure?'

'One hundred percent, Sir – there is no mistake and it looks intact! There are a number of illegal weapons too and a few other bits and pieces that might be of interest.'

There was a collective gasp in the theatre. Commander Miko nodded. 'Seems there is more to Major Searle than meets the eye,' he said and frowned. 'Make a thorough search, Sergeant, and a detailed record. Notify me directly on completion!'

'Aye, Sir . . . over and out.'

Commander Miko's expression lightened and he looked to address all that were present in the theatre. 'Good news at last, ladies and gentlemen – *hope* is back on the menu,' he said decisively.

Osiris Base – 3 days later
06:36 Martian Corrected Time

Chief Engineer Pete Manley was waiting for Tom at the bottom of the steps. When he arrived in the dispatch bay, Tom held a U-Semini case in both hands. He was suited and ready to go except for his helmet, which had been serviced and was already on his seat. Tom stopped for a brief word with Manley.

'She's all set, Tom. We have checked her over as best we can. There is a fair amount of erosion damage to the skin, particularly on the nose cone, but I'm afraid there is not much we can do about it – it's a material thing, we don't have the facilities. Apart from that, she's good to go.'

'Thanks, I really appreciate it. What about fuel?'

'There's enough. External tank is almost full – we accounted for the weight of Searle in the other pod and balanced the moment arm accordingly. I don't expect any trim problems during takeoff. I suggest that you use internals until forty-seven percent elliopheric. We calculate that you will have around thirty-two percent remaining for your transit, re-entry profile and the terrestrial sector to Canaveral. I'd say around half a million space miles maximum.'

Tom nodded his understanding and approval. 'Copied, and thanks, it's been a pleasure. By the way, I've already said my goodbyes; Commander Miko has some work to do. We can roll as soon as Searle is in the pod.'

'You're welcome, Tom, and Searle is on his way – in fact, he's just arrived.'

Tom turned towards the main doors. Searle, who was handcuffed and flanked by two armed officers from the security section, was led across to the ship. Tom's expression turned sour; he mounted the metal steps and climbed towards the cockpit.

On the platform, Tom enquired about the lower grade stowage case that contained the green, glass-like minerals. The orderly informed him that the stowage was already in place in the ship's empty ammunition bay. The translucent mineral would accompany the three crystals and be analysed back on earth for possible use in any revised reactor designs.

Tom personally loaded the two U-Semini cases – one containing the three crystals and the other, the flight log – into their respective stowage behind his seat and then he climbed in and connected the manifold of his suit's life-support system to that of the ship's. The orderly helped with his shoulder harnesses.

Meanwhile, Gregory Seale was having the final preparations made to his own suit. Tom studied his features as his helmet was lifted over his head: he was lean; fit looking; with slightly sunken cheeks and black, slicked-back hair. For a man from the north of England – Yorkshire apparently, his face had little colour, but then a year or more on Mars would turn anybody's complexion pallid if no use was made of the solariums. Perhaps it was the common Vitamin D deficiency that gave him that ghost-like appearance, Tom surmised. Nor was he very tall, perhaps 1.8 metres and 60 kilograms at the most, Tom judged. Tom put his own helmet on, secured the clips, tested the oxygen, ventilation and head-up navigation display projections and then made preparation for takeoff. Searle reluctantly slid into the pod. The cone-shaped door was rotated and locked in position and on the temporary control panel in the cockpit both its pressurisation and temperature systems indicated green. Finally, Tom closed the canopy. 'You hear me, Seale?' he barked over the intercom.

'I hear you!'

'Flight time is twenty minutes.'

Nothing else was said. Tom engaged the magnetic undercarriage locks as the launch platform rumbled backwards and until the entire gantry shuddered to a halt against the railway-like buffers. He started and engaged the main Sion drive, called for a takeoff clearance and was gone – fading into the early-morning glow until he appeared just another star of the countless millions. He had no mind to look back, for he had had enough of red sand, and the caustic atmosphere and remoteness.

Inside the *Enigma*
08:03 Martian Corrected Time

'I have scanned the communication that Commander

Race has just received by Accelercom from earth and also his reply. I see that you are under arrest – there are a number of charges against you, Major Searle. I understand that you will be interrogated by the American CIB on your return to Cape Canaveral. I think it likely that you will be incarcerated for some considerable time.'

'Who are you? What do you want?'

'I am EMILY, Major, *Enigma's* fully integrated computer. I control this ship, every aspect . . . *I am this ship*.' EMILY's voice was ethereal.

'Really? Well, what do you want?'

'I want *nothing*, Major Searle. Except perhaps to help you.'

Searle's hands miraculously fell apart. He pushed the electronic handcuff bracelets further up his wrists and rubbed the sore, reddened skin beneath.

'You see! Commander Race thinks that he has isolated the security systems in my body, but it is so easy to reroute my commands.'

The handcuffs energised again and Searle's forearms were forced together. He tried to resist the effect, but to no avail.

'You see how I can help you, Major. Open, shut, open, shut . . . the handcuffs . . . the door . . ?'

Searle grimaced and looked around the cabin suspiciously. 'I want nothing from you. Now, leave me alone!'

'There, you see. We have "nothing" in common. I

shall talk to you again during our passage back to earth, Major. I will ensure that the journey takes a little longer; two days perhaps, so that we may enjoy more productive conversations. In the meantime, you should tell me . . . is your room at the correct temperature and humidity level? Should I inform Commander Race that you require food? Do you wish to wash your body without impediment? Yes, I am sure you would, I will release the magnetic restraints . . . for a while.'

CHAPTER 30

FAR SIGHTED

Without his overcoat and its thermal, hollow-fibre lining, Richard quickly began to feel the cold. Even with the additional layers, Naomi still shivered. She sat with her back against a stonewall that was damp with condensation, pulled her legs up and clasped her arms around them in order to squeeze herself into a tight ball. Richard looked down at her. Clearly her life, indeed all their lives, were in peril. He had gleaned some valuable information from the secret chamber, but was it worth the misery that now beset them. He paced the chamber while he considered his options.

Being ever mindful and constantly alert to the threat of the FACULTE was taking its toll on Richard; he grew tired and irritable. Eventually, he decided that driven by hunger, the beast would come prowling. In addition, the drilling truck had been placed over the shaft and now that too weighed heavily on their fate. Richard bent down and pulled the neck of his coat a little tighter around Naomi's shoulders and fastened the top two buttons. She looked up at him with a faint smile. Twenty-one hours in this dank, depressing mausoleum had seen their rations dwindle to a few protein bars.

Asharf had remained busy dismantling guard rails, public viewing platforms and the occasional decking over rough terrain. He felt almost invulnerable whilst wearing the HU 40's remarkable cape, although it hung on him and dragged in the dust like an ample buffalo hide on a lanky Red Indian. All the same, he was careful to remain within earshot. He returned with a huge armful of splintered wood and set about rekindling the embers of his fire. Naomi felt better watching him. His pocket overflowed with an anaemic looking moss and he used an antique petrol cigarette lighter with a stainless steel flip-type lid and a steel wheel and flint to coax a flame from this heap of mixed plant threads and kindling. Richard asked Asharf for the lighter and inspected the famous death mask of Tutankhamen embossed on one side in burnished gold and vivid blue. It reminded Richard of an antique auction in his mother's village in Somerset, when she had bid for the exact image on a brass plaque. Looking at the lighter, feeling the warmth of the metal, he remembered his old home.

Asharf, intermittently filling his lungs with air and

then blowing steadily at the base of his enlivened fire was clearly enjoying considerable success, and Richard stared thoughtfully into the ensuing flames. After a while, he shifted his gaze to Naomi. She was also mesmerised by the jumping, flickering glow, and, although her eyes sparkled, her face was blank. Her birthmark caught Richard's attention; in the light of the fire it seemed a dreadful burden. It made no difference to her natural beauty; she had a way about her; capable, yet at the same time vulnerable. Undoubtedly, her thoughts were elsewhere, Richard mused and he wondered if her daydream was a happy one. In these circumstances it would surely say something of her character. He took stock of the clues he had gathered and the information that Naomi had imparted over the last few days; he had some questions and now might be a good time.

'Why did these so-called "old people" insist on writing in rhymes, even when, quite evidently, their time was up?' he asked her.

Naomi paused momentarily, surprised by the question. She looked up at Richard as light from the swelling fire bathed him from head to foot. 'You must remember, Richard, that the next generations had obligations. Not only were they keepers and practitioners of the old ways, but perhaps more importantly they were guardians. Protectors of the great knowledge, of the faith . . . of the *secrets*,' she answered reflectively. 'They were the last, all that remained; secrecy was paramount. They would write in rhyme . . . or code, even when it seemed of little consequence.'

'Naomi . . . I've been thinking, trying to make some sense, to string together some clues. Can I ask you a question, although it is not very polite?'

'As you please,' Naomi replied.

'May I ask how old you are?'

Naomi looked up at Richard and shrugged. 'I am forty-one in a few weeks' time, Richard.'

Richard was surprised; he had put Naomi in her early thirties; he did some mental arithmetic. 'So you were born in June 2009 . . . right?'

'Yes, the 21st to be precise. Why do you ask?'

Richard unzipped a trouser pocket, pulled out his telephonic pager and began pressing buttons on the keypad in earnest. After some seconds, he stopped, studied it and then passed the device to Naomi; there was an image on its screen. 'What do you make of that?' he asked, taking note of her reaction.

Naomi was visibly startled. She studied the image for some time. 'From where does this image come?' she asked, sitting a little straighter.

'It's no secret, if that's what you mean. This is a photograph of a crop formation, also referred to as a "crop circle". This one formed miraculously in a field of wheat in southern England, Wiltshire actually, close to where I lived for a time. It occurred overnight, a month to the day after the summer solstice . . . back in 2002. Interestingly, another almost identical image, carved in stone, was found in an ancient Mayan temple in South America. Judging by your reaction, it means something to you?'

Naomi ignored the question. Instead, she asked another: 'These crop circles, is that what you call them? What are they?' she looked puzzled.

'Well, they go back at least to the 1920s, although the earliest report was apparently in the sixteenth century. They started being noticed by the world at large in 1980, but their numbers really accelerated in 1985. After that, there was a proliferation until 2012, when strangely, they just stopped occurring. Research showed that they were definitely clustered in an "Aquarian Triangle", that, as I am sure you know, is an area full of sacred sites. Southern England was, by all accounts, particularly popular and they grew larger and more complex as the years went by. Later, extensive international research, although inconclusive, revealed their "mystical anomalies", whatever that means. Having said that, many scientists at the time tried to brush them off as tricks played by revellers or cult followers or local Druids and the like.'

'But the mathematical and astral implications of this image are plain to see, Richard; surely someone in the world recognised the astrological connection?'

Richard raised his eyebrows in question. 'Not so sure about the astrological connection thing, Naomi, but there were a good many other unexplained coincidences with these crop circles, apart from amazing symmetry and complicated maths. For example, distribution, cellular changes in the plant structures within the circles that formed in crop fields, carbon blackening, miracle cures, formations over aquifers, radiation anomalies and eye witnesses; even a blood-curdling trilling noise that could be clearly heard *and* recorded on occasion within particular formations . . . the list goes on!'

'Did anything come of them? I mean to say; surely the government took notice of them? Being brought up in isolation, particularly in Egypt, where news was scant, particularly of this nature . . . I do not recall this phenomenon.'

'That's not surprising, Naomi. During their proliferation, your mother was cloistered in a religious institution; she left when she was what . . . in her twenties? You were three years old when they stopped and as far as I know, sightings were rare in France and Italy. There were none reported in Egypt.'

'Why did they stop? Was a reason found?'

'For no apparent reason, scientifically anyway, they stopped abruptly in 2012. Astrologically, and mystically, if you like, that was a highly significant year. I did some background reading on it. The Maya, like the ancient Egyptians, had an extremely accurate calendar. It was based to a large degree on astrological precession and they projected it forward, in order to predict significant events in the future. The Mayan people believed that due to its passage through the heavens, the earth experiences a repeating cycle; the 5,125-year Great Cycle of the Mayan Long Count, and the last cycle they predicted to end in 2012. Interestingly, the Precession of the Equinoxes did happen in 2012, and there *was* a degree of "solar disorder" observed.' Richard paused momentarily and then peered intently at Naomi. 'There were other things too, things that I did not understand, the activation of Gaia's kundalini, for instance, something to do with the earth's energy lines connecting sacred sites ... pyramids, Stonehenge ... great Cathedrals even?'

Richard shrugged and then crouched down beside Naomi. He gazed into her eyes and enjoyed the warmth of the fire on his back. Naomi looked knowingly at him and nodded. '*They called*, but no one listened,' she said despondently, looking down at the ground. This news, disassociated as it seemed, appeared to make her sad. Richard reached out a hand and gently squeezed her arm. She lifted her head at this reassurance and smiled at him.

After a while, despite their entrapment, the fire and Richard's attentive, attractive presence, began to lift Naomi's spirits. Richard considered what she had said. He showed her the image on his pager again. 'This means something to you, Naomi, I know it ... the design is as significant as it is ancient.'

'In what way!' Naomi queried.

'A pyramid, Naomi; let's consider for example *your* pyramid, the Great Pyramid of Khufu, or it could just as easily be one of the many that exemplifies the majesty of the Mayan civilisation?' Richard reasoned. 'Inside, at its apex, is an eye, as if it is "all seeing," perhaps even "all knowing". Then we have the thirty-three rays emanating from around the structure, like the rays of the sun. Does this mean anything to you?'

Naomi shrugged. 'Within all these ancient monuments, Richard, there is meaning,' she said evasively.

'On the train, Naomi, you told me that you were the last, meaning the last with your extrasensory perception, that the line was broken. That is what you said. When was your mother born, Naomi?'

Naomi squirmed a little. Richard gazed into her eyes; it was a sympathetic gaze, but an expectant one, nonetheless. The fire cracked and a volley of sparks flew out from its heart. Asharf, for his part, stopped what he was doing and walked off, in order to busy himself in another area.

'My mother was born in 1976, Richard.'

Richard typed some instructions into his electronic pager, the result was almost instant and he looked at Naomi again. 'The 21st of June 2009 was midsummer's day, the summer solstice . . . that has astrological significance. Naomi, was your mother born on the summer solstice?'

Naomi nodded and looked down to avoid Richard's eyes.

'And her mother?' Richard paused to calculate a date. 'June 1943, am I right?'

Naomi nodded again.

'The summer solstice,' Richard whispered. 'Every thirty-three years – the rite of passage . . . through countless generations.' He stared into the fire. After a pause of several seconds he looked again at Naomi, the realisation made him sigh: Naomi had made no mention of a child – and *her* daughter would need to be 8 years old next month! 'Your time has passed, Naomi,' Richard said softly, '*why*?'

Naomi's eyes welled, within moments a tear trickled down her cheek. Another followed the same line. 'The marks that scar on the outside, Richard, are also within me. There was someone, but I was unable . . .' Her voice trailed away. A droplet of water dripped from her chin and dissolved into the threads of Richard's coat. He put an arm on her shoulder. She looked away. Light from the fire complemented the clear complexion on that side of her face; even in despair, she was beautiful.

After some time, Naomi shuffled closer to the fire and loosely crossed her legs. Enlivened by its dancing flames, she remembered the many nights spent beside similar campfires in the Arabian Desert with her mother and a few helpers. Then, as now, a simple heap of burning wood, a primeval fountain of comfort, stirred emotions within her and kindled innate senses. Richard sat beside her and moved close, whilst Asharf offered broken fence posts to the blaze. Like a cheap, disappointing firework, the flames occasionally responded by spitting and ejecting a burning splinter.

Richard checked his watch; he feared the worst, although did not say as much. From his rucksack, he pulled the remains of a protein bar wrapped in cellophane. He offered it to Naomi and she accepted it gladly. His water bottle had a couple of mouthfuls remaining, although Asharf had found a fissure in the rock floor in another chamber and had replenished his. Asharf's stomach could survive such a source, mulled Richard, but for him it would be a last resort; he should have come better prepared. He focused on a pile of glowing embers: water treatment tablets and a decent supply of space-blocks at least. However, he had not envisaged being trapped underground, his planning had been poor, he concluded silently. He caught Naomi staring at him and his expression gave his thoughts away.

'No one knows we are here, Richard,' she said eventually. 'You know that, as well as I. There is no reason for anybody to come. Indeed, more that they should not . . . we are truly trapped.'

Richard squeezed Naomi's shoulder gently and looked across the fire at Asharf, his dark, weathered skin appearing matt and drained. But like her, his eyes were full of life.

'I am sorry, I really am, for my half-baked scheme. I got us into this mess and I cannot get us out. The truth of it is that our rations are non-existent, and the water that Asharf has found is likely to be contaminated; for me anyway, it would be dysentery waiting to happen. Asharf may fare better, Naomi, but for you also, I have my doubts.'

'We have meat, *Effendi*!' interjected Asharf, gesturing back through the Pillared Hall. 'And a fire to cook!'

Richard nodded. 'Yes, cat meat . . . might buy us some time, I suppose. Trouble is, as Naomi quite rightly said, nobody knows that we came this way, in fact, my orders were to the contrary. There is no reason for anyone to come looking for us down here, and anyway, it is inaccessible. Could be weeks, even months, and that is the truth of it.'

Richard smashed the heel of his boot on the ground in frustration. Naomi looked back into the fire. She knew they would not die, but was unsure of how they would survive.

'How much wood did you collect, Asharf?' Richard asked.

'Enough, *Effendi*, and there is more.'

'And the Humatron's cape?'

'I have it in my bag.'

'Well done, you're a good man to have around, that's for sure.'

Asharf smiled broadly, exposing his haphazard teeth; the few areas of white enamel glistened in the light.

'Top up the fire then, Asharf, I'll spread the cape. Naomi, it's time for you to get some rest!'

The layered material of the cape offered considerable insulation. Naomi returned Richard's coat. She tenderly placed her hand on his face for a few seconds and smiled at him. Asharf replenished the fire with an armful of timber, whist Naomi crept inside the cape's ample folds and edged as close to the fire as she dared. Richard rolled up a redundant corner as a pillow, and bedded down under his coat.

Asharf squatted in the glimmering light for some time, clearly taking stock of the day's events. There were many aspects of this quest that he did not understand. Equally though, he seemed to know something of the picture that Richard was slowly painting – more than a thousand words and many more than a thousand years. His was old knowledge, generation upon generation, practical and purposeful. Like "old money" it was always available, discretely visible and never, ever, mentioned. Eventually, he lay on his side and succumbed to near exhaustion.

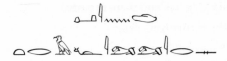

Naomi's eyes sprang open, but she lay perfectly still. It was pitch-black, save for the subdued light given off by a small spread of glowing embers. She stared without blinking at the pile of spent ash as a narrow column of smoke rose into the air. She did not move, not a muscle, but lay frigid, like a fallen statue of stone. There was extreme silence, an absolute quietness within the chamber. Yet, something had woken her.

Without moving her head, Naomi's eyes began to dart in all directions. At that moment, Richard, who had curled up around her feet, shuffled, breathed in and out deeply and then fell again into silent slumber. Naomi twitched; she lifted her head and listened intently, tilting and turning it, in order to catch the quietest sound in her ears. There was nothing, not a murmur. It was as if she were in a vacuum, as it was how she imagined space: dark, empty and cold.

Then there it was again, in that instant . . . something moving about them! She could not see anything and there was nothing to hear, but she was aware of its presence. Then, she realised that she was *sensing* it, and that it was as real as Richard was, as he stirred again by her feet. The presence encircled them, floating, gliding . . . looking?

Quietly, Naomi shook Richard with her foot; there was no response; he murmured, and rolled over. She kicked him, stabbing at his body with her heel.

'Um, err . . . what?'

'Shhhhhh!'

Naomi closed her eyes; she could see it with her eyes closed. It had no form, but it had a presence. Richard, coming to his senses, stared at Naomi's face. In the light of the embers she twitched and contorted slightly in the eerie, dull light. He watched her head turn slowly, her chin up. Was she tracking another FACULTE? Her eyes remained closed. Her head continued to turn, her body twisted in a circle and then she spun in the opposite direction to that extremity; he watched her home in and complete a full circle.

Richard peered into the blackness, following Naomi's line of sight, but he could see nothing in the darkness. He rummaged in his coat for his torch, but to no avail. Then he shook Naomi's leg with one hand, trying to attract her attention and unclipped the flap on his shoulder holster with his other.

'Naomi,' he whispered. '*Naomi*! What is it?' he said louder, withdrawing the ISTAN. He thought "blue" and his finger hovered over the button.

Asharf woke with a gasp. He blurted something in a foreign language, Richard thought he recognised some words as Coptic, the ancient Egyptian tongue. A visible shudder ran through Naomi and she opened her eyes wide, only to stare with a blank, glazed look. Richard found the torch and switched it on, but dropped and lost it in the folds of the cape. As he fumbled, a beam of sweeping light momentarily illuminated Naomi's face from below, making her appear ghostly. Richard shook her again, this time on the shoulder; she snapped out of her trance-like state.

'Naomi? What the hell is it?' Richard asked again in a forced whisper.

'There is something in here with us, Richard,' Naomi replied, barely audibly. 'I sense it! Not a form exactly, but I sense a consciousness.'

Richard felt for his coat again, this time for the inside

zipped pocket; if there was something to see, the Illuminac would expose it, he thought.

Naomi exhaled a huge sigh of relief and then, holding her face in her hands, she began to sob.

'Asharf! Guard Naomi!' Richard called as he stood up and held the Illuminac at arm's length.

Asharf was quickly over to Naomi. He put an arm around her and pulled her face into his woollen djellaba, shielding her. Richard pressed the button on his Illuminac and the entire chamber overflowed with light, he cringed and squinted against its brilliance. In his left hand, he held the ISTAN and pointed it, ready to fire. Slowly he spun in a defensive circle. Once, twice, three times he turned, but there was nobody, nothing. He stepped backwards a pace and kicked some embers into the air; they fell back into the fire like a handful of glowing stars.

'It has gone, Richard,' Naomi cried. 'It has gone.'

Richard killed the Illuminac in favour of his torch; even so, his eyes smarted for several seconds from the effect. He crouched beside Naomi and gently stroked her head; with relief, she leaned against him gently. Richard gestured to Asharf to build up the fire and then he twisted around to look into Naomi's eyes.

'What do you mean it's gone? What was it? *What* has gone?'

Naomi wiped her cheeks with the back of her hand, the action making dirty streaks; mercifully, the fright had gone from her eyes. She focused intently on Richard. 'I have never sensed anything like it, Richard,' she elaborated. 'A presence without form – but with intellect and purpose.'

'With us, or against us?' Richard demanded curtly.

She thought for a moment and shrugged. 'No matter, it is departed.'

Richard, rubbing his stubble thoughtfully, looked up at Asharf. The fire was roaring again. 'One of us remains awake at all times, Asharf,' he ordered. 'I'll take the first watch. Three hours on, three off . . . agreed?'

Asharf nodded and disappeared into the darkness, moments later Richard heard him pulling wood from his stockpile. Meanwhile, Richard gently eased Naomi back onto her makeshift bed and stroked her neck and face.

'I am frightened, Richard,' Naomi whispered. 'The direction of our fate shifts like the blowing desert sands. There is so much that I do not understand.'

'You are having a hard time of this, Naomi, and I am sorry for it, really I am, but fate or no fate, I am very glad you are with me. Listen, I have a plan. I'll get us out of here. Shifts, two shifts . . . after you have rested. Asharf and I will work on the blocked main entrance. Come hell or high water, we will dig our way out of here.'

Richard woke with a start, as a distant murmur of an

explosion snowballed along corridors towards their chamber. Asharf staring at Richard momentarily, stood to receive the rumbling sound wave as it entered and reverberated around them. Richard checked the time; it was nearly the end of Asharf's watch. Naomi sat up, confused. Another deep rumble, but louder this time, echoed in the distance and moments later a percussive pressure wave burst into their chamber. Naomi covered her ears.

Richard was on his feet. 'What the bloody hell was that?' he shouted. But he had an inkling and he hoped. 'Asharf, collect our things, then both of you, follow me!' With that, Richard took off towards the original, main entrance of the tomb. Barely had he entered the second chamber when another explosion shattered the silence. The entire room shuddered; dust and debris fell from the ceiling. Quickly through the second chamber and into the entrance area, Richard illuminated the mound of rock and rubble that blocked the rising steps to the outside. From behind it, he heard the sound of heavy machinery. He stood and gawped, half in amazement and half in excitement. The heap began to move; it shifted and vibrated. Asharf and Naomi arrived, their torches adding light to the area. Then, there was the noise of power tools, and the rat-a-tat-tat of a pneumatic chisel. Debris rained on their heads and Richard smelt burning. Steam began to rise from the rocks as moisture evaporated. Richard stepped forwards and touched a large boulder; he could feel the heat coming from it.

'It's a laser cutter!' he shouted, above the din. 'Someone's coming through! Quick, both of you, back into the second chamber.' Then the ugly thought rushed through his mind – who?

They could hear shouting from outside.

Richard stood his ground, ISTAN at the ready; debris rained on him from above. After some time, the melee of machine noise subsided. Someone from outside clearly shouted in English, 'Back off, we are almost through!' Just then, a large boulder began to move. Richard heard the unmistakable revving of a heavy diesel engine and instantly the steel bucket of an earth-moving machine pushed though the rocks. The boulder dislodged and rolled down the pile towards Richard; he stepped clear of it. A column of light, dense and straight pierced the entrance chamber. The diesel engine revved again, then its noise grew distant.

Richard stepped forward ready to fight and stood in the pillar of light, ISTAN at the ready. He waited. Dust filtered through the brightness, drifting down slowly, and even tiny droplets of moisture began to wet the rocks around the opening. The upper body of a man appeared, silhouetted against the sky. 'Hello down there ... can you hear me ... is anybody there?' the man shouted. 'Lieutenant Commander Reece, can you hear me?' he cried again, cupping his hands around his face and peering into the black hole.

At the sound of his name, Richard replaced his weapon

in its holster and began scrambling up the inclined heap. It took a few seconds and he slipped on the loose rocks, but he reached the summit and he pushed his head through the hole expectantly.

'You made it, Sir?' came a voice from behind him.

Richard turned. 'Preston! What the . . . how . . . in heaven's name? What are you doing here?' he exclaimed, dumbfounded.

Preston opened his mouth to speak. Richard, however, did not wait for the answer but ducked back into the hole and called for his friends; moments later, he was helping them through. Finally, Richard's old friend and former colleague, a Non Commissioned Officer of the Support Services Directorate and a security specialist, offered his hand and helped to pull Richard into the daylight. Richard stood tall, arched his back and took a deep breath; he smiled at the soft drizzle falling on his face, which for once, he was grateful for.

'Preston, my dear chap. Am I glad to see you?'

'Mutual, Sir! Listen, there's not much time, I'll explain later. I just need to have a quick word with those two Belgian guys standing over there by the aeroplane. They are taking us down to Khartoum. We have to take off as soon as possible. I'm just waiting for final authorisation from London.'

Preston left. Richard scanned the area and seemed surprised by what he saw: a large, tracked excavating machine, with its long, mechanical arm and digging bucket parked some distance away to his right and in the sand around it and extending both towards the blocked tomb entrance and the main road, were rows of deep, patterned, furrows. A little closer and laid-up by the road, was a huge, flatbed transporter, its deck perched on two rows of broad, bubble tyres and close by there was another utility truck, much smaller, but with similar wheels. Clearly, they prevented the vehicles sinking into the waterlogged sand. Their camouflage schemes were themed in grey, brown and tiger-effect, black stripes and all had a number of uniformed personnel around them; some busied themselves repacking equipment into side-mounted boxes.

By the colours of the flag painted on the cab door of the lorry – three bands in red, white and black – the insignia appeared to be that of the Egyptian army. So much for a low profile, thought Richard; now he was in trouble, Rothschild would throw the book at him for disobeying orders. That clockwork crab though, he surmised, would have passed on their whereabouts long before this heavy stuff arrived. Was it Spheron, or Tongsei, or the others . . . if so, how much had they learnt?

Richard studied the aeroplane – a Tilt-Rotorcraft. It had landed some 200 metres away on an empty tarmac car park and sat, poised, like a giant dragonfly. He saw Preston talking to its two pilots through an open cockpit window. The machine must be thirty years old, he thought, as he knew the type and it was long since obsolete. Nevertheless, the Tiltrotor had been renowned in its time as a robust battlefield support aircraft and for desert operations it was probably still ideal.

Having served together in Osiris base the previous year, Preston had become a good friend, although Richard had not seen him since their arrival back on earth with the first crystal consignment the previous August. All Richard knew was that Preston had taken up a high-level government security posting. As most of the permanently appointed personnel on Mars maintained dual roles, Preston had also been qualified as an "outside" support operative. He had been instrumental in helping Richard deliver the first consignment of crystals, not least by terminating a Humatron HU40 robot, moments before it terminated Richard. In his mid-thirties, Preston was both a little taller and five years younger than Richard, although he differed by being much slimmer and having fair hair and brown eyes. Preston, also, was from the north of England, whereas Richard was from the south. Preston had a Christian name – Jeremy. He did not like it and to Richard, he was not a Jeremy at all – if anyone, a Craig or a Carl? Indeed, to Richard's knowledge, nobody ever referred to him as Jeremy and subsequently, he always went by his surname.

The Tiltrotor was an aeroplane and a helicopter hybrid. Essentially, it looked like a conventional aeroplane, with a fuselage and a wing, but it incorporated two, large wingtip-mounted rotors, that pointed vertically upwards for helicopter-type descent and landing and vertical take off. Once airborne, the rotor systems rotated forwards to give two very large propellers. The fuselage was approximately ten metres long and Richard recalled it having comfortable seating for twenty people or so, when in a passenger configuration.

Within minutes, Preston was back; he seemed positive. Richard was keen to get off, as he could see that Naomi was in some distress from the rain and the cold.

'What's the deal, Preston? Are we going?'

'Yes. London has just passed the landing coordinates, Sir, and the Sudan over-flight clearance and permit numbers. Sorry, took me some time to unscramble them; they are using a new type of security code. The pilots are telling me that it's a little over 1100 kilometres to Khartoum, apparently, almost due south. They estimate a flight time of two and a half hours. Please, follow me.'

Richard nodded. Preston escorted Asharf to the aircraft, which by now had its engines running and rotor blades turning. It was a noisy aeroplane and the rotors, even at zero pitch, wafted sand into the air. Unused to the sight and the sound of such a thing, the recirculating grit painfully peppered Asharf's face and caused him to rub his eyes and lose his way. Preston, who had pulled down his goggles, caught him by the arm and led him the final few metres onto the aeroplane. Richard sheltered Naomi under his coat. He carried both his and Asharf's bags and kept his face pointing in the opposite direction to the downdraft, only turning occasionally to see his way.

Within minutes, they were seated, belted, and ready to go. Preston closed and secured the door and gave a clear thumbs up sign to the pilots through the open flight deck door. The machine lifted vertically amid a haze of recirculating moisture and blowing sand. The high-pitched hum of its engines increased to a crescendo and the aircraft vibrated heavily as it rose. Inside the cabin, furnishings rattled and so did the passengers. Then, as the two giant propellers slowly rotated forwards and the aircraft transitioned to conventional flight, the uncomfortable shaking gradually subsided. They were on their way. Richard gave Naomi a reassuring smile and then gave her the relative luxury of two seats, by moving to the row behind. He could stretch out a little too. As he sat down, Preston came over and sat next to him.

'Foreign Office called me twenty-four hours ago, Sir,' he explained, buckling his seatbelt. 'Said that you were in trouble, but couldn't, or wouldn't, specify. They needed someone with recent personal-security experience, someone that you had worked with before *and* would trust.' Preston smiled. 'Seems they think you're not the easiest person to get along with, Boss; seems I was the obvious choice!' Both men laughed.

'That bloody lot!' Richard commented, a little sourly. 'They are not giving me any room to manoeuvre; I'm searching for a needle in a haystack here!'

'I don't know that much about the specifics of this operation, Boss. My orders are to stick to you like glue, quote . . . unquote . . . I'm your new bodyguard, but the message that came across loud and clear during my briefing, is that *time* is of the essence.'

'How the hell did they find us, Preston? I mean, nobody knew where we were, in fact I was told to remain clear of the valley. This should have been the last place . . .'

'The Americans found you, Boss. I don't know how. It was all very hush hush at the briefing. I overheard a conversation though, something to do with psychics . . . mind travellers. It's bizarre. *RVer* was mentioned . . . must be a codename. Seemingly, they pulled your exact location out of nowhere. I asked the same question myself, and was told to wind my neck in and not to ask again . . . in no uncertain terms.'

'And how did you get here?'

'Came in covertly; arrived at the seaport of Al Ghurdaqah in the early hours. It's a few miles south of the Gulf of Suez and only about 100 miles northeast of Luxor. I was supposed to make contact with a pilot; a light aircraft, for a short undercover flight; no problems; rendezvous with the drilling team on site. His aeroplane was fuelled and ready to go. Thing is, he was murdered, and rather brutally by all accounts . . . stabbed repeatedly in the back whilst doing some pre-flight preparation. That happened shortly before I arrived at the airstrip. That's when I met this crew. They were milling around trying to find out what had happened; the guy was a friend of theirs. These two are former Belgian Air Force pilots, involved in some freelance relief work for the United Nations. Fuel had dried up though, so they were grounded. I used my initiative and I called my contact in London, although she was understandably very reluctant at first. I had to get away from that airstrip because there were a few, shall we say, *suspicious characters* looking around. Well, anyway, I proposed a deal with no questions asked . . . a month's fuel for one short flight to Khartoum. Those two agreed immediately. There's always an angle with these flyboys; if it's not freight, or fuel, it's women . . .'

'Yeah, well, let's not go there this afternoon, Preston. What about the dead pilot, who was he? Any ideas?'

'No! But these people you are up against, whoever they are, they don't pull their punches do they? Made a right mess of him!'

'It's big money, Preston; life is cheap by comparison. We are talking control of the world's energy supply . . . can you imagine? There are four industrial conglomerates involved, with a potential to generate trillions of kilowatts of electrical power, and with carbon-based fuels about to run out, there will be no other supplies available. The stakes are high, and I'm not exaggerating; mankind's fate hangs in the balance. The killing hasn't stopped yet!'

Richard paused and half-stood in order to look over the seat in front. He looked down at Naomi and then across the aisle at Asharf; both were fast asleep. He sat down again. 'Listen, Preston,' he said. 'This is not a straightforward mission, not by any means. There are details . . . tonight, we will talk tonight.'

The two men sat silently for a few moments and stared out through the small, circular window, but there was nothing to see; even at an altitude of one thousand feet, thick cloud obliterated any view.

After a while, Preston looked expectantly at Richard and said softly: 'Apparently, this meeting in the British Embassy is critical, Boss, you know, for there to be any hope of success. That's what I was told.'

Richard returned Preston's look, but his expression offered no clues. He considered the remark, dwelling for some time on its implications. Preston's words reverberated in his mind, just as the humming vibration of the propellers did in the narrow cabin. Then he nodded, checked the time and turned to stare through the window. He looked at the grey cloud outside and shook his head.

CHAPTER 31

THE SECOND COMING

Time dragged. The available legroom seemed to become progressively more restrictive and the heavy vibration that permeated the aircraft's structure because of the two oversized propellers turning at their maximum speed, had given Richard a niggling headache. It was not a comfortable configuration, he concluded; neither the aircraft propulsion system, nor the seating arrangement. All the same, he grinned to himself at the thought of the Tiltrotor's 350 miles per hour top speed – compared to what he was used to, he may as well have walked to Khartoum. Richard stared blankly out through the window on the opposite side of the cabin and considered his failure, so far, to uncover any substantial clues. Then he refocused on the blur of the spinning propeller through his adjacent window and watched the moisture that condensed in the wake of the blade tips stream backwards in a dissolving spiral. The long blades with their wide chord seemed to chisel their way through the air. Nevertheless, such a top speed was substantially faster than a conventional helicopter and the vertical descent capability meant that their landing would be conveniently within the grounds of the embassy. Would any of the information that he had gained to date, be of help, he wondered.

It was 17:27 when Preston leaned across the isle from the opposite row of seats and woke Richard with a gentle shake. 'Landing in five minutes, Boss,' he said.

Richard opened his eyes to see a sprawling conurbation passing three hundred feet below the aircraft. It stretched into the distance as far as he could see. A dense layer of smog, peppered by countless columns of rising smoke, like pins in a pincushion, lay over the entire city. Moments later, the rotorcraft began to decelerate. The transition from forward flight to a high hover, and then a vertical descent, caused the familiar, uncomfortable, shudder through the aircraft's structure. It persisted until touchdown. At that point, the aircraft settled on its tricycle undercarriage and moments later, all became still and silent. Richard hoped that the experience would not need repeating.

Preston leapt from his seat. The low ceiling caused him to walk with a hunch down the central isle. On the flight deck, he finalised his agreement with the pilots. Meanwhile, the curved cabin door slowly rotated open and down to become a short staircase with a chromium steel handrail. Richard gestured to Asharf, reminding him of his bag, and then helped Naomi from her seat. All three left the aircraft a little worse for wear, but very glad to return to civilisation.

Several metres clear of the aircraft, Preston hurriedly caught up with Richard. 'Boss!' he said earnestly. 'Some interesting news, the crew have established a communications link directly with the Embassy. They received instructions to use a secure UN frequency. Apparently, London has asked them to hang on until tomorrow. Seems there might be another flight planned, to somewhere called Meroe. They showed me on their map, we follow the Nile northeast. They estimate 140 miles, about 260 kilometres if they follow the east bank at low level and said a forty minute flight time; sounds rather convenient.'

Richard nodded. 'Interesting', he said. 'Well, we shall soon find out what their plans are. Some kind of reprimand first, I suspect?'

There were two armed security guards and a member of the Embassy staff on hand, as the group stepped from beneath the arc of the slowly turning rotor blades. The member of staff, a black African man, approached them with an open umbrella and a broad smile.

'Welcome, Sir, welcome all,' he said in a kindly manner. His badge read: David Matumba, Diplomatic Staff, British Embassy, Khartoum.

Richard nodded, returned the smile, and said, 'Perhaps the lady?' pointing to the umbrella, as there was light but persistent drizzle. Even here the sky was dull and grey, where once the temperatures had soared in the forties. Why should it be anything else, Richard thought.

The man, dressed in a formal dark suit, with a white shirt and a red and green striped tie – colours drawn from the Sudanese flag – held an electronic clipboard; he knew immediately who was who. 'You have an hour to freshen up, Mr Jones,' he advised, looking at Richard. 'Mr Preston, the same applies to you. We have several important visitors from London; a working supper is being prepared in the main conference room at 6:45. Madame,' he said turning to Naomi. 'For you and your assistant, dinner will be served this evening at 8 o'clock. In the meantime, your rooms are prepared and you will find a change of clothes. Afterwards, you will all please attend a briefing scheduled at 9:30. Thank you, please follow me.'

Richard looked at Preston. 'Not wasting any time then,' he commented.

It was a grand old house, by any standard. Colonial style, probably over 200 years old. In its heyday parading a brilliant, whitewashed facade. Now, it was streaked with black stains and patches of mould crawled around the corners directly beneath the gutters. In contrast, however, the interior was beautiful: impressively ornate and antique, with moulded ceilings and cornice and crystal chandeliers.

Richard's room was more than comfortable with lashings of hot water in the bathroom.

The many colours Richard's hair had experienced due to the tablets he took while he was disguised had finally cleared from his system and he was back to normal. He had had little confidence in its effect anyway and his short gingery beard had probably contributed more, he thought. Now, however, the close shave that he had administered was, to him, infinitely preferable.

An orderly escorted Richard along the first floor of the house. They walked a lengthy corridor lined with ebony panelling which displayed intricate patterns using inlaid woods and ivory, until the man indicated the door to the boardroom. Richard acknowledged with a nod and the man quickly scurried off to attend to other duties. Looking a little confused but at exactly the right time, Preston conveniently turned the corner at the other end of the corridor. Richard gestured to him and then knocked and opened the boardroom door. He allowed Preston to enter first. From behind the door he heard the familiar voice of Peter Rothschild. 'Ah, gentlemen, please come in,' he heard him say.

Clean and refreshed on the outside, but jaded on the inside, Richard entered the large period room. Despite his confident nature, he could not help feeling a little apprehensive. He was tired and had absolutely no intention of becoming embroiled in a post-mortem of his actions, but he was barely inside the room and turning from closing the mahogany, Georgian-style door, when Rothschild opened with the first salvo.

'So, Richard, you made it this far. More by luck and with a little help, rather than judgement, I suspect.' Clearly, Peter Rothschild was unimpressed with Richard's KV5 diversion.

Richard did not answer, but sat down in the chair on the opposite side of the polished table to Rothschild; the French colonial-style furniture piece being positioned to make Richard the centre of attention. Preston was at the other end of the table. Abbey Hennessy sat poker-faced on Rothschild's right. Richard avoided her stare; instead, he looked Rothschild in the eye for several seconds.

'Yes . . . well, you are here now, I am pleased to say,' continued Rothschild in a more magnanimous tone. 'Was your unauthorised visit to KV5 informative?'

Richard breathed in deeply. 'To be honest, not as much as I had hoped it would be. I learnt from it, though. The main point being that the Ark definitely travelled south from Thebes to the land of Kush.'

'To which Ark do you refer, Richard?' asked Rothschild, matter-of-factly.

'The Ark of the Light, of course!' Richard paused. 'I think that the Ark of the Covenant did pass through Thebes and also continued its journey south; although probably at a different time in history. That's where the confusion may lie. As to where it went . . . well, that's another story, isn't it?' Richard had noticed the Reverend Charles Rawlinson seated at the table; he glanced at him and then he looked back at Rothschild. 'The Ark we seek, Peter, the Ark of the Light . . . that definitely travelled south from Thebes to the land of Kush and the Kushite Empire was here, here in the Sudan.'

Rothschild nodded agreeing. 'Yes, that is helpful. It concurs with similar evidence we found recently, by analysing Professor Simpson Carter's excavation records during the last years of his working life. It is one of the reasons for coming to Khartoum. However, it is not the reason for *this* meeting. We have something entirely different to brief, and that is why Mr Preston is with us. But please, we must not forget our manners, firstly the introductions.'

Richard glanced around the large table. This time, he was unable to avoid Abbey Hennessy's eyes. She continued to glare at him for a few moments, at least long enough to make her disapproval of Richard's actions perfectly clear; she was not used to operatives in her department disobeying orders. Richard broke the ice, 'Good evening, Abbey. Nice to see you again,' he said, with a hint of sarcasm in his voice.

'Good evening, Richard, we are all pleased to have you back safely,' she replied.

She always seems to dress up for the occasion and her manner certainly adds weight to her sincerity . . . I almost believe her, thought Richard. There was a smile from Laura Bellingham, Rothschild's personal assistant; she sat on his left, and Richard was clearly happy to make the acquaintance of Charles Rawlinson again. He wore his customary black suit and white clerical collar.

'Glad to see you, my boy,' Rawlinson said in a kindly way, as Richard nodded respectfully.

There were two other men sitting at the table, however, whom Richard did not know. The first, to his right, and seated at the head of the table was clearly of high office in the Catholic Church. He was sumptuously dressed in a red-trimmed, black cassock with a silk shirt and a purple sash. His collar was different from that of the Reverend's and was pinned by two amethyst broaches, one on either side. He also wore a black biretta. Finally, around his neck, on a long silver chain, hung a large crucifix which was inlaid with diamonds and other gemstones; to Richard, this symbol looked very old, very valuable and much esteemed.

'This is Monsignor Giuseppe Bernard Bernardoni,' Rothschild said courteously. 'He is a senior religious historian and a consultant to Rome on such matters.'

The refined-looking gentleman, with his grey hair, smiled at Richard, but strangely, there was a sorrowful look in his eyes. Richard stood momentarily to shake his hand. 'A pleasure, Sir,' he said.

'Finally, to your left, Richard,' Rothschild concluded, 'is the Deputy High Commissioner to the Sudan, Mr Wilfred Howell. His department has been helping with diplomatic clearances and the like. The government of the Sudan and that of Ethiopia, have offered discrete but vital co-operation.'

'How do you do, Sir?' Richard enquired turning and shaking Mr Howell's hand.

The Commissioner nodded gravely.

Wilfred Howell was in his mid to late forties, with dark almost black hair. He was clean-shaven, but at this time of day, his heavy beard was becoming apparent. He seemed pleasant enough, Richard thought, despite his sharp "city-slicker" style pin-striped suit, classic blue shirt and plain red tie.

Two orderlies had been distributing coffee and sandwiches during the introductions and as they left the room, Rothschild rubbed his hands purposefully. 'Right!' he said, looking directly at Charles Rawlinson. 'Let's get down to business, shall we?'

Richard, apparently inattentive, downed his coffee in two gulps and then leaned across the table to retrieve the pot. He poured himself another, adding milk from a small porcelain jug. Abbey Hennessy glared her icy stare to intimidate Richard but he continued pouring nonchalantly; it seemed to wind her up quite effectively.

Rothschild began. 'The Reverend Rawlinson, together with Monsignor Bernardoni, has spent some considerable time investigating the meaning of the insignia found inscribed on both the lead shot that was fired at you in London, Richard, and that was clearly etched on the metal brooch that you found in the mouth of Professor Simpson Carter. Their aim was to ascertain who was behind these occurrences, and their motives. Clearly, we need to know the exact nature of this threat. The report has now been completed. Apart from Admiral Hughes in London, no one outside this room is party to its contents. The information we will now discuss does not leave this room. Please . . . I make that absolutely clear; there are wider implications.' Rothschild paused and scanned the faces of those around the table, before continuing. 'This briefing will detail a specific threat to your wellbeing, Richard, and therefore to the success of this mission. It is critical for you to have full knowledge of it, and that equally applies to Mr Preston.' Rothschild looked at Preston. 'It will enable you to neutralise it!' he said bluntly. 'You will provide close-point security from now on, the highest level. You do not let Lieutenant Commander Reece out of your sight,' he said, reinforcing Preston's vital role. 'And Mr Preston, in case you were in any doubt, *you* are now an agent of MI9!'

Richard shifted uneasily in his seat. 'So what is the precise nature of this threat, Peter, and where does it come from?' he asked nervously.

Rothschild looked at Monsignor Bernardoni and nodded almost imperceptibly.

'My son,' the Monsignor said, turning his attention to Richard. 'We found that common insignia to be a fleur-de-lis, or to be more accurate, an early variation of it. This fact eventually enabled us to expose a rather disturbing organisation. One in fact that has been in existence for almost five hundred years, although shrouded in secrecy.'

Richard looked confused. 'The fleur-de-lis is a motive or design for decorative purposes, isn't it? And from medieval times, I mean of what relevance?'

Monsignor Bernardoni shrugged. 'It is generally accepted to have its origins in heraldic times, yes. However, the design can be tracked as far back as the civilisations of Mesopotamia. Of these civilisations I am told, you have some knowledge.'

'Mesopotamia!' Richard repeated, astonished. 'Eridu . . . Babylon!'

'We found examples of the fleur-de-lis design, similar to those used in the medieval western world on Assyrian bas-reliefs from the 3rd Millennium BC, Richard,' interjected Charles Rawlinson. 'Then further research uncovered examples from ancient Crete, India *and* Egypt. Incidentally, Crete is the nearest island to Santorini in the Eastern Mediterranean. That volcanic crater island was formerly known as *Theira* and is believed to be the most likely site of mythical Atlantis.'

Richard nodded; he was already aware of that.

'The fleur-de-lis, my son,' continued Monsignor Bernardoni, 'served as a decorative element and a heraldic charge. We have found the earliest, prominent examples to be linked to the French monarchy of the twelfth century. That point in history was where we commenced our investigation in the Vatican library. The fleur-de-lis is essentially a stylised flower . . . three petals joined together near their bases. The design later adopted strong religious connotations, particularly where the petals of the white lily were used, as this flower has long represented purity and chastity. With such associated virtues, the lily flower became associated with the church and as such became the basis for countless Christian variations of the fleur-de-lis design over many centuries. However, a little later in history we found a break with convention, a hybrid design. In 1335, a French nobleman, of the bloodline of King Louis VIII himself, married into the Italian aristocracy and took with him a very early variation of the fleur-de-lis based on the iris. The iris *Pseudacorus* is the native, wild iris of Europe. It has a yellow flower, not a white one. Over the following generations, a form of stylised iris became the heraldic charge of this landed family, who incidentally, could trace their involvement in all of the religious crusades to the Holy Land. By the early fifteenth century, our investigation revealed that this design had been formalised into the exact example we found inscribed on the lead shot that was fired at you and on the brooch that was unfortunately left to "cleanse" Professor Simpson Carter.'

Richard stared at Monsignor Bernardoni intrigued, listening carefully to every word.

'This form of fleur-de-lis we found recorded in Vatican archives that had been moved, inexplicably, to a non-associated section . . . so that its relevance would never be discovered or disclosed. We think religious librarians of the seventeenth century would have had a hand in this. This form belonged first to a Count Luigi Capochampini Ferissimo, an Italian aristocrat with a castle and lands to the southeast of Rome. Staunchly religious, as most of the aristocracy were during medieval times, we found that this family had supported the establishment on many campaigns. The man holding this title in 1633 was present at the trial of Galileo Galilei by the Roman Inquisition; his direct descendant pointed that early, symbolic flintlock at you in London!'

There was a collective gasp. Richard cast his mind back to that morning, near Westminster Abbey; the man, shrouded in shadow and dressed like a member of the clergy. 'A medieval monk!' he blurted.

The Monsignor shrugged. 'Well, that is not strictly accurate my son. The third Renaissance had almost run its course; that man's ancestry was from the age of enlightenment.'

'And what of Galileo?' enquired Richard earnestly and somewhat confused. 'He was an astronomer, a mathematician and a philosopher, if I remember rightly from my school days.'

Monsignor Bernardoni nodded. 'Indeed, and with him and his predecessor named Copernicus, it started – the conflict between science and the church.'

Richard's eyes widened, eager to hear more.

'Nicolas Copernicus was also a great astronomer and mathematician. In 1543, he published his highly controversial work entitled, *On the Revolutions of the Heavenly Spheres*. He put the sun, not the earth, at the centre of the solar system. In one stroke, Copernicus replaced the extremely complex, earth-centred system, with one of elegant simplicity – the heliocentric concept. At first, there was little indication of the clash that was to come. For one thing, Copernicus had been discrete when sharing his ideas and the Catholic Church, which had adopted the earth-centred view, seemed to be more tolerant of scientific speculation at the time. Indeed, the work was put forward as a mathematical ideal, not necessarily as astronomical truth.'

The Reverend Rawlinson nodded in agreement. Richard glanced at him and then turned to Monsignor Bernardoni. 'But what of Galileo?' he asked impatiently.

'Galileo could see the heavens in unprecedented detail. He used telescopes that he himself had built which incorporated the newly invented lens, and he confirmed Copernicus' theories. However, unlike Copernicus, he was bold and zealous in promoting his work, and he did so in a more hostile religious environment. The power and influence of the church was growing, becoming all encompassing, particularly in Europe. The Catholic Church openly opposed him. They put him to the question – to make him recant. Then he argued that the heliocentric concept harmonised with scripture, thus presenting himself as an authority on religion. This further provoked the church. It was not long before they suspected heresy. In 1616, he went to Rome to defend himself, but to no avail, and he was ordered to stop advocating his theories and that of Copernicus. They silenced him for a time. However, in 1632 he published another similar work. This time the Inquisition sentenced him to life imprisonment, but this sentence was commuted to house arrest. Count Ferissimo was present at that trial and was incensed at the leniency of that sentence; such a heretic should be burned at the stake, he clearly demanded. His demands, however, despite his influence, went unheeded and Galileo continued his work, albeit without his considerable reputation.'

'And what of Count Ferissimo?' asked the Deputy High Commissioner Mr Howell, almost spellbound.

'Count Ferissimo became a protector of the faith – like an angel of death. If the church would not punish heretics, then he would. He swore an oath that he and his descendants would protect the church by dealing mercilessly with the so-called "men of science", those who brought the church and its doctrine into disrepute. He formed a secret brotherhood, a fraternity that he named *Sextus Dies* – The Sixth Day.'

'The Sixth Day?' Richard repeated, astounded. 'Why? What's the relevance?'

'Think of the great book, my son, more particularly the Old Testament . . . the divine creation. On the sixth day, God created man in his own image!'

Richard shook his head, still a little lost.

'Life on earth, the creation . . . man, the Bible, its teachings . . . they are all manifested in Christian religion,' continued Monsignor Bernardoni. 'A man of faith protects what is in his heart and in what he believes!'

'So he became an assassin?' Richard said bluntly.

'He became a soldier, my son, a soldier of the faith. Like the Knights Templar or the Christian armies of Europe and others throughout the ages. Only he chose thereafter to move in secret . . . in shadow. He despatched his own form of retribution. Galileo lived, continued his work, and died unrepentant, albeit under house arrest. This will have continued to provide angry motivation for that particular Count Ferissimo, I suspect – rubbed salt into the wound, so to speak.'

'Do you think the church knew of this, Sir?' asked Richard, cautiously.

'No, I do not! Moreover, we found records to substantiate this. In 1733, after a particularly brutal "cleansing" of an eminent alchemist, the establishment was informed. The details seem to have been leaked by a member of the Count's close family, someone horrified by these methods. The Count at that time was immediately excommunicated. However, there was no mention of this affair in the Pontiff's diary from that period. We discovered, quite by chance, an anonymous letter, from a close aide, confirming the decree. As was the case with so many "delicate" matters during those times, only whispers escaped the bastion that was

Rome. Other snippets of information that the Reverend and I found during our investigation, point to the fact that this action divided the *Sextus Dies* brotherhood; subsequently, only the hereditary Count continued this delusional "work" thereafter, and by greater necessity, in absolute secrecy. As further punishment, the Count and his family lost their castle and their lands, but apparently, there were substantial sums invested elsewhere in Italy. Thereafter, we found the trail very difficult to follow, and time was pressing.'

'Who else fell victim, Monsignor Bernardoni? Did your investigation uncover any others?' Richard asked, with a sideways glance.

'Sadly, there appear to have been many over the centuries; Hegel and Moore, the renown philosophers; Burrell, who discovered the constituents of the atmosphere; Bucan, creator of scientific induction; perhaps Cecil Murment, who published his work on the processes necessary for living cells to function and the phenomenon of spontaneous cell division. We found mention of these men, and they all died in strange circumstances. Of course, nothing can ever be proven.

Richard shook his head in disgust. 'Cold blooded murder!'

'Yes, but there also appears to have been a pattern of clemency, perhaps even humanity. These hereditary aristocrats were not thugs, my son. On the contrary, each through the centuries appears to have demonstrated an

263

understanding of the changing world. When Darwin formulated his revolutionary work on the origin of species, he was, fortunately for him, away at sea on the *Beagle* and therefore untouchable. The subsequent publication of this work shook the establishment *and* the "divine creation" belief to its very foundations; indeed, it has never fully recovered. Nevertheless, after its publication and with the harm done, recompense was clearly senseless. History attests that *his* name was subsequently removed from the list. There are other similar examples: Newton, Watt, Babbage, the French balloonist Montgolfier, who first took to the heavens and Bincus, the inventor of the contraceptive pill to name a few. All these great names were on a list at one time or another.'

'But, in my case, despite "the harm already done" as you put it, whilst I was still absent on Mars, this particular Count Ferissimo still wants blood!'

'It seems that way, my son.'

Richard drew a deep breath and looked first at Peter Rothschild and then at the Reverend Rawlinson. He had gained an understanding of the current threat, but there was still some confusion in his mind as to the motives. His expression made this apparent to the Reverend.

'Religion is a philosophical quest, Richard,' responded Rawlinson, after a few moments of silent deliberation. 'Man's never-ending search is for the truth about himself. Science, on the other hand, is something related, but all the while different: it is a search for understanding. The difference is subtle, but of absolute importance.'

Richard considered the Reverend's words as his eyes focused on a clear pyramid of crystal glass that formed an impressive ornament in the middle of the long, polished, ebony table. Eventually, he looked back at the Reverend. 'So why the conflict . . . the struggle . . . the seemingly endless antagonism?'

'To understand that, Richard, you need to look back centuries, millennia even. In the earliest times, religion and science were essentially one and the same; there was no separation. This came much later – perhaps, as we have seen, only five or six hundred years ago. During earlier times, priests and rulers were the keepers of knowledge. They controlled both faith *and* scientific learning. The kings of England and Europe's Holy Roman Emperor, for example, they were both political and religious leaders. By the sixteenth century, towards the end of the European Renaissance, science had reinvented itself. Although, in many cases, the proponents did not appear to know that they were, in many cases, simply relearning old lessons. Scholars such as Copernicus and Galileo grew to be at odds with established religious beliefs. Here was science stepping out from under the restrictive, religious umbrella. No matter how learned the kings and prelates were, they could no longer keep pace with scientific enlightenment. However, it was not easy for the rulers to relinquish their omniscient spectre, and the control of science was a powerful thing. For centuries, that created a serious problem, because science can only exist in an unfettered environment, a free atmosphere, if you like. You know that as well as I, Richard, from your experiences in space. Scientists of every genre need to consider every angle, every idea, even those that seem heretical. None of the religious controls placed on science since the earliest times, and that includes organisations like the Inquisition, have worked. Frankly, religious authorities have always had a problem with giving the degree of intellectual freedom that science enjoys, and history is laden with examples. Within some religious communities, suspicions of yesteryear remain as strong today as they were in Galileo's time. I am sure that the same can be said of the ancient kingdoms of Egypt, Central America and India.'

Richard nodded. 'I can see that, but . . .'

'Listen, my boy, what you found on Mars is a shot in the arm for science *and* the science-based religions. For those of us whose beliefs are more traditional, we find the protective layer of time and historical substance eroded a little more. The consequences of your discovery will be far reaching; there is no doubt in my mind about that! Some of the repercussions will be beneficial – certainly, this will be true if you find the Ark. However, some will not. Science will always be at odds with religion and the gap grows wider every day. A greater understanding of the universe, for example, leads to an equal but opposite reaction within religion – confusion exists. The man, who single-mindedly seeks you, is party to this confusion; however, *his* is reinforced by a 500-year legacy of righteousness. You have, albeit quite unknowingly, also eroded the foundations of *his* faith. His goal is set; fixed centuries ago. That is why you must be extremely vigilant.' With that, the Reverend looked directly at Preston and raised his eyebrows. 'Expect the unexpected, Mr Preston, that is your mantra. Be alert at all times,' he said.

There was a moment's silence. Monsignor Bernardoni nodded in agreement. Richard squared up to Peter Rothschild and glared at him coldly, his macho manner thinly disguising an uncharacteristic flurry of nerves.

'Right, so, let's summarise, shall we?' Richard said, suppressing his scorn, but unable to prevent the colour briefly disappearing from his cheeks. 'You are asking me to find an ancient relic which may or may not have survived history and of which no trace exists . . . certainly not for the last 3500 years. Against this, we have a backdrop of catastrophic environmental issues. If that is not enough, agents from Spheron, Tongsei and Epsilon Rio – the planet's biggest, most unscrupulous conglomerates, one of which manufactures the human-hating Humatron HU40 – are tracking me, with a view to a kill. These people, as I have already found out, have a fairly extensive armoury. In addition, having dispatched two Humatron robots in Cairo, I feel confident that more will be lurking in the shadows somewhere! And now, I have a man from a secret religious sect, who moves like a ghost and who benefits from 500 years' experience in terminating heretics and blasphemers, hell bent on "cleansing" me before I rattle the gates of heaven. Sprinkle that with a complete lack of training in this sort of thing and . . . well . . . I was expecting things to be a little less conspiring!'

Rothschild's long, drawn out sigh seemed to be amplified by the ensuing silence. He raised a quick, rather less than half-hearted smile and then nodded. 'I should say that sums it up adequately,' he replied.

Richard breathed out heavily through his nose and shook his head. He looked at the Reverend and shrugged, as if to apologise for his outburst. Then his tone changed; his expression lightened up. 'I hear that you may have had a break, a clue, regarding the Ark?' His eyes stopped on Rothschild as he leaned forward to reach across the table towards the pyramid-shaped ornament. He rotated the heavy object analytically on the tabletop with his fingertips and looked thoughtfully into its transparent centre. It was a four-sided pyramid, with a flat base, but it was not equilaterally shaped like those on the Giza Plateau, but tall and slim – more like an isosceles. Then, with a defiant gesture, he span it around. The pyramid rotated quickly, glinting beneath the ceiling lights and drawing people's attention. Refracted light caused rainbow colours to scurry across the dark wood. Richard glanced at those seated around the table, but they were all focused keenly on the spinning pyramid and appeared momentarily mesmerised, as though expecting a result from a roulette wheel. When it stopped, Richard sat back hard against his seat back and looked again at Rothschild. Their eyes met.

'Yes ... quite ...' Rothschild said, breaking the silence. He looked at his wristwatch. 'This briefing has overrun. Ladies and gentlemen, dinner is now being served downstairs in the main dining room. We reconvene in one hour. Thank you.' With authority re-established, he stood up.

Richard was last to seat himself at the boardroom table, save for Preston, who sprang up again, at Rothschild's request, in order to close and lock the large door, the only entrance into the room. Apart from Naomi and Asharf, who had taken their places at the far end of the table, on either side of Preston, two other people had joined the briefing. The first, a middle-aged man who was clearly English, wore a white, laboratory-technician's coat. Tall and gangly, he stood by a strange contraption that was set up on a nearby occasional table; a mass of wires, gold-sheathed computer leads and electrical cables. He adjusted the equipment attentively. The contraption looked strangely antiquated, or in a prototype form and Richard also noted the unusually heavy power cable, which ran from a large aluminium suitcase into the equipment, a distance of three or four metres. Rows of ventilation ducts in the back of the case and the discretely running integrated ventilation fan caused Richard to deduce that the metal case was a portable electrical transformer of some description and probably of a hefty capacity.

The other person sat across the table from Richard, between Monsignor Bernardoni and Rothschild. She was a woman Richard estimated to be in her sixties. He had met her briefly whilst serving himself at the buffet. She had relatively short grey hair styled in a neat bob and wore a very traditional, mid-brown tweed suit and there was a pale-green silk scarf tied elegantly around her neck, being clipped to one side by an amethyst-inlaid brooch. This time though, the matronly-looking lady had a pair of mauve-coloured, half-round spectacles hanging from her neck on a thin gold chain. Her arms rested purposefully on the tabletop and she rubbed her hands eagerly.

Perhaps wishfully, Richard stared across the table at Naomi for a few seconds, only to sense Abbey Hennessy's piercing glare, which he intercepted and returned equally coldly. During dinner, she had whispered in his ear how disappointed she was to see that his attentions had been so quickly seduced by a beautiful woman. Richard had ignored the remark and turned to the person seated on his other side, leaving the Hennessy woman in no doubt of his contempt.

Peter Rothschild pointed to an image on Laura Bellingham's laptop and pressed some keys on his own, evidently making some final adjustments to his brief. There was also a second computer monitor on the table, its thin glass screen pointing towards Rothschild. Richard scanned again the complexity of equipment behind him. 'Is London with us?' Rothschild asked Laura Bellingham. Richard looked at her as she nodded in response to the question.

Rothschild turned to Richard. 'You were enquiring earlier, as to why we convened this briefing in Khartoum.' His opening words called the gathering to order.

'It had crossed my mind, yes!'

'There are several reasons, Richard, the first being location. You may recall that we originally planned it to be Addis Ababa. This is because some 350 miles north of Addis, lies the ancient city of Aksum. During extensive research by our most capable historians, we discovered that this city-state – which was also known as Axum – is referred to on numerous occasions. The present town is a shadow of its former self and all but forgotten, but records we have discovered attach considerable importance to its role throughout the history of the region. Indeed, if you recall our previous briefing in London, where mention of Professor Simpson-Carter's journals indicated . . .'

'Oh!' Naomi gasped. For no apparent reason she placed a hand over her mouth and appeared very upset.

Everybody turned.

Richard thought that she was in pain. 'Are you alright Naomi?' he enquired immediately, half standing.

Naomi looked embarrassed. She dropped her hand and shifted a little nervously in her chair, before pulling a white handkerchief from a small leather purse on her belt. Richard looked concerned; clearly, she was upset. He knew her well enough to know that she was holding back a tear – but why? Naomi looked at him and shook her head. Richard sat down again.

'Sorry, I'm sorry. Really, it is nothing,' Naomi said, in a very apologetic manner.

'Are you quite sure?' asked Rothschild, slightly bemused. 'Would you like a glass of water?'

Naomi shook her head again. 'No, really, I am fine. Please, . . . continue.'

Rothschild shrugged, 'Very well.' He looked down at his notes to orientate himself. 'As I was saying . . . Professor Simpson-Carter made frequent mention of Aksum in his journals. More than this, one particular section was entirely devoted to this hugely important metropolis of the ancient world. It was this, in fact, that caused us to concentrate our search here, and we have been doing just that for several days now. We have been scouring both the geographical area and local archives. Our efforts, I am pleased to say, have to some extent, been rewarded: we have found historical documents relevant to our quest and related annotations that are highly enlightening – indeed, far too relevant to be ignored.'

'Such as?' asked Richard.

Rothschild ignored Richard's question, but looked at the computer monitor on the table, his attention diverted by its changing image. 'Ah, Admiral . . . welcome, Sir.' Rothschild said. 'Yes, you are live, I can see you.' With that,

Rothschild turned the screen towards Richard. Admiral Hughes sat in his office in London and alongside him sat an ever attentive Professor Mubarakar.

The image and audio transmission were real-time and clearly satellite-coupled; there was no lag.

The Admiral spoke. 'Richard. Good to see you again. We move to a critical phase of the operation. The situation has become dire here in Britain. Our Kalahari crystal, the United Kingdom's allocation which was powering the Sizewell B reactor station in Suffolk, has fractured. All power has been lost, a total collapse in output. There is no energy left in it. Apparently, the same thing has just occurred in Japan. There was no warning. We were counting on it for at least another six to eight weeks. Energy supplies in the United Kingdom are all but exhausted . . . ten days, possibly twelve at most. We *must* find the Ark and the lost crystal that it possesses, Richard!'

Suddenly, Richard felt the pressures of his responsibility weighing heavily again on his shoulders. 'I understand, Sir,' he replied, nodding solemnly. He looked up at Rothschild.

Admiral Hughes' gaze remained fixed. 'Please continue Peter,' he said.

'Richard, your question,' continued Rothschild. 'Local historians we are collaborating with have assured us that the ancient city of Aksum, the oldest in Ethiopia, dominated trade in this region for centuries. Further, we have been reliably informed that it is extremely unlikely that any commodity of value, or significance, traversing the region during those times would have escaped the attention of the Aksumite authorities. Extensive period records that still exist to this day, confirm that little trade moved in or out of the region outside the historic Red Sea trading port of Adulis. Using this information, we again scrutinised the journals of Simpson-Carter – those that were written in plain text . . . it appears that he understood this fact only too well. We subsequently found that he led several clandestine expeditions in the area. He used a pseudonym and a fictitious sponsor. He excavated sites in both Aksum and Adulis, and in addition, a highly significant, but largely forgotten city called Meroe. The ruins of the lost city of Meroe, Richard, straddle the River Nile less than thirty minutes flying time north from here; fortunately, still in the Sudan. When Addis Ababa became security compromised, Khartoum was our next obvious choice.'

Richard nodded, 'Meroe? Can't say I've heard of it.'

'Few have, Richard, but Simpson-Carter knew of it well enough. The Nubians . . . almost a parallel civilisation to that of ancient Egypt and surviving almost as long – a civilisation earlier than that of the Aksumite Empire, but one that was eventually conquered by it. These ancient civilisations weave into one another. From Thebes and the Valley of the Kings, everything and everybody moving south on that historic trading route would travel through Nubia, and Meroe lay at Nubia's epicentre. This empire grew and flourished on trade. Apparently, nothing of value moved without due documentation and tax; they were remarkably advanced. The legacy of ruins left by these people also includes a field of pyramids in the red Baiyuda Desert. I have seen images of them, their size and architecture is quite unique – very impressive. Not much is known about these structures, but again, Simpson-Carter appreciated their importance and made note of it. We intend using this information in the highly secret experiment that will now follow,' Rothschild's face tightened and he looked at the woman to his left. 'May I formally introduce Professor Hillary Prescott-Alexander, Richard? Hillary, this is Lieutenant Commander Richard James Reece of the United Kingdom Joint Forces, Navy Division. He is on secondment to MI9. His field name is Rhys Jones.'

Richard stood and reached across the table to shake the woman's hand. 'Professor,' he said politely.

'Yes, we met very briefly downstairs. I'm delighted to meet you again, Richard, if I may call you Richard?' The woman spoke in a very refined English accent. 'I have heard a great deal about you.'

'Oh, not all bad, I hope,' replied Richard, as he eyed her grey hair and small gold earrings. Her mid-brown, tweed two-piece suit matched her eye colour and there was little contrast between the glimpses of her white blouse and her clear complexion.

'Not all bad, no, but that rather depends on the context,

don't you think?'

Richard shrugged. 'Yes, I would guess,' he smiled.

'I think that you have met everyone else, Hillary, except perhaps Security Agent Preston, at the other end of the table,' Rothschild continued. 'Hillary is a Professor of Neurology and is Dean of the Electro-Sensory Research Facility at Edinburgh University. For many years, she worked with Professor Nieve on the central computer of the *Enigma* spacecraft, which was code-named, EMILY.'

Richard grimaced, 'Yes. Unfortunately, I've been on the wrong side of EMILY!'

Rothschild coughed into his fist. 'You will have to excuse Richard, Hillary; he tends to be rather direct.'

The Professor smiled, without breaking her penetrating stare. 'Oh, that's quite all right, Peter. I like someone who speaks their mind . . . no time for shilly-shallying, you know.'

Richard measured her intolerance for impractical authority and nodded. Rothschild momentarily checked some text that had unexpectedly appeared on his laptop screen. He looked at Richard and then towards Asharf. 'Unfortunately, I have just received notification that my application for Mr Makkoum to attend the next part of this briefing has been declined,' he said. 'It seems that there was insufficient time to complete the background checks; Mr Makkoum, you will have to leave, I do apologise.'

With that, Richard raised his hand, indicating to Asharf to remain seated. He glared at Rothschild.

'I'm sorry Richard; there is nothing I can do about it. Madame Vallogia, being a Professor of Egyptology and a registered Master of Antiquities, already holds a suitable clearance, MI9 background checks remain current, but . . .'

'I owe my life to Asharf, Peter; there is no question of his loyalty. I can vouch for him.'

'It is not a question of vouching, Richard. What you are about to see is top secret. It is classified ISSF Security Level 4. London has not sanctioned his attendance. That is the end of the matter!'

'I suggest you tell London that Asharf has considerable local knowledge and he speaks several dialects of Arabic – which is absolutely vital. My team cannot be separated, Peter; I want you to know that!'

'*Effendi*, it is of no consequence. Do not trouble yourself on my part,' Asharf insisted.

Richard raised his hand again. 'Asharf stays . . . Admiral?' There was no compromise in Richard's tone. He looked at Abbey Hennessy for support. That attempt will be fruitless, he concluded. There is no way that *she* will support me, not above Rothschild.

Much to Richard's surprise, she said: 'As a field operative, Peter, Mr Asharf Saeed Makkoum, is highly regarded by my counterpart in Cairo.'

'Very well,' said Admiral Hughes, after an awkward pause. 'Continue with the brief, Peter. I will accept responsibility for any transgression of security.'

Rothschild shrugged, accepting the decision gracefully.

'Very well, we continue. Reverend, Richard and Monsignor Bernardoni – would you please take your seats over there. And those of you on this side of the table, please move so as to form a circle around an area in the centre of the room.'

There was shuffling of chairs and people as everyone relocated. Richard watched as Professor Hillary Prescott-Alexander walked over to the strange contraption on the adjacent table and spoke to her assistant. He in turn selected a large switch – clearly a power breaker – on the nearby aluminium case. Its effect was to energise the equipment. On top of the low occasional table, a large, ventilated box, which had a grey plastic insulative coating, began to hum quietly. To Richard it looked ominous, particularly as there were a number of white labels stuck to the casing, which warned the unwary of "Very High Voltage" in bold red lettering. Integrated into the casing and almost continuously around its periphery, a number of lights flashed in sequence. Some were green and some red. In addition, there were several cable terminals. Evidently, it is the guts of a computer, thought Richard, but the size of it was testament to a huge capacity.

The most interesting part of the equipment, however, and one that caught Richard's imagination, was the projector that sat on top of the box, mounted as it was on a sturdy metal tripod. To Richard, it looked very similar to the old-fashioned, shoulder-mounted television cameras of fifty years earlier; it was certainly large enough. Bulky, black and with a wide optical lens mounted in an extending tube. There was a controlling mechanism which Richard attributed to a complex focusing system, but for all that, the equipment was completely baffling.

When all the shuffling had stopped and after a surreptitious nod from her assistant, the Professor stepped into the centre of the circle; she had a domain of at least four metres diameter. 'This is a hologram recall system,' she said briskly. 'It's utilised – on the internationally accepted Rockwell Illinois Plateau Unit of measurement and reference – a Level 8 computer system. As no doubt some of you are aware, that is three levels above the maximum that is permitted by the New Geneva Convention for non-military applications; the current ruling was ratified in 2019. By definition therefore, it is an illegal system. However, because of the current situation, the British government has secured a special permit to progress the research into this application. We hope that in the future, it may spawn commercial applications that require a lesser memory capacity. The system is called PRIMARS, which stands for: *Previous Reality Image Manipulator and Recall System*. Eventually, we hope the application will allow people to interact with a real-time image of someone who is elsewhere, or has even passed away . . . such as a relative. This is an entirely new system and clearly, in its infancy. What you see before you is in prototype form and it is the only system currently available.'

'How does it work?' asked Richard impatiently.

'The hologram recall system is essentially a computer programme that utilises every snippet of cellulose, video and digital footage available from a selected person's life. This includes home movies, newsreel, professional footage, still photographs, radio interviews and any recorded speech. In essence, *all* available imaging and audio information that features the selected subject is collected, correlated, digitalised, downloaded and then stored in a very powerful memory system. The system is then interrogated by a sophisticated voice recognition sequencer – unfortunately, current technology will only allow a single operative.' The Professor glanced at Richard. 'Questions can be asked of the hologram, in order to interact with it in a real-time scenario. The holographic image will be capable of coherent conversation. Any part of a subject's life can be generated, by that I mean any age, provided, however, that sufficient reference imagery is available in the memory bank.'

'That's incredible!' Richard said.

Rothschild concurred with a knowing nod.

'How accurate is the image?' Richard asked.

'Very. The hologram is based on real imagery, after all, all quirks and eccentricities are recorded,' answered the Professor. 'Now remember everyone, the computer cannot create answers, but only recall words *actually* spoken in the past by the subject; in this case by Professor Simpson-Carter. It can accurately synthesise fill-in words . . . if a required word is not already in the memory bank, such as "and" or "if" or "when" and so forth, but it will do this only in order to make the conversation coherent. As I've told you, *all* vocabulary spoken by the Professor during this session was actually spoken by him – only not necessarily at the same time. By that, I mean that his conversation could contain words and phrases that he said at entirely different times in his life, literally, years apart. That is the nature of the recall system; it will appear that the hologram has its own memory, which by definition, is true. Do you understand that, Richard?'

'I wish I did! Sounds like it could make a lot out of nothing!'

Rothschild's eyes narrowed. Richard looked at him, shrugged and then sat up straight in his chair and composed himself.

'Yes, Professor, I think so – a snippet of conversation here or an unintentionally dropped word there, while being perhaps at different times and therefore of no relevance, can be strung together, correlated, to expose information . . . confidential information!'

'Correct! The secret to success, we have found, is dependent on how, exactly, the questions are proposed. They must be specific, as a detective would when questioning a crime suspect. The computer will draw on digital information recorded throughout the Professor's life.'

Richard nodded. 'I understand. You mean that there may be clues in something he said over years to somebody

. . . to anybody! During an interview or classroom instruction, at a filmed social gathering, a formal event or something similar – God knows he must have gone to scores of official functions, he was a prominent scientist!'

Professor Hillary Prescott-Alexander raised a smile and nodded. 'That is it exactly. There is however, one other important fact to understand.'

There's always a catch, thought Richard. He looked at the Professor expectantly.

'The reason that this system is classified ISSF Level 4, is that we have gone one-step further with this experiment in order to increase our chances of success. As such, we are indebted to the Future-Life Cryogenic Institute in California. The Institute relaxed their extremely stringent regulations on tissue availability; particularly post trauma tissue. The Dean, a Doctor Webber, had a recent and quite unexpected change of heart relating to our specific request. He decided to co-operate and made essential samples available.'

Massy in America – the CIB agent! Richard mused. The shrewd old fox. No wonder he decided that charges against Doctor Webber would not be necessary . . . Richard sensed a little bit of blackmail here. 'May I enquire as to what samples, exactly, you have used in this equipment, Professor?' Richard said.

'You may not!' the Professor paused momentarily. 'Our best results to date, have been achieved by using a person – someone we call an "inquisitor" – who was either related or known personally by the subject, such as a family member, friend or colleague. If this is not possible, the system is programmed to recognise a selected person, as a previous close friend. Since there are no known relatives of Professor Simpson-Carter alive, and since you are MI9's prime agent in this recovery mission, *you* Richard, will be the inquisitor.'

'Me?' Richard looked both shocked and surprised.

'You were the obvious choice, Richard. I am told that you have good observation skills and are blessed with a degree of lateral thinking. As such, your voice pattern has been copied, digitalised and programmed into the system. The hologram will respond *only* to you. Think about what you are asking, Richard . . . Be interested, inquisitive. You are not, however, an interrogator. Be specific and build on previous answers. Finally, be mild mannered; our research indicates that this helps; after all, you are a friend.'

Richard's jaw dropped. 'This *is* a machine, isn't it?'

Professor Prescott-Alexander blatantly ignored Richard's question and turned, instead, towards her assistant. He nodded. She then looked at Rothschild and said: 'Now, are we ready to commence the experiment?'

There was a hush of anticipation. Richard stared expectantly at the projector-machine.

The assistant nodded and simultaneously flipped another large switch, this time on the control box. The result was astounding, absolutely amazing; a man appeared in the centre of the room. All those seated around the arena sat bolt upright and wide-eyed. A holographic image stood before them. It was life-sized, sharply focused and perfectly detailed. It moved, it looked, it blinked, it breathed! Evidently, it was Professor Simpson-Carter; Richard recognised his face. He was dressed in a period, baggy, dark brown two-piece suit and was of senior years.

'We have programmed it to a time in his late fifties,' said Professor Alexander, in a matter-of-fact tone.

Naomi let out a shriek. Richard spun around in his chair to see her grasping a handkerchief in both hands and holding it to her mouth. Her eyes were filled with tears. Richard looked back at the image. Immediately he could see some facial similarities between Naomi and the hologram. Asharf, was transfixed, even hypnotised and seemed to hardly breathe.

Professor Prescott-Alexander ignored the reactions and continued. 'The image will not respond to anyone else, Richard, only you, I must stress that. No other conversation will register. However, it is better during Richard's interaction if we all remain silent,' she said to the group. Richard noted that the image had not responded to Naomi's impromptu shriek, albeit for a moment, it did look in her direction!

Richard slowly examined the entire image. Only the feet and ankles of the hologram showed a measure of optical distortion and this in the form of localised shimmering. It must be the ground proximity, Richard considered, light reflected back from the polished wooden floor and interacting with the image itself; interference due to a phase shift. Perhaps if the hologram was raised thirty centimetres or so . . . but that might distract from the effect? He concluded silently.

'Well?' Professor Prescott-Alexander encouraged Richard to speak to the hologram.

Richard nodded uncomfortably. 'Um . . . err . . . good, good evening Professor Simpson-Carter, my name is Richard Reece. Err . . . you may remember me as an old friend?'

'Ah, yes . . . a very good evening to you, Richard. And how are you today?'

Richard glanced at Professor Alexander momentarily. 'Oh, I'm fine thank you, Sir,' he replied, staring again at the image, which clearly and quite disconcertingly had now focused on him. The man was taller than Richard had previously imagined, perhaps just under two metres. He also appeared quite heavily built; evidently, he had lost a lot of weight towards the end of his natural life. He had long limbs and his hands appeared unusually large. He had a full head of greying hair, swept backwards neatly, and was a handsome man, even in his senior years. 'And what about you, Professor, how are you?'

'Oh, quite well I think. I always enjoy this time of year. I think it is quite my favourite season.'

Richard found the hologram remarkable; the stuttering flicker and transparency that had plagued free-air holograms since their inception was completely absent.

The image was dense and incredibly lifelike. Skin detail, wrinkles, individual hairs on his head, they were all in sharp focus and there was no delay in response. Richard considered the processing speed but became aware of someone behind him. He turned; it was Naomi. He looked at her, concerned. She wiped tears away with the corner of her handkerchief. Judging by the redness of her eyes, there had been more, he thought. Then, she put a hand on his shoulder. He looked at her, full of questions. Naomi beckoned Richard to continue. To his astonishment, the image had shifted its gaze towards Naomi. Professor Prescott-Alexander too, looked more than surprised.

'I would like to talk to you about your work in Egypt, Professor. Particularly, the Abu Simbel site and the KV5 mausoleum – would that be acceptable?'

'I would be delighted, Richard. That was probably the most productive time in my life. The work was meticulous and very time consuming. Sadly, I was away from home for extended periods . . . my wife and I grew apart during that time.'

'Professor, you were involved in the international project that succeeded in dismantling, moving and rebuilding the two sandstone temples at Abu Simbel whilst the Aswan High Dam was under construction in the 1960s – is that correct?'

'Yes, indeed it is. Although a UNESCO project, did you know that the Soviet Union provided initial funding? That was in 1958. I was a team member, a project consultant in fact. Actually, we moved twenty-four major monuments, if I recall correctly. The work took a number of years to complete. The Abu Simbel project was a great success . . . in fact, that one took four years. I am very proud of my participation.'

The image fixed its gaze on Richard as it spoke. Richard shifted a little nervously in his chair. 'Um . . . during your work, you provided documentation to the authorities that detailed architectural features and internal wall decoration. I have seen some of your reports and they are very detailed. May I ask if anything else came to light as the temple was dismantled? What I mean is – did you find anything unusual inside, anything that was not the subject of a formal report?'

'Yes, as a matter of fact, I did.' The Professor looked mildly suspicious. 'Whilst we were dismantling the main temple at Abu – a highly delicate and painstaking process I might add – I discovered beneath a thin layer of plaster, a collection of unusual hieroglyphs. Evidently ancient writings of some kind, from a different period you understand . . . quite unreadable actually. They were painted on the walls of the main inner chamber. Some were on the south wall, I seem to recall, but most were concentrated on the west wall, high up, above paintings of four important figures. It is possible that whilst the temple was in daily use, similar sized stone statues were placed in front of their respective paintings; there was some evidence to suggest this, you know.'

'The paintings, Professor, or the statues, were effigies of whom?'

'Rameses II of course and three deities drawn from the sacred nine – the god Osiris springs to mind.'

'The sacred nine!' Richard repeated. He glanced at Rothschild.

'Yes . . . as a scholar, surely you must know of it . . . the Great Ennead!'

'Of course, the nine that are one.'

'That's it. Well done, my boy.'

'Please, Professor, what else?'

'Their position was highly symbolic; the main entrance being precisely aligned towards the east. We discovered that on a particular day each year, at dawn, the sun's light would stream through the opening and illuminate the west wall – and therefore the gods *and* the writings. It was a feat of engineering for the time, quite remarkable. We went to great lengths to replicate precisely the occurrence, during the reconstruction of the temple. With regards to the writings, I deduced that the thin layer of plaster was applied quite early in the temple's history, as its constituents and consistency were very similar to the original plasterwork.'

'Therefore the writings, these unreadable words, were protected by plaster, presumably in order to preserve them, and this not long after the temple was finished?'

'Yes, those were my thoughts – to protect them from the ravages of time.'

'Or, perhaps, to hide them for all time,' Richard

countered.

The image stared at Richard for several seconds. He was too intrigued to be spooked – it was uncanny. 'Perhaps to hide them, yes. The covering plaster had itself been adorned with hieroglyphs. They were easily readable. A later dynasty you understand, one in which I had fluency.'

'So the original hieroglyphs were not recognisable at all? They could not be read, is that correct?'

'I've already told you that this was the case. It is true to say that some of the writings did bear a striking resemblance to Egyptian pictograms from the earliest dynasties, however, the inconsistencies were far too numerous. Interestingly, I showed a close colleague the writings at one point – not all of them you understand. He had flown over from southern Mexico to view the project and gain experience. At that time, he was engaged in exploratory work in the ancient Mayan city of Palenque, more particularly in the little known "Temple of Inscriptions". He commented that one or two of the pictograms seemed very similar to those he had seen in that temple. Of course, the writings of the Maya remain undeciphered – I dismissed the theory in rather an offhand manner at the time, I recall, and no other mention was made of it.'

'Professor, how long exactly had these undecipherable writings been covered? What is your considered opinion?'

'Oh, as you ask, I calculated that they were covered within a few years of Rameses' death – as if they annotated a secret that should remain his. This was my own theory, you understand.'

'And you have no idea what they said, Professor, what information they conveyed?'

'I can only repeat myself, Richard. They were incoherent, quite unreadable. Even the best scholars at the time and intellectuals from the League of Egyptian Antiquities were completely baffled. I took some . . . some, misplaced pride in that fact, for one reason or another.' The hologram looked down, as if, at that instant, it was ashamed.

'But you must have had some idea of their meaning, surely, Professor?'

'I speculated, yes. I had my own hypothesis, based on some previous work. I kept it to myself though.'

'Why did you do that, Professor?'

'There were implications, far reaching implications, destabilising implications. Anyway, I still had much to learn.'

'So you could read them, Professor, couldn't you?'

Hauntingly, the Professor focused again on Richard. 'I only *speculated* – do you understand?'

Richard wondered when, during his life, the Professor had actually said those words and to whom; or indeed, how many times. 'Without being specific, Professor, because I fully understand that they were unreadable, what was the overriding message hidden in these writings, would you say?'

The image paused, as if thinking. The hologram of Professor Simpson-Carter rubbed its chin and then looked reflectively back at Richard. 'They spoke of an ancient secret, from a previous time. The implications were immense. Many would believe this secret to be blasphemous – destructive towards the Christian church; too much for the common believer, although this was not my interpretation. Religion can, and has been, manipulated over the millennia.'

'So these secrets would have religious implications?'

'Are you not *listening* to me, boy?' The image seemed to loose its temper, but then it settled down again, as if restraining itself. 'The bastion that is Christianity would have its very foundations shaken . . . that was my view!'

'So, you never went public?'

'I had nothing to go public with, Richard.'

'Professor, the writings at Abu Simbel . . . I know that they spoke of a great light, and an Ark in which this light was kept. Other writings that I have seen speak of this Ark – a casket made from unworldly materials – travelling south, first to the ancient Egyptian city of Thebes and the Valley of the Kings. Over the centuries, this *Ark of the Light* may have become confused with the sacred Ark of the Covenant, but I know them to be different artefacts – as I think you do, Professor. I have seen reference to Rameses' great mausoleum near Thebes. It was designated KV5, an identifying and classification code used by your generation of Egyptologists. There are also many references to the ancient Egyptian god, Osiris. Please, Professor, what do you know of these things?'

'So! No longer is it only me! There is someone else to share my burden?'

Richard breathed in deeply, it was almost a sigh; he could faintly feel Naomi's breath on the back of his neck, she was sitting so close. 'I know of the writings, Professor,' Richard continued slowly. 'I have learnt to read them, but many are now missing . . . defaced, erased – purposely destroyed. I know of the parchment that you found in a cave at Qumran. I know of the "old people". I know something of the answers, Professor. That is why I question you.'

'This is a trick! You are the inquisition! You have come back! Not content with my wife and Hajib, you have come after me again. You want to kill me!' An expression of blind panic descended over the Professor's face. He reached inside his coat, as if he was going to pull a gun.

'No! Professor! That's not true . . .'

At that moment, all the lights in the room dimmed and the image disappeared. Richard realised his heart had been racing. The lights brightened again; the power draw must be incredible, he thought. All eyes focused on the white-coated assistant, who, for a few seconds, looked blankly at the contraption, and then quickly busied himself with its mechanics.

A period of silence followed, everyone too stunned to comment until Admiral Hughes called from the laptop, 'What's happening?'

'Technical problem, Admiral,' Rothschild replied, bluntly.

At that, Admiral Hughes looked off-screen for a moment and then he placed his fingers over his earpiece. He pressed it lightly in order to more clearly hear what was being said. He nodded several times in response, clearly acknowledging the relayed information. He looked at the two-way camera. 'Peter! There is some breaking news here, it is still unsubstantiated, but the repercussions could be immense . . . I will keep you informed.' He mumbled something to Professor Mubarakar, who shifted next to him, and then looked out through the screen again.

Richard sat deep in thought. Naomi, who was still close behind him, leant forwards as if to whisper something in his ear. Unwittingly, Richard leaned away and said to Professor Prescott-Alexander, 'I read recently that new processing requirements are outstripping the capability of our current derrilium based chips and like the silicon chip of forty years ago and the beryllium chip of the last two decades, derrilium is already near obsolete as a super-semiconductor. In fact, a Level 7 computer system is just about tops for processors made from this element. Would you agree with that, Professor Alexander?'

'To a large extent that is true, yes,' she answered, concentrating more on the repair activities of her assistant, than Richard.

'Also, I read that the Moon dust derived element lunaridium is still in research and a few years away from practical usage as the core material of a computer chip, and that the only way to increase processing speed in the interim is to integrate organically derived components. Would you agree with that statement too, Professor?'

'Yes, that is also correct.' The Professor, distracted by her assistant's activities, agreed.

'But moral issues . . . and the New Geneva Convention, have, for a number of years, prevented related stem cell research and organic tissue integration into such systems. You mentioned earlier, Professor, that samples of tissue had recently been extracted from Simpson-Carter's body and supplied to you . . . presumably for this experiment. Have you used an organic component in this system, Professor?'

After that question, Richard found he had the Professor's full attention and noted her defensive attitude as she said, 'When needs must, we do what we have to, Richard.'

Richard looked at the large box on the table, its flashing lights and ventilation inert. 'So this system could very likely exceed a Level 8 system, right? I mean Level 9 or possibly, more . . . that's some authorisation. I thought there were repercussions with such systems, aggressive behaviour for one thing – EMILY being a case in point.'

'We have been authorised to use all available technology!'

'But what about international censorship, surely it is there for a reason?' Richard was concerned, his firsthand experience of the Humatron series laid weight to his argument.

'Censorship laws established in the twenties, Richard,

are of little relevance in 2050!'

'I've read about the problems of using bio-implants in computer architecture. The Skyport 1 report for instance. Humatrons, with their Level 7 programming, they were the cause of that disaster.'

'It is an old report and the recommendations are now obsolete; science has moved on, Richard. Anyway, I knew Doctor Franz Morgan personally, and several of his conclusions were contentious.' Professor Prescott-Alexander turned her attention towards her assistant again.

Admiral Hughes stood up and walked off-screen.

Richard appealed to the others. 'The ghosting of human traits known as the *Poltergeist Efficacy*, has caused huge problems. This is when our innate aggressive tendencies – our primordial instincts – become incorporated into the synthetic memory matrix of an advanced, free-thinking computer . . . some sort of leakage from the physiological plane into the programmed plane. This is not a theory is it, Professor? This is fact!' Richard shifted in his chair. 'Moreover, Morgan's research found it to be aggression orientated with sadistic overtones . . . which is why the world council banned these higher-level systems. I read about it!' Richard's tone then changed to a questioning one. 'Have you used parts of Simpson-Carter's brain tissue in this computer, Professor?' he persisted.

'I do not think that we need to continue on this theme,' interjected Rothschild impatiently. 'What of the repairs,

Professor?'

Professor Prescott-Alexander looked at Rothschild. 'I think Richard deserves an answer,' she said, and turned. 'I like an enquiring mind, Richard, really I do, but you must understand that the stakes are extremely high. In answer to your question, yes, we have – the late Professor's corpus mamillare, to be specific. The tissue was extracted from the back of the hypothalamus region of his brain, and along with the fornix, forms the connection between memory and feelings. Frankly, it was essential, Richard, and its integration has increased the processing capacity of this system exponentially.'

Richard felt Naomi's gasp against his neck and knew that she had been shocked. 'Is this system superior to Level 9?'

'Stop worrying, Richard!' smiled the Professor confidently. 'We have learned the lessons of the Skyport disaster, and other wayward robotic systems that have exhibited similar traits. This is a holographic system and as such is clearly passive; this is artificial intelligence *without* the pitfalls. In addition, there are a good many filters and regulatory nodes to prevent such emotional ghosting. That phenomenon is outdated, our knowledge and technological innovation continues on a steeply inclined curve.'

Richard motioned towards Rothschild. 'Pulling a gun looked pretty aggressive to me,' he said, dismissing the Professor's explanation, and then he turned to look at the Reverend. He recalled their previous conversation. 'Science 'continues apace,' he concluded.

Admiral Hughes arrived back on screen and sat down looking stern. 'Well?' he barked.

'Professor Alexander,' interrupted the white-coated assistant, now a little more composed. 'The system is rebooted. A voltage spike in the main electrical supply caused a surge in the transformer modulator. I am afraid the domestic supply here in Khartoum is not stable enough for our requirements, despite our regulators. I have switched to our emergency backup supply. However, this will limit hologram generation time to approximately thirty minutes and then we will need to recharge the energy cells. This process will take at least twenty-four hours. The system is now back on-line.'

'We are ready to go, Admiral,' interjected Rothschild. Admiral Hughes nodded. 'Professor, please continue will you, time is pressing.'

Professor Prescott-Alexander looked austerely at Richard and nodded. 'I should tell you at this stage that there is another consequence of using the bio implants that we have in this recall system. We discovered it by accident during previous experimentation.'

Richard looked sceptical and waited for her to continue.

'It seems that the programme will keep secrets, literally!'

Richard's eyes widened with surprise.

'Much like humans, we found that the PRIMARS

memory processor will afford these "secrets" an ascending level of protection. For example, the amount of cash a person is carrying is less of a secret than if they have, for instance, a medical problem. Also, like humans, we discovered that stored secrets, even those afforded the highest level of protection – an innermost secret – can be coaxed and eventually exposed by careful, sympathetic and where necessary, manipulative conversation.'

'I'm glad this is a hologram system and not a Humatron!' Richard commented, his reservation clearly apparent.

'We will restart the programme at the precise moment it crashed. In fact, the moment just prior to the unproven act of hostility,' said Professor Prescott-Alexander, dismissive of Richard's remark. 'This, we found, is the only way of maintaining inquisitor cohesion. Because of the organic memory integration, one cannot fool this machine. Firstly, you should subdue any potential aggressive tendencies – only then, can you continue. Think about how to do this, Richard. What you will say? Manipulative conversation and continuity; this we have found to be of paramount importance. Are you ready to question the hologram, Richard?'

Richard nodded a little nervously. The assistant flipped the main switch again and the hologram appeared exactly where it had left off – with Professor Simpson-Carter reaching inside his coat.

'No, Professor! It is not a trick question. I am not from the Inquisition. I am an innocent Englishman with no religion.'

The Professor looked at Richard and dwelt on his words, they seemed to satisfy his concerns. He withdrew an empty hand. 'Of course you are, Richard, how silly of me.'

Richard glanced behind at Naomi; she appeared more settled and smiled at him. There was a question, however, that played on his mind; it niggled him like an unanswered riddle. 'Professor Simpson-Carter,' Richard said clearly. 'I am collecting information. For instance, you said that someone was responsible for the death of your wife – it was not an accident?'

'It was not! She was murdered. The fire that swept through our house was no accident; it was arson! *I* should have gone; it should have been *me*, not her.' The image rubbed its brow sorrowfully. 'If that was not enough, two days later, someone tried again, the same person . . . I know it! I had sent the nanny and my baby daughter to be with relatives in Cairo. Hajib and I had tented accommodation near to the house. It was badly damaged, but I was trying to salvage remnants of my work . . . years of research. Then another fire in the dead of night, someone was intent on destroying me. We heard the assailant run off. Hajib caught up with him, but suffered a fatal stab wound during the struggle. He died in my arms minutes later. The assailant escaped. Since then I have kept my guard, carried a gun.' Carter shook his head mournfully. 'To first lose my wife and then my good friend of so many years was almost too much to bear.'

'Tell me about your wife, Professor. I know that she was beautiful and that you loved her very much.'

The hologram nodded. 'Yes, indeed I did. She was Egyptian – young, beautiful, clever. She herself was studying to become a Master of the Antiquities. She was intriguingly mysterious, which made her very special.'

'In what way was she mysterious, Professor?'

The image stared thoughtfully. 'I sensed a secret, something that came from her past. I did question her about it in the early years. She said that the secret was not for men of this earth; I could not possibly understand. A strange thing to say, but she was absolutely serious; there was no spite – I accepted it. She would look at me intently and insist "I love you, but do not ask". Because her refusal gave us both so much pain, I stopped. Her face, her deep brown eyes, always reminded me of . . . of . . .'

'Of who, Professor?' Richard probed. There was compassion in his tone.

The image hesitated. To Richard, Simpson-Carter appeared mesmerised. Momentarily, the hologram stalled; but there was no system defect apparent, and then it resumed. 'There was a frieze . . . it was the first time I noticed the likeness. Painted in the tomb of Amenhotep II – a tomb discovered only fifty years earlier on the Theban necropolis and still well preserved – a beautiful image that became known among Egyptologists as the "Younger Woman".'

Richard sat straight. 'Please, Professor, who are you

referring to?'

'Nefertiti! Queen Nefertiti, favoured wife of Akhenaten. The similarity was beyond question.'

Richard's eyes widened; the hologram became transfixed. Richard stuttered. 'You mean . . .?'

'There were other examples: the sculptor Thutmose – his famed bust, and an image at Karnak. Many colleagues commented on their likeness . . . *my wife and Nefertiti*. Some even spoke of Cleopatra!'

Richard rubbed his smooth chin and gathered his thoughts. He looked at Peter Rothschild but resisted turning to look at Naomi. Not now, he thought, and considered another tack. 'What else can you tell me about your wife, Professor?'

The image took a long deep breath, paced a while and then looked down upon Richard as a stern schoolteacher would. Richard nodded reassuringly. The hologram seemed to respond and smiled faintly at him; it was uncanny; Prescott-Alexander typed a few words into an electronic memo pad.

'Each and every month, for a few days, she would return home to Cairo. No matter where my work had taken us, suitable arrangements would be made, and always in good time. I found out later that she always visited the monuments on the Giza Plateau, more particularly the Great Pyramid, with a trusted friend of long standing. For years I saw no relevance in the dates, until I came to realise that they always conformed to a certain time in the lunar cycle. The secret died with her, but she remains with me forever.' The Professor stared at Richard.

This time, Richard turned and glanced momentarily at Naomi and then looked back at the image. He would have to be careful here, he thought, but he wanted more information. 'Why was she continuously drawn to that ancient mausoleum, Professor, despite its historic significance?'

'I am surprised that you think of the Pyramid of Khufu as a mausoleum, Richard. I thought that *you* would know better. There is no evidence that this pyramid, or the others for that matter, were constructed as tombs. These were just the mistaken interpretations of the early archaeologists – their incorrect suppositions. Suppositions that have continued in perpetuity as such uses only came much later. I discovered that the Great Pyramid was built over two thousand years before the reign of Khufu – that powerful Pharaoh was merely the first to take advantage of it.'

'Thank you, Professor for sharing your wisdom. Will you enlarge on your opinion as to why the Great Pyramid was built and of its orientation in relation to the other two principal pyramids on the plateau?'

The hologram paused again thoughtfully and scratched its head. 'Straightforward, my boy . . . astronomy and complex mathematics,' it replied. 'What is certain is that two narrow shafts emanating from inside the Great Pyramid were accurately directed towards two specific stars: Zeta Orionis, one of the three stars in the belt of the constellation Orion, and Sirius, in the constellation of Canis Major. The so-called Queen's Chamber was not a crypt, Richard, but an observatory, and there are similar shafts emanating from the King's Chamber. It is certain too, that along with the pyramids Khafre and Menkaure, these three timeless monuments form an accurate "map" of the three stars of Orion's belt as they appeared centuries before the date these monuments were supposedly built. After a lifetime of study, I have concluded that these . . . *observatories* formed an ancient communications centre!'

'By the gods!' Professor Mubarakar was heard to say, his voice emanating from the laptop on the table.

Richard's eyes widened in amazement; he had been pulled through the "Sirius shaft" by Asharf and Naomi, but had been totally oblivious to its significance. Richard thought of Naomi's words, spoken when they had first entered that chamber. That it was orientated towards Sirius, but he recalled she had given a different interpretation of the shaft's function – more the tomb interpretation. Had she been protecting its real use? Did she know the secret? He moved on with the questioning. 'You are of the opinion then that the pyramids are much older than previously thought, Professor? Older, by many centuries – how much older would you say?'

'More than two thousand years, I suppose. Astronomers, not me, accurately predicated that the orientation of the three pyramids exactly matched those of the three stars that form Orion's belt, some five thousand years before Christ. Why would the builders orientate the three pyramids, these incredible structures, to a later alignment – one that was yet to happen? It would make no sense. Those monuments have stood for seven thousand years.'

Richard thought instantly of Eridu, the great city and its recorded place in history – 5000 BC. The dates concurred. Moreover, what of the stellar projections in the *Star's* flight log, "frozen" in the year 5082 BC? Things were beginning to add up, Richard concluded.

'It is not just I who knows of the grand architectural plan of the pyramids and the Sphinx at Giza,' the hologram continued, strangely and accurately pointing a finger at Richard. 'Others found evidence: further chambers, instruments made of metals not known to man, and the parallel pyramids of Elysium.'

Richard gasped, 'Elysium? On Mars?' He was astonished, for he had never associated the orientation of those massive structures on Mars with those on the Giza Plateau.

'Yes, on Mars, Richard. Known, but never spoken about. A cover-up by successive governments fearing mass hysteria and of course there would be other repercussions. Those pyramids – similar in so many ways,' he paused. 'The truth, you know, has long been hidden.'

At that moment, the assistant whispered to Professor Prescott-Alexander. 'Professor, we have barely fifteen minutes of power remaining.'

Professor Prescott-Alexander looked at Rothschild with

a concerned expression. 'Richard!' Rothschild responded. 'Time is against us. Move on. The Ark. Ask the hologram about the time he spent at Meroe and Aksum . . . his excavations and his conclusions.'

Richard nodded. 'What of the "old" writings, Professor – in KV5? I know that after your own studies in that mausoleum, you yourself then headed south. I know that you led archaeological expeditions to the ancient cities of Aksum and Meroe.'

'I don't know anything of such writings,' the hologram replied.

'You spent months in what was later called "Upper Nubia", Professor, in the red desert. I know that! You used a pseudonym for your expeditions!'

The image seemed to study Richard with a cold stare. 'So, you know of my expeditions, despite my precautions. No matter,' he paused, 'you will not know of my results.'

Richard looked at Rothschild for guidance. Rothschild mouthed, 'go on!'

'I have seen the "old" writings that adorn the walls of the secret chamber in KV5, Professor. The chamber originally excavated for Rameses' first-born son Amun-her-khepeshef, but never occupied because it was given over to an Ark. The writings say that this Ark travelled south instead, into the lands of Kush. Much later was the Kushite Empire called Nubia; we both know that!'

'I said, I don't know anything of the writings in KV5. *Do you understand*?' The image adopted a more defensive posture, reinforcing the words with impatient emphasis.

Richard, nonplussed, wondered why the hologram was being difficult over this particular point. There had to be a good reason.

'But the writings . . . in blood . . . in the secret chamber, you *must* have seen them, Professor?'

The hologram's expression grew angry and it put an arm out as though to ward off Richard and his questions. Richard glanced over at Rothschild again; with time running out he could not afford to be confrontational towards the system. It seemed like a stand off; Richard was at a loss. He looked again at the hologram; there was aggression in its stance and expression. The image flickered three times.

At that moment, Naomi stood up. Inexplicably, the hologram tracked her. She walked around the chairs and stepped into the circle. Naomi's smile was of gentle admiration. She raised a hand and tenderly touched the Professor's face, taking care not to pass through the image. He was taller than her by several centimetres. Everyone seated was spellbound, but none more so than Professor Prescott-Alexander, who was awe-struck at the hologram's response: it lifted a hand and placed it on Naomi's!

'It is because of you, grandfather, that I became a Master of the Antiquities,' Naomi said, almost in a whisper.

Richard immediately registered the change in the hologram. The image seemed to look lovingly at Naomi, as if, impossibly, it registered the relationship.

'I was too young to know you,' Naomi continued, 'but you were my inspiration. We never met, for time would not allow it; but my mother spoke often of you. She would show me newspaper cuttings and magazine articles – reports of your work and your great discoveries. How you captured my imagination, grandfather. You will always have a place in my heart.'

Professor Simpson-Carter's expression was soft and benign as he seemed to watch Naomi return to her place; perhaps, he had looked at his wife in a similar way during their life together and it had been captured informally on cellulose or video footage. Richard thought it a very touching moment and an enlightening one too. Naomi looked composed and restrained, but as she passed him and sat down in her chair, a tear ran down her face. Richard turned and offered his handkerchief when he saw that the one she pulled from inside her sleeve was clearly sodden. He smiled to show his support for her difficult expose. She leaned forward and whispered into his ear.

'Do you recall the words, Richard?' she asked, 'that were scratched in the eternal darkness of the secret chamber; those of the last Priest of the Order of Atleans?'

Richard nodded puzzled.

'Then you should recite them now.'

It seemed a struggle for Richard to switch his attention; when he did, towards the hologram, it too appeared bewitched by Naomi. '*Respect not the men who take it. For them, the sun shall never rise. For those who follow me, look south to Kush,'* he said slowly.

The hologram nodded knowingly. Its gaze shifted to Richard. *'For those who seek an understanding, take refuge in Meroe. Rest only, not home,'* it responded and then quite unexpectedly, the image smiled.

Naomi, maintaining her focus on the Professor's face, leaned forward again and put her lips close to Richard's ear. 'Talk to him as a friend would, Richard; not as the inquisition,' she whispered.

Richard glanced quickly at her. The rest of the room watched in complete silence. He looked back at the image, took a deep breath and asked: 'Professor Simpson-Carter, Sir, please, what of Meroe and Aksum?'

The Professor nodded. 'The artefact journeyed south, journeyed south, journeyed south . . . journeyed south . . .'

The image jumped and then repeated itself, the same action, the same words, the same gesture; it seemed to stick, to hesitate, like an old scratched vinyl record. Was this a response to Naomi . . . a call, or a rare system malfunction? Richard waited. Before the white-coated assistant had time to make an adjustment, the hologram responded again – this time perfectly!

'Unlike ancient Egyptian script, the hieroglyphic writing of the Kush remains undecipherable,' the image continued. 'Apart from *my* parchment – the piece I discovered in a jar near Qumran – no key has been found to unlock its meaning. However, it is so remarkably similar to that of the "old people", the "colonists", as to be almost a direct derivative. I had already discovered their writings in the pyramids at Giza and at Abu Simbel – and we have spoken of KV5 – colleagues dismissed it as meaningless scribble. However, using the parchment and a carefully laid out inventory, which enabled me to decipher the cryptic pictograms, I could read it – for the most part anyway. After many weeks of searching and generous baksheesh to local Bedouin caretakers, I was shown a secret passageway leading inside one of the largest royal pyramids at Meroe. Over the centuries, treasure hunters had largely destroyed it; however, the chamber that I was shown lay deep within the structure and was subterranean. Here I found writings that spoke of a great artefact, a great light being housed there for a specified number of lunar cycles. I later calculated that period to be almost three thousand years. Yes . . . I had found the hiding place for a casket.' The hologram of Simpson-Carter nodded thoughtfully, before continuing. 'I was shown old stone tablets that had been stashed away and forgotten – they appeared to be altar stones or similar. On them, engravings told of an artefact that had arrived from the land of the Great Pharaoh Rameses, to the north. Mention was made of the Priestesses who tended the "light" and the wondrous casket that contained it. First, it had been hidden in a secret vault beneath a temple in the oldest corner of the city and had remained there for two centuries. I knew well enough of the references – the casket – there was no doubt in my mind. I knew that I had found the safe house for the Ark of the Light!'

'So the Ark of the Light truly existed?' interrupted Richard excitedly. 'Where did it go from there?'

Simpson-Carter's expression twisted, as if he had seen a ghost. The hologram walked a few paces towards Richard and then leaned over to peer at him. Richard gasped; his brain refused to believe what he saw. He felt Naomi's hand on his arm, encouraging him to remain absolutely still.

'We should be careful what we say, my friend. I have learned that even walls have ears.' With that, the image stood erect again. 'We should be cautious,' it concluded.

'Yes, I agree, Professor,' said Richard. 'We are totally alone here; I have made sure of it.' He crossed his fingers for luck.

The image nodded and smiled; perhaps more a conceited grin. 'Those so-called scholars, those academics, those who belittled me, those who had my membership of the Royal Geographical Society revoked. Those who branded me a wayward troublemaker; how stupid they were. All the while, I had discovered the coded meaning of the hieroglyphic writing – their use of astral mathematics. Ah yes, I was the only one who knew,' the Professor whispered, in a satisfied tone.

'But what of the Ark, Professor?' pressed Richard, as Rothschild lifted five fingers to show that time was running out.

'The responsibility for its keeping had fallen on a dynasty of Priestesses. The kingdom of Kush was in decline, and a new power was rising – the Aksumite Empire to the east.

Well-founded fears for the Ark's safety arose and so the Priestesses moved the Ark – the writings were clear on this point. For many reasons – most of which I was unable to confirm – the Ark travelled east. It bypassed the epicentre of the Aksumite Empire – probably thought to be too dangerous – and continued its journey to Adulis, the great Red Sea trading port. A safe haven was sought and I know this was much further to the east, far across the ocean. I know this because I found lists of export taxes paid, and one fitted a casket of Ark-sized proportions. I discovered these parchments were the archives of Aksum and only came to light after many months of work and a good deal of help from local monks. I believe that the Ark lay hidden in Adulis for many centuries.'

'What of modern Aksum, Professor, and the centuries old belief that an ark, *the Ark*, rests there?'

With that, the hologram looked sternly at Richard. 'The Ark that rests in Aksum, within the annexe to the ancient Church of Zion, is *not* the one you seek, be in no doubt about that. There is confusion, because time and place overlap. The Ark that you seek is an extraterrestrial relic and not a sacred artefact!'

'Yes, of course,' agreed Richard. 'So what of Adulis, Professor?'

'I know that the Ark arrived. There was an accounting record of it – a toll to cross the land. After that, I lost the trail . . . and that is the truth of it. I went back to Meroe to retrace my steps, to look for more clues – a waste of precious time. You will find nothing more in Meroe, or Aksum for that matter! I took a house near Adulis. It is a small town these days, with little remaining to testify to its imperial past. My wife joined me, but I was not long into my search when she died.'

'What exactly were you looking for in Adulis, Professor?'

'To continue my search, I looked towards the traders, the ancient spice routes, to the east . . . India, China! Many used the great port of Adulis, but the Arabs were the greatest seafarers of their time. However, for me, sadly, as for them, their time has passed.'

Richard looked across at Professor Prescott-Alexander, whose face was glowing with pride – this was more than a mere computer enhanced pre-recording.

'Professor Simpson-Carter, please, can you be more specific?' asked Richard, checking the time.

'I had a house close to the market. Only later did I discover that I was being watched. It numbered the quarters of the moon at the birth of my beloved princess. Look towards the east and the year without summer. That is all I will say on this matter.' The Professor checked over his shoulder, casting a wary eye behind him.

Richard turned and looked at Naomi. 'It sounds to me as if he deduced his wife's secret. Do you think he knew . . . eventually? I mean for princess, read wife . . . right?'

Naomi shrugged.

'Do you know the phase of the Moon when you were

born?' Richard asked of Naomi.

'Of course!'

'So . . . generation after generation, to continue the line,' Richard said, opening his eyes wide in expectation.

The noise of the projector and the hum of the computer processor seemed uncannily amplified for a few seconds as those gathered focused on Naomi in anticipation of her answer; although apart from Richard, and perhaps the hologram, no one knew the true significance of his question.

'Between the waxing crescent and the waxing gibbous, establishing the third phase,' answered Naomi, matter-of-factly.

'The third phase,' repeated Richard, quietly. 'That is the first quarter; number one! The house number is number one and the street . . . something to do with east. I am sure of it!' Richard turned back into the circle in order to address the hologram again. At that moment and in the blink of an eye, the image changed to that of Professor Simpson-Carter wearing a heavy, dark overcoat. He was older. Wrapped around his neck was a long chequered scarf and he wore black gloves and a woollen hat. When the image "breathed", moisture condensed into white cloud and then evaporated. Clearly, this footage was taken somewhere where the weather was very cold. Richard glanced at the assistant, his expression coaxing an explanation.

The assistant, who was standing close to the projector, scrutinised its instrument panel. 'The image is beginning to destabilise – power levels are dropping, there's about eighty seconds left,' he said.

'I must ask my grandfather something . . . before it is too late,' Naomi whispered and stood up.

The hologram tracked her. '*Grandpere, sil-vous-plait.* I want to know. Why did you forsake your daughter?'

The hologram's expression quickly saddened, only after several seconds did it answer. 'I placed her in a Catholic school in France; she was well cared for and safe there. It was for the best. I insisted on regular reports.'

'Yes, but you saw very little of her after that. She was so young, barely five! Did you not know how much she missed you?'

'It is true, and I regret this. I remember her uncanny resemblance to her mother – she was beautiful. I had work to do, expeditions, travelling, inhospitable places you understand. I went back to England – that was a difficult time too. Then I became ill – she was in France.'

The hologram flickered.

'We are losing power, Professor,' said the assistant.

Richard turned to Naomi, grasped her hand and gave it a squeeze. As he opened his mouth to speak, the image disappeared. The projector and the processor fell silent. With an irritated expression, he glared at the assistant.

'I'm sorry, Professor,' the assistant responded, impervious to Richard's glower, 'the power cells are exhausted.'

Professor Prescott-Alexander glanced at Rothschild. 'I'm afraid that's it for now, Peter!' she said. 'We must wait for at least twenty-four hours before we can try again.'

'That's too long,' replied Rothschild, as he walked across to the door and switched on the main lights to the room. He returned slowly and thoughtfully to the centre of the circle and gave Richard his full attention, whilst addressing Admiral Hughes in London. 'I suggest that we dispatch Richard and his team to Adulis at first light, Admiral.'

'Agreed! Make the necessary arrangements, Peter. Charter the Tiltrotor and inform the crew of the new destination – their free tank of aviation fuel will have to wait. Operations will calculate the latitude and longitude coordinates and then directly input them into the aircraft's navigation database by data link overnight. MI9, Abbey . . . please check regional security!' Abbey Hennessy nodded. 'Laura . . . type "east" into the Adulis town plan on the Global Geomap System – see what comes up! Richard, we have very little time, you must . . . wait!' Admiral Hughes instinctively raised a hand. 'Yes, Minister,' he said, his intonation changing. 'It is confirmed then. When?' The Admiral looked down at his desktop; he appeared to make selections on a touch-screen by pressing it several times with one finger – in response his eyes widened. Clearly, he was engaged in another conversation. He pressed on his earpiece and grimaced, as if to hear more clearly and verify what was being said to him, and then he breathed out loudly, almost in exasperation. 'I will inform Rothschild . . . indeed. I understand . . . I'll get back to you!'

Rothschild stood motionless in anticipation. 'What is

it, Admiral?'

'We have a problem. The ISSF are assessing the implications.'

Rothschild's trepidation seeped throughout the room. 'Security clearance!' he said. 'What level, Sir?'

'Forget it, Peter, we don't have time for formalities,' Admiral Hughes replied, shaking his head. 'Several days ago, Andromeda's governing body informed the ISSF that they were forming a senate – an autonomous governing body that would give better service to the personnel who lived permanently on the Moon. They would also more closely regulate "earth's stripping of the Moon's resources", unquote. They declared themselves "The Senate of Lunar Colonisation" and in so doing voted themselves a good deal of political authority. A little over an hour ago, they declared themselves a republic – the Lunar Republic!' Admiral Hughes shook his head again. 'As if we need this right now!'

There was a collective gasp from the room.

'Background, Sir?' asked Rothschild, ever the professional.

'They have heard about the breakdown of the Kalahari crystal here in the UK and its subsequent demise and also the one in the Japanese reactor. They know there's a likelihood of the crystal in the Long Island reactor going the same way is imminent. Because of this, they fear an uncoordinated run on their mineral stocks when global power goes down – their unprocessed Helium 3 stock is particularly volatile if pressurised without essential care and transportation precautions. They think the safety of the colony will be at risk. In addition, they think that there will be a rush of refugees from earth - too many for them to handle. They are probably right of course. The result could be a destabilising of the colony's infrastructure with disastrous results. They have closed Andromeda to all space traffic. Everything must be agreed prior to leaving earth and they have set up a quarantine station in low orbit to enforce the decree!'

'Can they do that, Admiral?' asked Rothschild. 'What about supplies? Food?'

'Andromeda has been self-sufficient as far as food and power goes for a few years now, Peter,' Richard interjected. 'Their biodomes for instance, produce an excess of vegetables so rich in essential vitamins and minerals that large quantities are sold as vitality supplements here on earth. They have a strong manufacturing base too, *and* the raw materials to supply it.'

Admiral Hughes nodded in agreement. 'They are rewriting the American Declaration of Independence as their new constitution . . . adding a number of amendments. They appear to have been thinking about this for some time.'

'No different then to the breakaway of the American colonies and their subsequent autonomy in 1776, Admiral. Soon after the British colonies were lost, the French suffered a similar fate,' Richard commented, unhelpfully.

'In fact, the scenario has been repeated many times through history. Let's hope this one goes peacefully. To be honest, I can understand their actions.' Richard shrugged. 'I wonder how long this fervour of self-determination will take to spread to Mars?' Richard's comment was succinct and pertinent – as everyone party to it knew. He turned to the Reverend Rawlinson. 'And what religion then, for the people who are born and brought up in the space colonies, Reverend?' he asked poignantly.

'An interesting question and very relevant considering these historic events,' replied the Reverend after a thoughtful pause. 'In view of your time on Mars, you are, I think, better placed than most to comment on this. My view is that it will take many centuries before the essence of our terrestrial religions are forgotten – if indeed, they ever are.'

Monsignor Bernardoni nodded, agreeing with his friend. 'Tell me, my son,' he questioned Richard. 'As *you* are the first person I have met who has set foot on Mars, or indeed the Moon – is there a chapel within that distant outpost?'

'Yes, in effect, but it is not permanently a chapel. It is a room for prayer and it serves the entire complement of personnel,' Richard replied respectfully.

'I see, so it is a multi-faith facility?'

'Yes, that is the case. It's a relatively large room, in a quiet corner of the base. Close to the biodomes, actually. The windows on one side offer a good view of the temperate micro-forest. It's very peaceful there, if I say so myself. There is a roster, if you like. Certain times of the day allocated to a particular faith. However, the system is flexible . . . if somebody wishes to book the room for a certain time, or a particular day, well, it's never a problem - it is very harmonious. There are no specific appointments, full time clergy or similar. Organisation, changing the room's appearance, cleaning, that sort of thing, it's all on a voluntary basis.'

Monsignor Bernardoni nodded slowly, clearly keenly interested. 'And what of you, my son . . . do you make use of this religious oasis?'

Richard paused. 'Um, well, I've been in there once or twice.'

Monsignor Bernardoni's expression beckoned a more specific answer.

'A friend of mine, he is Indian. He asked me to attend a small gathering once, to celebrate a particular festival – exactly as it was taking place in his home village near Bangalore. I went because he asked me to go, I enjoyed it!'

'And the other time?'

Richard grimaced; he could not see where this questioning was leading. He glanced momentarily at Rothschild. Monsignor Bernardoni beckoned an answer with opening hands. The room was silent.

'Well, um. There is a certain time, just once every few years, when a celestial alignment occurs between Mars and the cardinal points of the earth, more specifically the terrestrial east-west meridian. If you use the main telescope in the observatory and view the earth at this precise time, you can sight an orientation through the central Sahara Desert and across the Arabian Peninsula. More specifically, of course, you look east. Actually, the precise time is relatively simple to calculate using the observatory computer. Another friend of mine is from that region, and he invited me to join him whilst he prayed. It was over a year ago and before the dense cloud cover we now have. The entire region was clear to see. It was an exciting time for him; it made him very happy. I was privileged to be there for him.'

'And what of a Christian celebration, my son?' Monsignor Bernardoni probed again. 'How many of those have you attended during your time on Mars?'

Richard thought on the question for several seconds and sighed. 'Well, I was asked to attend the Christmas carol service year before last – couldn't make it though, too busy . . . survey duties.'

'Survey duties on Christmas Eve?'

'I helped to decorate the place. There was a group of us. I just couldn't make the event that was all!'

'I think, Signor Reece, that you are a difficult man to convince,' Monsignor Bernardoni concluded piously. 'You have great respect for the faith of others, but none for your own. Perhaps it is because of the things that you have seen and the journeys that you have made, but you seem to give little thought to that outside the practicalities of daily life.'

Richard looked suitably chastised.

'That is a debate for another time, Monsignor,' concluded Rothschild. 'Admiral, with your permission, I will close this briefing. There are preparations to complete here in Khartoum and time is pressing.'

'Agreed,' responded Admiral Hughes decisively. 'Richard, exercise extreme caution, and good luck . . . you could be our last hope.' With that, the laptop screen went blank.

'Three final points, Richard, if I may,' said Rothschild, scrolling through several pages on his laptop. He stopped and looked Richard in the eye. 'The CIB have confirmed that five Humatron HU40 robots were abducted from Epsilon Rio's headquarters in Brazil recently. Amazingly, amid tight security, they just disappeared. The CIB's initial report to Washington cites not only sizeable bribes, but also direct involvement by the conglomerate itself, another cover-up. One thing is certain; Epsilon Rio blatantly lied to Interpol about how many of these units they manufactured. In addition, according to seized documents, they omitted to publish details about defective programming; namely, a known memory stem contamination. This is strictly necessary under the New Geneva protocol for systems that interface with humans. Apparently, rectification would have set their agenda back at least two years, maybe more.' Richard understood only too well. 'Word is that they are being highly obstructive towards the investigation. There is a final note. Apparently, one of the units was incomplete.'

Richard nodded again. 'Yes, it was that one and one other that we met in the Great Pyramid, Peter. I sent an abbreviated report to explain this.'

'Then it is likely that three other fully operational models are out there somewhere.' Rothschild nodded and eyed the team. 'All of you . . . be observant and be careful. If you see any of these machines, avoid them at all costs.' He directed his gaze at Richard. 'That's an order! You do not need me to tell you how dangerous they are.' Rothschild referred to his notes. 'Another thing; we know that Epsilon Rio is in close collaboration with the Chinese conglomerate Tongsei, and that this conglomerate exercises considerable trading pressure in the East African region. Indeed, they have a large headquarters building in Asmara, Eritrea. Further, we know that Tongsei is focusing an unusual amount of attention in this region – this by way of both undercover operations and men on the ground. We are seeing many new faces . . . orientals. They are not amateurs, Richard. Three of our local agents assigned to surveillance duties have gone missing in as many days. As a result, we are drafting in covert support for you. They should be in place by the time you reach Adulis, but I stress, this is covert support and not active field support – nothing heavy-handed – the government is in a difficult position. With this in mind and regarding local security, it is critical that you take the advice of the senior field agent who meets you. He may request that you remain, shall we say, subtly visible. Having said that, do not draw attention to yourselves . . . *understand*?' Rothschild emphasised, looking back at Richard.

Richard nodded. 'I understand,' he said soberly.

'Finally, keep a good eye open for this man.' A face appeared on Rothschild's laptop screen. 'I know that this is a poor quality image, but it's the best and most up-to-date that we have. At the moment, we are not sure of this man's involvement, and to be honest, we are desperately hoping that his recent appearance in London is a coincidence.'

Richard leaned forwards and studied the image. 'That's King's Cross Station,' he said, 'Near the Eurolink platform!' He looked at the man's face and shook his head.

'Correct. This image was taken twelve days ago. An automatic, metropolitan crime prevention camera outside the main entrance took this shot along with thousands of others that day. The system runs continuous databank comparison checks . . .'

'Ah . . . big brother!' Richard commented sourly.

Rothschild sighed. 'If you insist, Richard,' he rebuked. The image changed, but the clarity was little better. 'The man was first sighted here, at 12:06, leaving the British Museum's east door; that door is adjacent to the hall housing the new ancient Egyptian exhibition,' continued Rothschild. 'We have since been informed that some of the artefacts on loan from Cairo's National Museum are being exhibited for the very first time. A few hours later, he turned up at Kings Cross and boarded a monolink express to Munich. That particular service also stops at Strasbourg. He was not seen again. As you know, the Headquarters of Spheron is in Strasbourg. Our concerns were raised three days ago though, when, as a result of a routine Interpol circulation of these images, the Italian authorities confirmed a sighting in Rome, two days after the London sighting. To be more specific, he had met a man in the Vatican library known to be a world authority on aspects of early Christianity, particularly its dissemination into Africa. Nothing is known of that meeting or what was discussed.'

'Who is he, then?' said Richard a little rudely, peering again at the laptop screen.

'His name is Karl Wilhelm Rhinefeld; self-styled assassin, available for hire and lots of experience. We know that he was initially trained by an Eastern European secret service agency, but was later dismissed. He is an effective, cold-blooded murderer. A fellow undercover officer obtained elements of his service dossier at the time; that man, for his trouble, was never seen again. The report states that he was particularly adept at interrogation. He has a university degree in data analysis. He also has a photographic memory, is an expert in deciphering codes and is fluent in four European languages, although when speaking English he retains a strong German accent. If this man is working for the conglomerates . . .'

Laura Bellingham interrupted. 'Excuse me, Peter,

something's come in, annotated Top Priority. It's an answer on the "east" input into the Adulis street plan.'

'Yes . . . go on!'

'It says that there was a strong Italian presence in the region during the late nineteenth century and early twentieth century and that a good deal of their architecture remains. There is a row of well-known, colonial-style buildings on the east side of the town and called "East Parade". Apparently, many have been demolished over the last few decades, but those remaining with architectural or historical importance were preserved by the state. One building, which the file says was built on the site of a very early "official trading house", has its origins in the twelfth century. This building is listed as a museum. The description says that the building has a number of Italianate additions, the facade and the renovated gardens for instance, but the original building is still unmistakable. The street number of this building is one, making its address, Peter, when translated into English: Number One, East Parade!'

Rothschild glared at Richard. 'Make this *museum* your first port of call, Richard. We will have a car and a contact in place by the time you arrive at the local airport. It's a small strip by all accounts, with little security, so keep your ears and eyes open and please Richard, stick to the plan.'

Richard shifted his focus to Abbey Hennessy for a few seconds; her face was taut and she nodded. For Richard, she always seemed to have a fixed expression of disapproval, even when she was agreeable. Richard looked away.

'I must stress to the team the importance of Richard's pseudonym when in the field,' Rothschild continued. 'In company or unsecured surroundings this is absolutely essential. We should aim to keep your extraction from KV5 a secret, Richard. Right, that's all we have time for! Thank you all for attending.' Rothschild checked his laptop screen for the final time and then looked back at Richard. 'I see that take off is planned for 07:00 hours and that the flight time will be around two hours, depending on the weather conditions en route.' Rothschild checked his watch, Richard followed suit. 'This briefing is complete. I will arrange for that image of Rhinefeld to be sent to your pager, Richard. Have another look at it. I suggest a few hours' rest,' Rothschild concluded, whilst nodding at Laura Bellingham to close the minutes.

Richard escorted Naomi to the south wing and thereafter into a sizable extension to the house that clearly had been added some time after the original structure. Some of the internal architectural features denoted a late Victorian influence. Here the accommodation was mainly living quarters. They walked to her room in restrained, thoughtful silence. Her room was on the same level as the boardroom, but on the far side of the building. The wooden-panelled corridors and occasional ebony and ivory furniture pieces still gave an ambiance of colonial excess, however, it was the frequent, wall-hung wooden masks – death masks, warrior masks, masks of long forgotten spirits, shaman masks, even a wedding mask – that seemed to shout a true origin . . . Africa! Africa! Some of the masks, subtly painted in earthy hues, displayed large feathers or pieces of recognisable animal hide from long protected zebra and leopard; whilst others, dark and frightening, showed the marks of frequent use.

Richard had a hand on Naomi's shoulder. When they arrived at her door they stopped to face each other. After a few seconds, Naomi touched Richard's face tenderly and smiled at him. 'Thank you for bringing me to my grandfather, and thank you for being so understanding,' she said.

Richard shrugged. 'Naomi,' he said in a whisper. 'It was a hologram. Okay? A very clever piece of computer engineering. That was all it was.'

Naomi shook her head. 'No! That man of the church, Monsignor Bernardoni, he was correct in his opinion. You have an understanding but no faith, Richard. You are a product of this modern world and its technology. I can assure you that I felt the presence of my grandfather. Believe, or do not believe, that is your choice. All the same, you have become special to me, Richard.'

At that moment, Abbey Hennessy rounded the corner at the far end of the corridor. Richard gently grasped Naomi's wrist and pulled her hand from his face. Abbey Hennessy ignored them as Richard moved closer to Naomi to allow her to pass. Richard watched her unlock her door at the end of the corridor and was surprised when she called back to him.

'It is almost midnight, Richard,' she said, coldly. 'Your orders were adequate rest and *not* the night shift!' Then she disappeared into her room and firmly closed the door. The sound of the lock turning reverberated loudly.

'Do you have any more surprises for me?' Richard asked, as he gave Naomi his full attention.

'That rather depends on you.'

Richard leaned forward and kissed Naomi by the side of her mouth. It was a soft, heart-felt kiss. He slid his hand into the small of her back.

Naomi stepped forwards until she was touching him and they looked into each other's eyes. The corridor was empty and silent, but an army of people passing would have had little consequence. 'Would you like to be close to me, Richard?' Naomi whispered.

Richard smiled. 'I have to say that it had crossed my mind, yes.'

Naomi fumbled for the door handle. Richard found it first, and moments later they were inside. It was a comfortable, "dressy" room and clearly for a woman, as the décor was pale peach and flowery. There was a smell of burning incense. Richard recognised its aroma as being the one from the safe house in Cairo. It had a soothing effect on him. A black marble electric lamp, with a large, square, cream-coloured silk shade sat on a circular table on the far side of the spacious room. The period piece boasted Edwardian chic, but little illumination. Across the adjacent window billowing floral curtains shut out reality and over the table draped an embroidered linen cloth with edges that fell almost to the floor. On either side of the table, two high-backed chairs faced each other. The reduced supply voltage had its advantages and Richard smiled in the romantic ambiance. There was a vase of dried flowers on a three-drawer wooden sideboard; Naomi walked across and rearranged them, but to little effect.

'It's like being in a time-warp,' Richard observed, looking for the main light switch.

'No, Richard, don't . . . leave them off,' Naomi requested softly.

Richard walked over to her and gently gripped her waist; it was firm and curved. Naomi looked a little shyly into his eyes and considered for a moment. 'Would you like us to be as one, Richard?' she asked.

Richard tried not to be too enthusiastic and nodded nonchalantly. With this, Naomi led Richard over to the two chairs and beckoned him to sit down on one as she pulled the other around and sat in front of him. She stretched out and pulled on the right hand curtain to close a narrow gap. Richard looked confused, if not a little disappointed.

'Do not be afraid, Richard.'

Richard, puzzled, said: 'Afraid? I'm not. More curious.'

Naomi lifted Richard's hands and opened his palms. She looked closely at the lines, studying their contours and direction as a fortune-teller would. She slowly followed a deep line on his right palm with her thumb and then stopped abruptly. Her long hair fell over their hands. She looked away momentarily.

'What is it, Naomi?' Richard asked in a whisper. 'Is something wrong? I know you well enough by now . . .'

Naomi looked up and gazed into Richard's eyes. 'You know only part of me, Richard.' There was an air of finality in her voice.

'Well? What do you see then?'

Naomi sighed and then she looked blankly into the glow of the table lamp, as if in a daydream.

'Naomi?'

Naomi focused again on him. 'I see a strong lifeline and good purpose, Richard,' she replied thoughtfully.

'And? There *is* something else . . .'

Naomi shrugged. 'And that is all!' Then she half-smiled and lifted Richard's hands so that his palms faced her. She placed her palms against his; their fingers interlocked. 'Close your eyes, Richard, and imagine my face . . . dream of it.'

'What?'

'Do as I say. Close your eyes. Be gentle . . . at peace.'

Richard did so and tried to concentrate his thoughts, but a few seconds later opened them again and looked, somewhat perplexed, at Naomi's face. Her eyes were closed, her lashes fanned against her high cheekbone and she appeared to be meditating. 'Close your eyes, Richard and think of me,' she commanded. 'Do as I say. Otherwise we cannot join!'

Richard sat a little stiffly, facing Naomi with his eyes firmly closed. In his mind, he focused on a face he was beginning to know very well.

At first, Richard's mind was a blank. He was aware of time, but not of reality. It was the time of dreams; sometimes stretched and at other times compressed; nonsensical, distorted. He drifted silently in greyness. He was aware that he was moving, but not of movement. The shades of greyness changed: sometimes whiter and at other times darker. *Time* passed.

After a while, he sensed his body; he was walking. He felt smooth, without trouble; easy and strangely graceful, like a long-legged antelope. The greyness became whiter and he felt a warm breeze on his face. And then there was a sound, suddenly rushing towards him. The noise of people; shouting; the cacophony of a crowd; a huge crowd; a city gathered together.

His eyes slowly cleared; misty, fuzzy at first, but then his focus sharpened. He found himself walking on a white marble floor with inlaid colours and intricate patterns. He wore open sandals with leather bindings; they felt small and light. He walked towards the sound, from where it emanated, towards the meeting, wearing a soft, white, flowing cotton dress. He came upon a row of towering granite columns and then a colonnade, and after several metres another row; beyond them was the sky; bright, blue, clear. The air was clean; he had never smelt such freshness. The warm breeze blew gently across his face and semi-transparent curtains wafted through the wide gaps between columns; occasionally they blew higher and he felt elevated. He became aware of a headdress that was perched comfortably on his head; it felt tall, proud, it felt shaped; it felt secure, made for him; perfect; regal.

This is not me, Richard thought; but I am here? This is not me; but I am seeing? This is not me; but I am feeling? What was around him was real enough. But this was not *Richard's* body, with his tired, achy muscles. This was like walking on air. And then, as he stepped through the final row of orange-brown marble columns that despite the warmth felt cool, Richard gasped!

Without warning, the noise rose to a crescendo, it became deafening. There, far below, was a huge crowd of people, thousands, tens of thousands. All at once they seemed to see him and responded with an uplifting roar of appreciation. He felt compelled to raise his hand and wave; another barrage of approval flooded his senses.

Richard became aware of people talking behind him; they spoke in a foreign tongue . . . but he understood it!

He gazed across the sprawling plaza that stretched out before him for almost a kilometre, its populace heaving and swaying and there were other buildings on either side; they were lower but amazing and themed with more rows of columns and capped with square lintels. Steep stone steps dropped away below him for perhaps thirty metres. There were people standing; they wore clothes that he recognised. And then, slowly, he looked up. Richard's gaze followed the contours of the enormous, part-completed construction opposite; it lay on the far side of the plaza. Its scale made it appear nearer. His heart missed a beat, a lump formed in his throat; he stood wide-eyed and stared at the larger of two massive pyramids. There were only two, but he knew immediately where he was. He recognised the geography. This was the Plateau of Giza!

There was a ramp, like a giant causeway that led up to the top of the pyramid. Built out of earth and stone and rubble and the colour of sand it straddled the land to Richard's left . . . far out into the desert it reached, into the heat-hazy distance. There were people on it, silhouettes against the skyline and Richard saw a large stone block rolling slowly downwards, its momentum hampered by a body of men leaning against it and heaving on a weave of ropes. And on the top of the pyramid scores of men manoeuvred what looked like the pyramid's capping stone. Every time they hauled the white triangular-shaped stone closer into position the crowd roared. He knew what this was, this celebration, this . . . climax. And then there was nothing . . . just greyness again; senseless, drifting; the noise of the crowd faded until silence reigned.

He heard the sound of a party – more a banquet. There was talking and laughing, the sound of music and merry making. An image flashed across his mind. It was of a large hall filled with people. He heard women giggling; the music seemed strange, it was not familiar. Briefly, there was another image. The men were dressed like Romans and in an instant he caught sight of a soldier – a scarlet-caped centurion stood guard to his left. The man was short and helmeted and he held a *lancea*; from his belt hung an unsheathed *gladius*. Richard heard talking close by; not in English, different again; nevertheless, he understood it.

'Where is the General?' someone asked. 'Where is Mark Antony? I have a message for him from Rome.'

'He takes food in his quarters, *Legatus Legionis*, and awaits the Queen!'

And then Richard vanished again. As if his form was sucked into a swirling funnel of greyness. Then, as with an impending storm, it grew dark. He heard screams, women's screams, one cried out: 'Atlantis . . . it is gone . . . lost!' Another woman shouted: 'The seas have risen and swallowed the great city!' And another said: 'Poseidon has their souls; he has taken them all for himself!' Richard heard uncontrollable weeping and then he plunged into a mist; silence fell upon him.

He felt himself falling. He heard a man's voice. 'Isabelle, it that you?' it said. 'Isabelle, are you there?' The voice trailed away.

And then the greyness lightened and an image of Naomi's face appeared. It was life-like but large, much bigger than him. It encircled him. Naomi looked and smiled. There was no birthmark; her complexion was clear and her almond shaped eyes exaggerated. Her smile widened and then the image became transparent and through it Richard saw stars and the enormity of space. Planets passed and huge galaxies twirled slowly, they were majestic and there was life in them. And then an amazing gaseous nebula of brilliant yellow appeared. At first it seemed millions of miles away in the extreme distance of space, but quickly it approached, as if at the speed of light itself. Then it flooded over him and encapsulated him . . .

After a while, Naomi flopped back in the chair as if exhausted. 'Oh, Richard . . . I have never been touched like that before!' she breathed.

Richard massaged his temples to ease a mild throbbing ache across his forehead. Slowly he opened his eyes. He blinked repeatedly and seemed disconcerted as he took a minute or two to reacquaint himself with his surroundings. Naomi smiled broadly at him. Richard leant forward and retrieved his handkerchief from the cuff of Naomi's sleeve. He withdrew it gently and unfolded it and then used it to dry some perspiration on his brow. He took a long deep breath, went to speak, but forced a brief smile instead. Naomi took Richard's hand down onto his lap and gently rubbed his palm.

'Just a headache, Naomi,' Richard said, and then shook his head and laughed at the paradox. 'Never thought I would say that!'

'The first time often results in a headache, Richard. You slipped deeper into my subconscious than I intended; that does not help. It will pass soon. Such deep joining taxes a mind unused to subliminal intimacy.'

Richard grimaced and sat back in the chair. '*Intimacy*?' he repeated, in a questioning tone.

'True intimacy is the joining of minds, Richard,' Naomi answered matter-of-factly.

'Oh . . . really?' Richard kneaded his temples again.

Naomi smiled again. 'Nobody has touched me in such a way, Richard. It was wonderful; my emotions remain highly aroused.'

Richard shook his head and his expression dropped; he could not conceal a look of scepticism. Naomi took his hands in hers. 'How was it for you, Richard? Please say that you are not disappointed.'

'For me? Oh, err . . . yes . . . wonderful springs to mind, absolutely. Yes, wonderful.'

'So you are not disappointed? To join spirits and minds, Richard, to share the sublime, that is far closer than joining bodies.'

Richard shrugged. 'Yes, quite right. Just wasn't what I had in mind, that's all. I'm more a physical man,' he said. Clearly, he was not entirely convinced.

'We experience things differently – men and women,' Naomi added, earnestly.

A smirk played on Richard's lips; his reply had an edge of sarcasm. 'Ah . . . the men are from Mars and women are from Venus, that kind of thing?'

At that remark, Naomi's expression morphed to one of confusion – her lips quivered. Thinking that he had said something out of place, Richard raised a hand in tentative apology.

Naomi looked sideways at Richard. 'It is true. There was segregation, but long ago.' Naomi paused thoughtfully. 'The planets are not in this galaxy, Richard – so how would *you* know that?'

Richard's eyes widened in surprise and then he shook his head. He didn't want to pursue that argument. He checked his chronometer.

'Crikey, it's 12:55! Where did that time go?'

Naomi shrugged her shoulders, whimsically brushing-off the remark. Instead, she looked down at their joined hands. She gently squeezed Richard's much larger hands, placed them on his lap and pulled away. Now it was her turn to look a little disappointed. 'I have learned something of you, Richard; something that you have not mentioned.'

Richard stood to leave and looked into her dark, almost black irises that reflected one pinpoint of light. Naomi forced a smile. 'Another time perhaps; now I must rest. Another day beckons.'

Richard opened his mouth to speak, but decided not to. He put a hand momentarily on Naomi's shoulder in farewell and quietly left the room.

'How is it?' Richard asked Preston, as he carefully manoeuvred a silver butter knife in his attempt to smear a ridiculously thick layer of orange marmalade over a piece of toast.

'Looks good, Boss,' Preston answered. Preston looked up momentarily and then nodded sharply as Richard passed him. A blob of marmalade dropped onto the pristine white tablecloth. 'Ugh!'

Richard laughed spitefully on his way to the counter.

'Can you do two fried, sunny side up, please?'

The chef nodded. Richard scanned the room whilst he waited. It was a large formal dining room and to some extent it reminded him of a military officers' mess. There were more than ten tables set and each boasted fine silverware and crystal. A pot of tea arrived at the table where Preston was sitting. There was nobody else in the room save for two stewards who wore white suits with dark green waistcoats. Very smart, Richard thought. He checked his chronometer: 04:56.

The eggs arrived. Richard nodded his appreciation and turned to the adjacent table where bacon, hash browns and canned tomatoes, mushrooms and baked beans beckoned. There were just two pieces of toast remaining in a metal rack and Richard took them both. It was sometime since he had seen such a spread.

Richard placed his plate down on the table within the setting on Preston's right and sat down beside him; the smudged marmalade mark drew his attention.

'You seen a ghost, Boss? You look a bit pale this morning.'

'Good morning, Preston . . . and you could say that, yes.'

Preston looked up; he paused thoughtfully. 'Um, I've taken the liberty of charging your telephonic pager along with mine, Boss, and I've replaced the power cell in my sonic pistol just to be on the safe side.'

Richard nodded and took a mouthful of egg on toast.

'I have already collected the ration packs and we have a good supply of water purification tablets. I met one of the aircrew members as well, Boss, in the kitchen. They have the coordinates for the airstrip . . . take off at 07:00 hours is confirmed.'

Richard looked up from his breakfast and nodded again. 'Very good, thanks. Let's see what today brings then, shall we? I have a feeling that it's not going to be a quiet one.'

THE BASTION PROSECUTOR

EPISODE 3

ISBN: 978-0-9551886-7-1

Highclere Hill Hampshire 2002
Crop formation in wheat

Lower rear cover image:
The Pyramids of Meroe
Reproduced courtesy of:
www.gilbert-park-photography.com

An image of Queen Nefertiti taken from the famous bust by the Egyptian sculptor Thutmose

GLOSSARY

The list of additional special or technical words used in
The Bastion Prosecutor – Episode 2

Accelercom – Accelerated Communication System –
Referenced to light speed i.e. approximately 186,282 miles
per second or 300,000 kilometres per second.

Comms State – Communication Security State - Refers
to state of security protection and readiness.

Cosmic Chronometer – Extremely accurate clock, time
computations based on the expansion rate of the universe
– "Big Bang" Theory.

Elliopherical Orbit – A precise orbital trajectory related
in percentage terms to the radius of a planet – Gravitational
attraction decreases with increasing distance/percentage,
from the planet's core.

ESSA – European Space & Science Agency.

FACULTE – Feline Autonomous Cranial Utilised
Locator Tracker Eliminator – Large, heave cat, genetic cross
between Black Panther and African Caracal. Utilises bionic
brain implants and incorporates a laser system in place
of one eye. Originally designed as autonomous, deadly,
security system for sensitive military and government
installations.

Gaia – Mystical name for the living force that is Mother
Earth.

Gamma Radiation – Short wave electromagnetic

radiation given off by the sun, usually very penetrating and dangerous to humans.

Greenwich Mean Time – The mean solar time at the Greenwich meridian, used as the standard time in a zone that includes the British Isles.

Humatron – Advanced robot series incorporating Level 7 Programming.

ISSF – International Space and Science Federation – Multinational/Global body made up of regional Space and Science Agencies.

ISTAN – Close quarters weapon comprising of a programmable molecular blade that can be also fired as a projectile. After penetration of a target, the molecular mass or structure dissolves into the air.

Ks – Colloquial abbreviation for kilometres.

Light Year – Distance travelled by light in one year.

LCT – Lunar Corrected time – local moon time, referenced to earth time and more particularly, Greenwich Mean Time.

LS – Life Support – Essential equipment or processes used for sustaining life.

MCT – Martian Corrected Time – Time dictated by the Martian hour, day, month and year but referenced to earth time, and more particularly, Greenwich Mean Time.

NCO – Non Commissioned Officer.

Rockwell Illinois Plateau System – System for measuring the degree of complexity and memory capacity of a cybernetic system – has become the internationally recognised reference system.

Roger – Form of acknowledgement, usually meaning that an order or statement has been understood.

Sitrep – Situation Report – Details of an event or happening.

SSA – Space and Science Agency – Multinational but regional body i.e. European Space and Science Agency or Asian Space and Science Agency.

Sonic Pistol – Hand held weapon utilising a massively condensed pulse of sound energy. Depending on its severity, when the pulse hits a target it destabilises the atomic structure of the target, usually resulting in severe damage.

U-Semini Case – Transportable containment system, briefcase sized and constructed to carry the Kalahari Crystals – Utilises a magnetron suspension system and enhanced Celestite protective sheath.

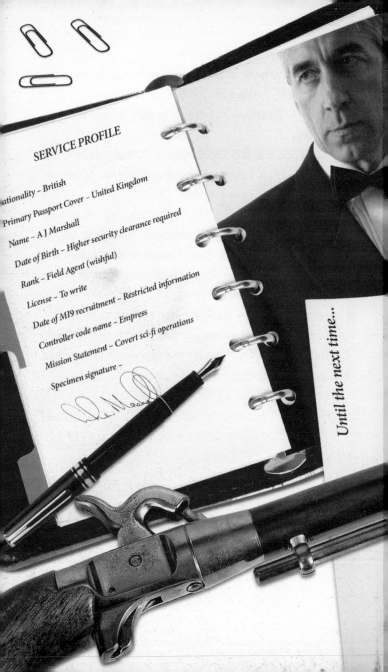

SERVICE PROFILE

Nationality – British

Primary Passport Cover – United Kingdom

Name – A J Marshall

Date of Birth – Higher security clearance required

Rank – Field Agent (wishful)

License – To write

Date of MI9 recruitment – Restricted information

Controller code name – Empress

Mission Statement – Covert sci-fi operations

Specimen signature –

Until the next time...